HOMECOUNTRY

T. W. LAWLESS

First published in Australia in 2012 by Campanile Publishing

www.twlawless.com.au

ISBN: 978-0-646-58469-0

1. Fiction

The characters and events in this book are fictitious and any resemblance to real persons, living or dead, is purely coincidental.

Cover painting, 'Cheetham Salt Works', reproduced with kind permission of James Yuncken

Cover design by Gregory Alex-Vasey

Cover photograph by Simon Woodcock

Edited and produced by Christine Nagel Literary Services

Typeset in Palatino 11/14pt

For my wife Kay and daughter Alex

PART ONE

1

Melbourne, 1987, Monday

Peter Clancy drifted along Lygon Street, feeling hung over and tattered from last night's drinking binge at the Tote. He was barely aware that he was running late for an appointment at a coffee shop nearby, but more aware that he couldn't give a fuck at the moment. He'd have felt better if he could have gone back to bed, but this appointment was too important. Last night's events flashed like a row of alternating strobe lights through a dense fog. He remembered going to the Tote for a celebration, for what he couldn't quite recall. Something to do with Collingwood? Then a drunken argument on the footpath. There was a fight. Peter couldn't recall if he was in it. He felt his jaw. *Must have been*. It ached every time he opened his mouth.

Peter couldn't remember why he had been in a fight. He didn't like fighting; he wasn't good at it and it didn't solve anything. Maybe he'd been an innocent non-combatant. It would also explain the blood on his shirt when he had woken up on the couch this morning, face down in a pizza. Despite having over a decade's experience of excessive drinking, he still hadn't cured the after-effects, which was why he always planned his hangovers for the weekends. During the week he stuck religiously to his nightly limit of twelve cans of VB. He found that was his optimal level to ward off hangovers and still maintain his clarity for his job. In Peter's job you had to be sharp; if not, you missed out on the fine details, the hidden gems, the non-verbal cues.

He reached into his aged beige, polyester suit pocket to retrieve an apricot-coloured tie. He didn't usually wear ties. The last time he'd worn one was in primary school. *The reserve of Toorak toffs*, he thought, as he stopped to examine it. The tie was the unusual request of a prospect he was meeting this morning and, totally out of character, he'd acceded to the request. A lot of prospects weren't your Bruce or Beverley Average. He tried to tie it as he walked but all that achieved was a huge jumbled knot with two little stumps hanging off it. He stopped and tried again. Same result. *Running later.* An attractive female passerby stopped to offer her assistance but Peter declined with a wry smile and a laconic, 'No thanks,' and continued walking.

Despite his overall unshaven, unironed appearance, thirty-year-old Peter looked rakishly handsome. His thick brown hair hung across his finely chiselled face and moody dark blue eyes. He was also seemingly blessed with good genetics, with a lean, well-proportioned body, though he hadn't exercised since leaving school, seen much sunshine or eaten balanced meals since leaving home. But a few more years of maintaining his current lifestyle would probably send his youthful appearance to a well-earned grave. The tremors or the bleary-eyes that met him every daybreak he put down to collateral damage.

This morning he had a 'date' with a woman named 'Rachel' who was going to tell all on her former lover, who happened to be a prominent married businessman. She said she would be in disguise and, for ease of recognition, Peter was to wear an apricot coloured tie. He didn't know what was worse, the repetitive drilling in his head or the tie that he was struggling to knot as he neared the designated rendezvous. In the end, Peter hung it limply around his neck.

The tell-all with Rachel was just the sort of fleshy sex scandal that his employer, *The Melbourne Truth*, relished. *Sex, sleaze and scandal sells*, that was *The Truth's* mission statement. *If you don't want to work here fuck off to* The Age *where you can write prose for the silvertails to read*, Peter's editor had so eloquently told him eight years ago when he'd accepted the position of journalist. *The Truth* was an institution with a healthy circulation of four hundred thousand, though no one ever admitted buying it. If anyone did, it was only for the racing guide. Certainly not the ample breasted Page Three girls or the lurid stories.

Peter had taken to the freewheeling honesty and mayhem at *The Truth* like an alcoholic to a drink. After working for a newspaper in Queensland that was essentially a propaganda platform for the long serving autocrat, Joh Bjelke-Petersen, *The Truth* was an epiphany. He had broken some big stories, particularly an exposé on corruption in the Victoria Police, which got him short-listed for a Walkley Award. Some stories stretched the truth a wee bit; the one he had spun about the man attacked by a kangaroo in his yard was one of his favourites. Photographs taken by the victim's wife of the mauling incident, however, did not make it into the paper, the kangaroo being stuffed. His only disappointment was that the Page Three girls weren't Australian but were sourced from the *Sun* in London. There were no live auditions, unfortunately. He was still comforted by the fact that he was part of a panel that chose the Page Three girl from a shortlist of seven photographs every month.

Exotic, inviting cooking odours emanated from the restaurants as he passed them. The crowd of largely well-groomed, well-heeled professionals sipped their cappuccinos at outdoor tables and conversed with an air of detachment, as Melbourne bustled about them. Peter loved the vitality and the bounding heartbeat of Melbourne. He was a long way from the entrenched inertia that had threatened to drown him in Queensland.

The culture, the ever-changing weather of Melbourne, the sport and even the sleaze enveloped him. Melbourne kept him alert and informed. Peter openly admitted he needed to see an art show or play every now and again, rather than piss up with his mates at the Tote, or at a Collingwood game, or a race meeting, and Peter was keenly aware that Melbourne had many layers he hadn't discovered yet. He would get around to it one day. His long suffering girlfriend, Michelle (a mousy lab technician at the Howard Florey Institute), was able to coax him away from his mates every week for a meal at an Italian restaurant with the promise that she would pay for the meal and give him fellatio (she liked to use correct medical terminology), when they got back to his flat on Johnston Street.

His mind drifted back to the business at hand. 'Rachel' was conspicuous by her inability to disguise her identity; an ill-fitting brunette wig and large dark sunglasses alerted Peter as he entered the coffee shop. Her chagrin was palpable when he sat down without introduction and removed the tie.

'How did you recognise me?' Rachel asked coyly.

'You used to be the weather girl on Channel Seven a few years ago. When you were blonde and called Christine,' Peter countered rapidly. Peter ordered two coffees from the hovering waitress, stressing that his short black be extra strong.

Indeed, Christine McGuiness had been the breasty, bubbly, blonde weathergirl whose report had rated highest with male viewers. Unfortunately, her career had crashed like a shower of hail when she had been caught in *flagrante delicto* with a newsreader by his wife at their South Yarra house five years ago. *The Truth* had been about to run the story but it was quashed at the last moment by the channel's legal department. Since her sacking, Christine had earned a lucrative income as the mistress of an

Italian chain restaurateur until he had allegedly beat her and locked her out of her Toorak townhouse one night and replaced her with a younger, bustier blonde named Skye. Vindictive and desperate, Christine/Rachel was now selling her story to *The Truth*.

For a brief moment he was aroused by her voluptuousness but that soon ended when she took off her glasses and started to bemoan her plight. He did feel sympathy for interviewees; those who had been destroyed by the system, those who couldn't get justice. In this situation, it was just another bread and butter story, good for the circulation figures. As she whined away, Peter sipped his coffee and wrote down keywords in his notebook. Christine stopped momentarily to dry the small tears that she had been struggling to turn into a torrent without success.

'Am I going all right?' Christine cooed. 'This has all been so traumatic. It's so depressing.'

'I'm sure it has,' Peter remarked dryly without looking up from his notepad. Peter was already composing her story of torment for tomorrow's edition. The headline would read, *Ex-weather girl's life of kinky sex with Italian stallion.*

He loved me would be transposed into *He loved rough sex.*

His wife confronted me would become *took a contract out on my life.*

He wanted to have a three-way would turn into *He held wild orgies every weekend at his love nest.*

Christine looked deflated when Peter wrapped up the interview in thirty minutes. She did suggest, however, that they continue the interview at her new residence, a flat in Williamstown, but Peter declined, citing a busy schedule. Peter had made a pact with himself not to get involved with interviewees. Not anymore. Not for two years. Not since the time when he had had a brief, deep and meaningful physical relationship with a stripper named Amber from St Kilda he had interviewed for an exposé. Her enraged boyfriend had beaten him senseless outside the Espie.

'I'll be in contact if I need more information,' Peter said as he stood to leave.

'Are you going to take your tie?' Christine asked, appearing deflated. 'It looks good on you.'

'I only bought it for today's interview. Besides, it's not my favourite colour.'

'I don't want to end up on the scrap heap, Peter. I hate the thought of being alone.' Christine looked longingly enough at Peter that it unsettled him.

'You'll meet someone. You're attractive. You're smart,' Peter lied. Peter had interviewed these women before. Once young and desired by their high-flying husbands or lovers they had found themselves superseded for a younger model. Maybe Christine would rise above this and go to university and study social work, or she would do what many others had done and drown their misery in a drug or alcohol haze.

Shazza, *The Truth*'s receptionist, hollered from behind the counter at Peter as he came through the front door.

'Pete. That girlfriend of yours has rung twice already. She must be tonguing for it. Better feed her the veal dagger tonight mate.'

'Thanks, Shazza. Why don't you tell the whole office,' Peter replied, embarrassed.

'I already have,' Shazza barked with laughter. She was a no-bullshit girl, full of red hair, freckles and booze. Peter always wondered how she kept her job but then again he wondered how anyone at *The Truth* did. Full of rebels and misfits. Another reason why Peter loved working there.

'Pete, come here,' Shazza got up from behind her desk and beckoned Peter closer. Peter walked with a sense of trepidation to the counter.

'You're looking under the weather, mate. I've got a cure for that,' she whispered as she produced a small flask from a drawer.

'What's this?' Peter asked cautiously. 'This isn't going to kill me?'

'It might kill you later. But today it'll put lead in your pencil. Have a suck on this,' Shazza unscrewed the cap and handed the flask across. Peter carefully took hold of it and sniffed at the contents through the neck.

'That reeks of alcohol.'

'No, no,' she argued, 'it's a vitamin drink. Drink!' Peter slowly lifted the flask, put it to his lips and swallowed.

'More than that!' Shazza laughed. 'You're not a flipping girl.'

He felt a spasm of searing heat burn its way down his throat, course through his body and squeeze the air out of his lungs. Peter put the flask down and gasped for several moments before he felt able to breathe normally again.

'Makes you feel good doesn't it?' Shazza declared, taking the flask from Peter and returning it to her drawer.

'Frig!' Peter panted, 'That stuff's poison.'

'Best hangover cure I've ever had,' Shazza replied drily.

Feeling strangely revived, Peter was thrashing away on his word processor when he heard a familiar wheeze and hacking cough approaching. Peter looked up to see his editor, Big Bob Connolly steering his corpulent frame like an oil tanker in heavy wind, up the corridor past the other journalists, the ever-present cigarette dangling from his mouth. Bob stopped several times to catch his breath and gather momentum before continuing. Bob Connolly had been the editor of *The Truth* for two years and in that time had increased its circulation with a winning formula: more sleaze, sluts and sex, drop the police/union corruption stories. Bob's mantra was, *we want the public titillated, not bloody educated*.

The more career conscious journalists had jumped ship as a result, including his mate Gavin, who he was meeting for a drink tonight. Peter didn't wear his convictions on his sleeve like them; convictions required a useless expenditure of energy.

Peter was hoping that Bob wouldn't stop to talk to him today. Bob loved to regale anyone in his line of vision with his latest grisly sexual encounter, usually with a prostitute and occasionally with a woman he had picked up at his football club. Peter didn't want his imagination assaulted today. Unbeknown to Bob, the staff had started a betting sheet on how Bob would die. Peter had wagered fifty dollars that Bob would die on the job. *Do a Snedden. Billy Snedden. Die on the nest.* Peter looked up when he noticed that the audible breathing was hovering above him like a helicopter. Bob was standing over him, his gut resting comfortably on Peter's desk.

'You've done it again, Pete,' Bob complained.

'What's that?'

'These made up words of yours. I found one in your copy. What's *negimous* supposed to mean?' A length of ash fell from Bob's cigarette onto Peter's desk.

'A negative celebrity. Famous for all the wrong reasons,' Peter replied.

'No more,' Bob laughed. 'What's that other silly word of yours? *Frex?*'

'That's just a combination of friend and sex. It means a friend you have casual sex with. I like that one. I reckon that could get popular.'

'Forget it. Sounds like a fucking cat. Even though it's *The Truth* we still have to use correct English.'

Peter relented.

'How did it go today?' Bob asked.

'Rachel is Christine McGuiness.'

'The horny ex-weather girl? Great,' Bob said. 'That's a lead story. I remember she had great tits. What's she look like now?

'Tits are still okay but she's looking long in the tooth. She's on the market if you're interested,' Peter joked.

'Bugger that!' Bob coughed out the words, the cigarette nearly coming out of his mouth. A shower of ash fell onto Peter's desk. Bob had three failed marriages under his ample girth and had no desire to *travel on the highway to hell again*, as he always said.

'We'll send a photographer around to her place today. Good work Pete.'

'No worries, Bob,' Peter started to type again. 'By the way, she's a *negimous*.'

'Shut up.'

Peter was meeting Gavin for a celebratory drink after work. Gavin had just left *The Truth* and had secured a position at *The Age*. Gavin Jenkins and Peter had done a Bachelor of Arts together at Central Queensland University, majoring in journalism, media and getting pissed. They were close friends then, living together in a rat-infested flat in third year. They were close associates in their first few years at *The Truth* but then Gavin had become the competitive one, the one who harped on about being editor of a prestigious paper in the future. Peter was happy to remain languid and unambitious.

Gavin had dismissed Peter's usual meeting place, the Waterside Hotel, out of hand, instead telling Peter to meet him at a trendy wine bar in Hardware Lane. Peter entered the unfamiliar surroundings to find Gavin and two men he didn't know sitting at a table drinking red wine. Peter was expecting others from *The Truth* to be there, but the wine bar and lack of *Truth* staff reflected Gavin's current self-elevated status. Peter was starting to wonder why he had been invited when he approached their table and introduced himself. Did Gavin want to rub his achievement in his face? The two men with Gavin turned out to be journalists from *The Age*. They were Melbourne Grammar types, an air of self-importance emanating from them. Gavin introduced them as Derrick and Spencer. Peter took an immediate dislike to them. Gavin attempted to pour Peter a glass of wine when he sat.

'No thanks. Beer for me,' Peter drawled as he caught the attention of a waitress.

'It's a good merlot. You should try it,' Gavin advised.

'So you're Peter Clancy. Gavin's old mate from *The Truth*,' Spencer asked as he sipped at his wine. 'Gavin says you're a good journalist.'

'I've had a few winners in my time,' Peter replied curtly.

'Peter and I went through university together,' Gavin added.

'Melbourne or Monash? Spencer asked.

'Central Queensland,' Peter replied, glaring at Gavin.

'It has a good journalism course.' Gavin was defensive.

'I'm sure it has,' Spencer said. There was a long period of silence. Derrick finally spoke.

'Intending to stay where you are?'

'Why not? *The Truth* has its merits.' Peter drank his beer as quickly as possible.

'Usually on Page Three,' Derrick guffawed. Gavin and Spencer laughed, Peter didn't. Peter drank the remains of his beer and slammed the bottle on the table.

'Another one?' Gavin asked.

'I'm going. I don't like drinking with upper class wankers. Remember I work for *The Truth*.' Peter stood to leave the table.

'There was no offence intended, old man,' Derrick said.

'What are you? A fucking English lord? I'd rather drink with the derros down at South Melbourne.'

Peter was outside the entrance of the wine bar when Gavin caught up with him.

'Are you trying to embarrass me?' Gavin asked. Peter laughed.

'You already sound like those fuckwits. It didn't take long, did it? You'll be joining the Melbourne Club soon.'

'You're jealous of my success.'

'You call this success?'

'I'll be editor of *The Age* in the next few years and you'll be still doing stories on celebrity orgies and alien abductions. You have no ambition, Pete, just a big chip on your shoulder'

'You win, Gav. You made it to the top of the shitpile. Happy?' Peter said as he stormed off to the comforting surroundings of the Waterside Hotel.

Feeling pissed and hungry, Peter wandered into the Apollo Café on Johnson Street at seven to pick up his customary Greek dinner. Living above the Apollo was like having a home cooked meal every night. Another advantage was that it was within staggering distance of the Tote. Con and Roula, the café's proprietors, greeted Peter. They were like a family to him. Or more like the family that Peter had wished for as a child. He celebrated every Easter and Christmas at their house. Thank God for the Greeks and Italians, Peter always told everyone. Without them we'd still be eating steak and chips.

'You want moussaka tonight, Peter, or the usual? Roula asked as she rolled an order of fish and chips in newspaper.

'I'll try the moussaka. I've had souvlaki for the last week.'

'You look tired, Peter,' Roula said. 'You need a good woman to take care of you.'

'I haven't met any women like you yet, Roula.'

'That girl, what's her name? She has been in here asking about you. I think she's waiting upstairs.' Con interrupted.

'Great,' Peter said dryly. 'Better make that two moussakas.'

'She looks like a good woman.' Roula handed over two plastic containers of moussaka, 'You'd have beautiful children.'

'That sounds frightening,' Peter said quickly as he grabbed the food and left.

'Think about it, Peter,' Con advised. 'You have to settle down soon. Be responsible.'

Michelle was dozing at the top of the stairs. She woke with a start when Peter nudged her. *Poor Michelle,* Peter thought, *why would she hang around a dickhead like me?* She was more suited to an academic type, a teacher or scientist. Someone stable and dependable. Everything that Peter wasn't. Peter had made feeble attempts to break up with Michelle, or rather he'd thought about it. Peter couldn't summon the courage; the sex was too fantastic. Despite her quiet, unassuming demeanour, Michelle was a demon in the bedroom.

'I thought you'd be here at six,' Michelle said as she stood up. Michelle attempted to kiss Peter but he turned away to open the door to the flat.

'I had an important meeting at work.'

'I wish you'd tell me.'

'Are you my mother? And can you stop ringing me at work. They'll start thinking you're a psycho,' Peter snapped.

'If you want me to. I just get worried about you.' Michelle said in a hurt tone of voice. Another reason why he couldn't follow through with breaking up — she always looked hurt when he raised his voice. It was like yelling at a puppy dog.

Peter entered the flat and turned on the light. Michelle followed and sat on the couch while Peter went to the kitchen and opened the lids of the plastic containers. The flat was spartan but clean. Another skill of Michelle's that Peter utilised every week.

'Do you want to go out for dinner? Michelle asked. 'I'll pay.'

'I got food downstairs. Are you fine with moussaka?' Peter flopped on the couch and handed an opened container to Michelle with a fork. Peter tucked into his food with gusto.

'I'm not sure,' Michelle asked, eyeing the food.

'There's nothing wrong with it. Tastes great. If you don't want it,' Peter snapped the container and placed it on the couch next to him, 'more for me.'

'I'll make some toast,' Michelle sighed as she got off the couch to go to the kitchen. The wall phone near the refrigerator rang. Peter ignored it.

'Aren't you going to answer that?' Michelle asked.

'You're up.' Peter was wolfing down the contents of the second container. Michelle picked up the receiver and spoke tentatively.

'Peter's phone. Michelle speaking.' Michelle listened briefly before calling Peter.

'It's your cousin. Says it urgent.'

Cousin? Peter thought as he removed himself slowly from the couch and went to the phone. He tossed an angry look in Michelle's direction as she hung around next to him.

'Peter Clancy. Who's speaking?' he asked brusquely. He seemed surprised at the reply and shooed Michelle away with the wave of an arm.

'Douglas Clancy? Of course I remember you, but why are you ringing me? I haven't spoken to you for ten years.' he blurted. From where she sat, Michelle could hear the buzz of Doug's voice but not his words.

'What's that?' he cried out. 'Oh, God, no!' Peter leant against the wall and ran his hand through his hair. Michelle got off the couch and came over to him, sensing something was very wrong.

'But she was fine when I spoke to her three months ago,' Peter retorted, 'Oh, God, that's terrible! I'll get there as soon as I can. Of course I'll be there.' Peter replaced the receiver and briefly wiped his eyes before going to the fridge to retrieve a beer. Snapping open the can, he took a long drink and walked back to the couch. Michelle followed and tucked herself in beside Peter.

'Is everything all right? You look upset.' Michelle attempted to touch Peter's face but he pulled away from her. Emptying the contents of the can with a deep swallow, Peter was off the couch and beating a path back to the fridge.

'My mother died yesterday,' Peter stated as he dived in for another beer. The fridge beer was depleted. Only a six-pack left. He looked in the pantry for reassurance that there were more grog supplies. Safe. There was another carton of VB and a bottle of Bundy if he got desperate.

'Peter, I'm so sorry. When did you last see her?' Peter returned to the couch and sat away from Michelle. He opened the can and only took a sip. He found a place for it on a gnarled coffee table, festooned with footy magazines.

'Ten years ago. We weren't very close,' Peter replied finding his vision drawn to a framed Monet print that hung on the wall to the left of the television. Why was he looking at it now when he always did his best not to. He hated it but never disclosed that to Michelle. She had bought it as a gift to celebrate their first year together. Peter remembered that he had bought nothing. Michelle had been so upset that he had taken her to the Tote for a counter meal.

Looks like someone spewed everywhere. That doesn't look like a garden.

'I'll stay with you tonight. You look upset,' Michelle said as she slid across the couch to Peter. She squeezed his hand for a response but Peter didn't reciprocate. His eyes remained fixed on the picture.

'I'm fine. I just have to ring Bob and tell him I'll need time off for three or four days,' Peter remarked

'It's no trouble, Peter. I'm always here for you. You know that I lo...' Michelle leant across to kiss him on the lips. Peter was off the couch before she could reach him.

'What's wrong? You're acting like your grandmother tried to kiss you.' Peter went to the Monet picture and removed it from the wall. He handed it to Michelle.

'Why did you do that?' Michelle asked in a confused tone of voice.

'This picture is really annoying me at the moment,' Peter stated as he paced about.

'That's our picture.'

'I need space at the moment. I don't like you clinging to me. It's annoying.'

'I want to help you. I know what grief is like. I lost my grandfather last year.'

'Michelle, I don't want your sympathy, all right? I just want you to leave me alone.'

'I don't understand,' Michelle replied, hurt.

Peter sat on the couch with arms folded. He turned to Michelle. 'I want you to leave. Please.' Peter's voice quivered. 'I need space.'

'It helps if you talk about your grief, Peter. Don't bottle it up.' Michelle sat closely to Peter and attempted to hold him. Peter jumped off the couch again.

'I don't want to talk. I want to be alone. Don't you fucking get it?' Peter snapped.

Michelle burst out crying then removed herself from the couch. She grabbed her handbag and the Monet picture.

'Fine. If you want it like that. Fine. I'm tired of your moods, Peter. I want some commitment. I'm tired of you treating me like this. I don't know what happened between you and your mother but this is not how you deal with it.'

Michelle headed for the door. Peter sat back on the couch.

'You won't see me again, Peter,' Michelle warned as she opened the door. She hovered for a moment in the doorway as if waiting for a change of heart from Peter.

'Fine,' she said before she finally slammed the door.

Peter lay down on the couch and stared at the blank television screen then at the space where the Monet picture had hung. An emptiness came over him. He had felt like this many times in his life. He reached for the beer that had grown warm on the coffee table. He took a deep drink, vainly hoping that it might fill that emptiness. It didn't. It never did.

2

Townsville basked under a sweltering, clammy pall as Peter walked across the blazing tarmac towards the comfort of the terminal, removing the layers of Melbourne clothing as he went. He felt like he was a cold sausage dropped in a scorching fry pan. By the time he had reached the terminal his clothes were already sticky with sweat. *What a place to have a hangover. A man could die of dehydration on the tarmac.*

A large sign assaulted his sight as he entered the airport lounge, 'Welcome To Townsville: Capital of North Queensland.'

Has anyone not told these people? It's not a separate state. Then again? Maybe it is. I wouldn't know. I left this place behind a long time ago. Thank God.

After retrieving his bag from the carousel, Peter surveyed his surroundings. He observed that most people were wearing clothes they'd wear around a pool. They weren't bustling, rather sauntering. Meet the locals. To the outsider they could have been tourists but tourists went to Cairns. Cairns was the tourist Mecca but Townsville seemed to be the thong capital of Australia, Peter observed as he walked towards the car hire counter. Already feeling intimidated by the strange surroundings and the curious stares from the locals, which said, *What are you doing here? And why are you dressed in long slacks and a long-sleeved shirt?* Peter would have made a quick exit after picking up the hire car but then he spotted a bar.

A quick reviver before hitting the road. No harm in that.

'Not open yet, mate. Another half-hour,' an extraordinarily hirsute man slurred from a chair near the front door of the bar.

'Going to the Isa. I need a drink. Hate planes,' the hairy man complained.

Peter noted that the man was wearing a casual tropical ensemble: singlet, torn shorts and a pair of worn-out thongs, and a large scar across his forehead. A PFO scar, most likely. *Pissed and fell over,* in medical parlance. Peter once dated a nurse. He knew the medical jargon. Peter thought of waiting but when the man approached him to engage in conversation Peter decided against it. He wasn't an alcoholic. He didn't need a drink as much as this bloke.

Peter had nearly called Michelle in the morning to apologise after he had rolled off the couch and stepped into a flotsam of empty beer cans. He had changed his mind after having a hair of the dog and realising that he had to be at the airport in thirty minutes.

Clarkes Flat was two hours from Townsville via air-conditioned hire car, which he had booked from Melbourne. He remembered the road. A long monotonous pot- holed bitumen strip running through a vista of monotonous bushland. The only visual relief was shot-out advertising signs and dead kangaroos killed by hurtling road trains carrying their cargoes of cattle. He was dreading the drive. At least the car would be air-conditioned and a cold six-pack as a travelling companion would get him there in a measure of comfort.

'No. We don't have air-conditioned cars. They should have made you aware of that in Melbourne,' an officious man wearing a scratchy toupee lisped loudly at Peter from behind the car hire counter. If Peter had have not been so annoyed he would have found the man's apparel amusing: tropical shirt, white hipster shorts and long white socks. Formal tropical wear.

'Why don't you have air-conditioned cars? This is the tropics,' Peter argued. The officious man was trying to serve the next customer but Peter was in his face again.

'Sir, if you're after air-conditioning, I suggest you roll the windows down. You'll get used to it. We have,' the clerk declared looking at the gathered queue behind Peter for affirmation.

Peter would have liked to emphasise to this jumped-up little clerk that he was born in the North, his family helped develop the North, but the next customer was growing impatient. Peter was sure someone said, 'Bloody Mexican,' as he slunk away from the counter with a key to an un-air-conditioned car in his hand.

How bloody ironic. An outsider in the land of my birth.

Feeling like he had arrived in a hostile country, Peter was happy to be leaving Townsville. But not quite yet. As soon as he could touch the scorching-hot steering wheel that had threatened to burn the skin off his hand he'd get the fuck out of here. The only thing that Peter remembered with fondness about Townsville was that his grandparents used to live here, and he would visit them from the station on holidays. He enjoyed the walks along the Strand with his grandfather. He didn't remember how fucking boiling hot it was.

A fucking cauldron. It's the winds of hell blowing through this oven of a car.

After grabbing a six-pack from a seedy hotel on the Strand, he was on his way, chilling his hands on an icy can and cooling himself with each sip, as he emptied the contents down his throat as he drove. Peter touched the dashboard. So hot you could make toasted sandwiches on it.

The trip to Clarkes Flat was, in a sense, both eventful and uneventful at the same time. Peter's awakening to the deafening horn of a road-train as it tore towards him when his car meandered along in the middle of the road was decidedly eventful. His overcorrection of the steering wheel as he dodged the heavy metal missile, careered off the road and then came to a halt centimetres short of hitting a large ghost gum, was indeed eventful also. The counting of dead, marinating kangaroos as Peter drove along the unbending road wasn't, neither were the micro-naps he had taken. *Roo count: twenty (including skeletons). Micro-naps: ditto.*

He felt grave with apprehension. It increased with each kilometre that he drew closer to Clarkes Flat. It wasn't only because his mother had died. Peter was going back. If Peter had had a mantra it would have certainly been: *Don't look back. Never look back. That's what rear view mirrors are for.* Going back to Clarkes Flat would be like going back into an empty room to look for something that you wish had been there. Peter wished that he had bought more than one six-pack for companionship. The one he had brought was now empty and the cans were strewn across the floor of the passenger side.

Peter was relieved when he saw the Clarkes Flat welcome sign on the outskirts of town. He didn't have another micro-nap left in him. If he fell asleep again, he wouldn't wake up for a day. And he was out of beer. A bullet-pocked sign proclaimed in faded lettering, 'Gold Heritage Town, population 2000'. Graffitied underneath were the words, 'Too many Abos.' Nothing had changed.

King Street looked more threadbare and dull since he had last seen it. Several shops were boarded up, including Clarkes Flat's only non-alcoholic entertainment venue, the Regent picture theatre. In its heyday in the 1890s, Clarkes Flat had been a bustling gold mining town boasting fifty hotels and a population of twenty thousand. Now it survived on the local meat works and two boarding schools. It did have a brief resurgence during World War Two when American servicemen were based here. Myth had it that the town had the easiest gals in Australia, especially the married ones. In the 1950s a forgettable Australian movie called *The Wallaby Boy* had been made around the town starring a forgettable actor, who had gone on a bender during the shoot.

Peter slowed down as an inebriated white woman staggered across the street in front of him followed by a wailing barefooted boy. They had just come from the Royal Hotel, an infamous landmark of the town. The Royal was the only pub for many years where the Aborigines were allowed to drink. It was the scene of many fights, including the town's last murder when the publican had shot a male Aboriginal patron in the public bar in the 1960s. Peter stared at the ragged boy who was now trying to help his mother across the road and onto the footpath. Peter was going so slowly that the car was stalling. He changed gear and sped up, still looking at the boy helping his mother negotiate her way along the street.

3

Clarkes Flat, Tuesday afternoon

Peter remembered his mother's house, Arkinholme, as he turned into the street. Once a Scottish mine-owner's house during the gold rush, it had emitted stately charm and class distinction. With Victorian splendour and the tropics in mind, the house was double-storied and surrounded by a wide veranda where you could sleep on hot nights. Its best feature was an English oak staircase with an ornately carved balustrade. The house was known as the Grand Lady. Peter wondered what state Arkinholme would be in now.

His mother Irene had purchased the house after selling their station, Cornish Downs, when his father died following a fall from a horse. The grounds had been covered in a lush lawns, bottles brushes and a line of jacaranda trees. A large palm had stood in the front garden with a marble birdbath underneath. A Grecian-style statue stood watch near the wrought-iron front gate. Irene had enjoyed entertaining the elite of the town until a series of bad investments. The elite drifted onto more fertile pastures, and Irene's alcohol dependency had increased and her behaviour more accusatory and depressed. The Grand Lady fell on hard times. Irene was unwilling to sell and unable to afford maintenance. Peter had no interest in maintaining the house. What should have been a stately solace from the stifling town and the regimentation of his school became a place of detention and Irene his jailer. He had to escape. Break out. Move far away from Clarkes Flat and forget he had ever lived there. If Arkinholme had been in Melbourne he might have felt different about it. If his mother had been different? If his father had not died? All ifs. He stopped the car out front and got out. He was not prepared for the state of the house. Worse than he had could have imagined. Years of neglect and advancing age had further taken its toll on the Grand Lady. The statue's head was broken. The wrought gate was gone. The yard was denuded of grass, the jacaranda trees were lifeless stalks, the palm tree now a stump. The fountain gone. The house was covered in peeling paint. Guttering falling down. It was a gloomy, dying façade.

Peter climbed the front stairs that shook as he tentatively ascended. He had just stepped over a missing tread when he realised that he did not possess a set of keys. Peter walked gently on the veranda, observing that some of the flooring cracked under him. The front door was locked. Peter started prising a familiar window; the same one he used to open when he came home late and Irene had locked him out. An elderly woman's voice calling from the bottom of the stairs startled him.

'Can I help you?' Peter turned and walked gingerly over the veranda to the top of the stairs. Peter recognised Maud Larsen, an effervescent, blue-rinsed widow who had been his mother's long-time neighbour.

'Mrs Larsen, it's Peter.'

'Peter,' Maud said cheerfully, 'I'll go around the back. Those stairs are due to collapse any day now. One of those Jehovah's Witnesses fell through them and injured himself. He reported it to the council. They have to be pulled down. The cheek of him,' Maud recalled without drawing breath.

'Don't worry,' Peter replied, 'I'll come down.'

Peter negotiated his way back down the broken stairs to meet her. Maud hugged Peter and he reciprocated by carefully patting her on the back.

'I didn't recognise you, Peter. It must be ten years. You poor thing. What a reason to come home. You…'

'I don't have any keys,' Peter was able to interrupt Maud's rushed announcement.

'I have a key with me,' Maud gave the key to Peter and continued talking.

'I'm so sorry about your mother. I found her dead in bed. She must have had a heart attack. What a shock. When you're going to go that's the best way. I used to check on her everyday. Make sure she was eating and taking care of herself. The Blue Nurses used to visit…'

'When…' Peter's attempt to interject failed. Maud had regathered her momentum. 'But your mother's at peace now. She'll be up there with your father. Always spoke about Dick. Oh, and you, of course. She was so proud of you. A job at *The Age* in Melbourne.'

'It's *The Truth*, Mrs Larsen.' Peter reply silenced Maud momentarily. Peter was afraid that Mrs Larsen was only gathering impetus for the next verbal onslaught. Could he ever escape? A half-breed dog ran excitedly to Peter from under the house and sniffed him. Peter pushed the dog away.

'That's Bindy. Your mother's dog. I bought her from the pound to keep your mother company and keep the house safe.'

'She's not a very good watchdog. She didn't bark at me.'

'She knows you're a friend,' Maud replied.

'Mrs Larsen, I'm very tired. Can you tell me when the funeral is?

'You didn't know? I thought your cousin would have told you. It's at Saint Anthony's tomorrow at eleven.'

'I'll see you there,' Peter was already ascending the stairs before Maud could reply.

'Did you want to come for dinner? There's little food in the house'

'No thanks,' Peter replied before closing the door.

A curtain disintegrated in his hands as he pushed it aside to open a window in the kitchen in a hurried attempt to illuminate the house and remove the foetid air. The house reeked of mothballs, rotting food and animal fats. The stove had a frying pan sitting on it with a greyish sausage drowned in a lump of sebaceous, rancid-smelling fat.

Mum's last meal. Ate a sausage and a chop with boiled peas and beans for sure. All by herself. This sausage was for later. Supper. After another beer.

Peter looked in the sink for confirmation. A saucepan with green water sat in it.

Peter poured out the saucepan. The stink of the frypan was overwhelming. He grabbed it, opened the window and threw it out, hoping the dog would take care of it. He plodded over to look in the fridge and found it filled with deposits of leftover food in Tupperware containers, pushed in among the full beer bottles and half-drunk ones. Peter took out one of the full bottles, opened it and walked around the house drinking. Not his brand but it would help allay his overwhelming thirst.

The furniture and carpet were shabby and tired, worn out by the years and neglect. He remembered his mother having the house renovated with the most modern touches that the 1960s could provide. Peter opened the lounge room that was covered now in cobwebs and gloom. The wooden stereogram sat in the corner as if waiting to be played. Peter brushed off the dust and opened the lid. A record sat on the turntable. It was by one of her favourite singers: Tom Jones. How many times had he heard the oily-voiced singer thinking he was being tortured? She had played it every time she had had a few too many. Too many was when she wanted to dance to Tom Jones.

'Dance with me,' Irene would slur as she bounced into his room unannounced to grab him away from his homework or reading. She would press him into the lounge and push him around in a jive. Peter's reluctance to follow would soon frustrate Irene and she would cut him loose to go solo. Occasionally she would knock over a table, sending an ornament crashing.

Having moved into town and feeling alone, Irene's attention was strangely comforting. It was the only occasion Irene ever made physical contact. When he grew older he wanted nothing more to do with his mother; he didn't even want to be in the same room as her. The last time she had tried to dance with him was when he was fifteen. He was lying on his bed reading when she had attempted to grab him off the bed. Peter had refused to move. He had laughed when he had seen her cry. He was still laughing when she ran from the room.

Mum's last dance and nobody was there.

Peter took the record off the turntable and returned it to its battered cover. He closed the lid of the stereo.

Three photographs still hung proudly on the lounge room wall despite the years of decay around them — his parents wedding picture, his graduation picture and one he had not seen on display before. Peter tentatively removed the mysterious photograph from the wall and inspected it. It was a black and white photograph of his parents and him as a boy. His father was holding his hand. Peter turned the photograph around and found an inscription on the back in his mother's copperplate writing: *At the show 1968, our last photo together*. Peter stared at the inscription for a moment then returned the photograph to its place.

Irene's bedroom door was closed. Peter opened it and peered in from the doorway. He had never set foot in this room. The room smelt of mothballs, lavender and port wine. An empty glass sat on the bedside table along with a bottle of anginine tablets. The bed had being remade after Irene body's had been taken away, but the pillow was still creased. Peter closed the door.

He was starting to feel exhausted and was hoping that his room was habitable enough to sleep in. He opened the door to his old room was instantly transported. He was a teenager again. He had not been in this room since he had finished university. Posters of his 1970s favourite bands still hung on the wall — Led Zeppelin, Deep Purple, Black Sabbath — the dinosaurs of rock.

Peter looked closely at the posters. It appeared that fresh sticky tape had been applied to them to keep them attached to the wall. Those very same bands that his mother had referred to as a mob of crazed drug-addicts. His favourite books still sat on the shelf — all of the Leon Uris books; *Ulysses* with a bookmark sticking out of the pages (only half-read); *Lord of the Flies*. Peter's ancient typewriter still had paper in it. The bed had a clean bedcover. Peter opened the cupboard to find his old clothes still there. Overwhelmed by the thought that Irene must have cleaned this room regularly, Peter put down the unfinished beer and collapsed on the bed, sinking into a deep sleep and dreaming of a past he had long forgotten about.

PART TWO

4

Maxwell Hillard had only just returned to his parent's farm on the Atherton Tablelands after a series of phone pleadings from his mother. He wasn't bothered that his father was dying and wanted to make amends. The old bastard could rot in hell for all Maxwell cared. It was for his mother — his long-suffering, placating mother who had had to suffer his father's wrath for thirty years. He only came home for her.

At least, he had being able to escape the drudgery of the dairy farm to join the police force and limit his visits home to once a year. Poor mum. Wanted his forgiveness? *Too late for that,* Max thought, as he drove down the muddy driveway, past the Friesian cows grazing in the paddock and towards a wooden farmhouse that always seemed covered in mildew and despair.

Max's mother, Gertrude Hillard, or Gerty as everyone in the district called her, was standing at the rusted front gate as if he was coming home for Christmas holidays when he pulled up. Getting out of the car, Max thought that she looked like a fragile doll. His mother had always been a diminutive woman; in fact Max had outgrown her by the age of eleven. But the Hillard men were big men and most people looked small compared to them. The Hillards were descended from tall and proud Bavarian stock; broad-shouldered and broad angled faces with long noses and piercing blue eyes. Enormous heads topped off with blond hair, sitting on a bear-like body.

Max gave his mother a sympathetic look as he came towards her. She appeared more stooped and grey since the last time he had seen her, still wearing her apron like a uniform. *Still keeping the ship from sinking.*

'Did you have a good trip?' Gerty asked meekly as she went to embrace Max. He reached out and enveloped her tiny body, his bear-arms wrapping themselves around her osteoporotic back until she all but disappeared.

'I needed that,' she said, patting him on the sway of his back as Max loosened his embrace. They continued together towards the house, Max in a brisk, marching walk, his mother trotting behind.

'Much as can be expected when you have to drive overnight from Mackay,' he finally remarked as he scraped his boots on a wire mat. He glanced back when he noticed his mother was immediately behind him. He stood aside to allow her to go ahead of him into the house.

'Not forgotten your manners, Maxwell, I see,' Gerty chirped proudly.

The front of the house reeked with the familiar smells of stale tobacco and damp as he entered straight into the lounge room. Shabby furniture positioned around a cold, brick fireplace. A pipe sitting in an ashtray on a table signalled his father's domain. An ancient sepia picture of his grandfather, Otto, sporting a bushy moustache hung above the table.

Gerty kept walking in the direction of a ray of light that entered through a pane window in the kitchen at the back of the house. The scent of baking and doughy warmth grew stronger. Mother's domain. An Aga stove radiated heat and comfort as they entered the kitchen. She turned off a transistor radio that sat on the window ledge and opened the oven door, taking out a tray of scones. She placed them on the table then attended to a kettle that was starting to boil.

'Cup of tea and scones?' Gerty asked as she deftly served the scones, pot of tea, jam and butter all in a series of sharp manoeuvres to Max, who sat cross-legged at the table.

'I'm glad you could come,' she continued. 'He'll be happy to see you. Cup of tea?'

'No thanks. Not yet,' Max said brusquely, 'I'll get him out of the way first.'

'I've baked scones,' Gerty said.

'How's he going?' Max asked as he looked at the inviting tray of scones. Gerty ignored Max and poured him a cup of tea, added the milk and sugar and served him a scone. She then sat down to serve herself.

'You have to eat something, Maxwell,' she admonished when she noticed Max was only sipping at his tea. She cut his scone, buttered it and smeared it with jam, placing the plate in front of him. After watching his mother perform this custom, which he had known since childhood, Max finally relented and placed half a scone in his mouth. Gerty nodded with satisfaction.

'The doctor said he has only days to live. The cancer's in his brain,' she replied as she popped a morsel of scone into her own mouth.

'What's he like?' he asked as he chewed. 'Still being a mongrel?'

'Mind your language,' Gerty chastised. 'The morphine keeps him quiet.' Her gaze softened.

'Maybe he should have started morphine years ago,' Max replied bitterly, looking away from his mother.

'He wants to make amends. He told me. It's time to forgive.' Gerty patted his knee.

'We'll see.'

'For me. Please?' she implored.

The ringing of a bell and a loud groan emanating from the bedroom interrupted their conversation.

'That's him.' Gerty stiffened. 'Probably wants to be turned.' She clenched her hands and rose from the chair. Max motioned for her to sit.

'Sit down. I'll take care of it, Mum. You need a rest.' Gerty looked puzzled for a moment then sat down again.

'He doesn't look like the man you knew. He looks like a skeleton.'

'It's fine, Mum,' Max replied as he stood and reached to his full height of six feet three inches. 'I've seen some messy things in the police force.'

'It may be upsetting,' she continued. 'I'll help you.' The bell rang again.

'Still impatient I see,' Max remarked. 'No, Mum,' he insisted, holding up his hand to block her from following him. He smiled at her and continued towards the bedroom.

Herman Hillard, or what remained of him, lay propped on a layer of pillows, his waxy, pale skin illuminated by a bedside lamp which cast shadows around the semi-darkened room and against the closed curtains. Herman was staring upwards with eyes like luminous pools in a head that looked as if it had decayed around them. Herman cranked his head in Max's direction as he entered the room. He was suddenly consumed by spasms of coughing as he tried to speak. He motioned for Max to grab the bottle of water from a bedside table. Max stood over him, ignoring Herman's request momentarily, but relented when Herman's withered arm waved more frantically. Max was surprised at how frightened his father looked. Max reached for the bottle and placed it in Herman's hand. He tried to lift it to his mouth but his hand fell. The coughing started to subside. Max took the bottle and placed it in Herman's mouth. He sipped a few mouthfuls delicately then stopped as if expended of all energy.

'You're here,' Herman croaked. 'Good.'

Max continued to stare at the cadaverous spectre of the man who had routinely flogged him from a very young age until the age of sixteen, every Saturday afternoon with a belt. He remembered the beatings his mother had received. He remembered how she cowered like a dog on the kitchen floor as Herman lay into her with his fists. He recalled the day he had grabbed the belt from his father and thrown it away. The fight that erupted had Max having the better of Herman, until Gerty had thrown herself screaming between them. Not long after that, Max had left the farm to join the police force, but not until he had warned his father that if he ever hit his mother again, he would kill him.

'You were right to join the police force.' Herman motioned for Max to sit beside him on the bed. Max sat down slowly at Herman's feet. 'There was no life for you on this miserable farm. I was a bastard to you and your mother. A right bastard.'

He started to weep, leaving Max taken aback. Herman allowed the tears to run down his face. Max had never seen his father cry or even laugh, only anger and brooding silence. He tried to touch Max's hand but it was too far to reach.

'My father was the same,' Herman continued. 'A hard man. He nearly killed my brother once.'

'And that's your excuse for how you treated Mum and me, you old cunt,' Max fumed. He rose from the bed, clenching his fists and moved towards the head of the bed.

'I wanted to say sorry, son. I want your forgiveness,' Herman said, sounding frightened as he looked at Max towering over him.

Isn't this all a bit too late? Max thought as he continued to clench and unclench his fists. I thought of killing you so many times. It was only mum that stopped me. I didn't want to see her sad.

He sat with Herman into the night, moving the pillows from time to time.

'Get your mother,' Herman gasped as he clawed for the bell. Max leant down and pulled the bell from Herman's spindly fingers, as he tried to move his wasted legs but only managing a rubbing motion under the sheets before collapsing. Herman opened his mouth to yell but merely emitted a muffled cry. His withered arms struggled and scratched vainly against the pillows. In time the struggle grew less.

'You don't deserve a peaceful death like this,' Max said calmly, 'But I didn't want you to die without me being part of it.' Herman's arms fell limp.

Good riddance, Herman. Rest in hell.

5

Cornish Downs Station, 1964

Peter at age seven didn't know or care that he was the fourth generation Clancy at Cornish Downs and that he would one day inherit a vast cattle station. Until that day, the station would remain in the capable hands of his father, Dick Clancy.

In his younger days Dick had been a keen fighter, carouser and drinker but his wife had gentled him. Occasionally, when he was displeased, that dark mood could still flash across his face like fire and cause men to wither under his gaze. The locals always blamed Dick's temperament on his Irish-Catholic ancestry but, of course, did not dare say as much to his face. They knew he was descended from sterner stuff.

Dick's great-grandfather and great-grandmother, Patrick and Bridget Clancy, had settled in the area a hundred years earlier, after a long and perilous journey on a bullock dray all the way from the Hunter Valley. They had survived the horrors of the Irish Famine and were determined to do all in their powers to never again be penniless and starving. So while Patrick operated a bullock dray supplying the stations inland from Bowen, Bridget operated a hotel. They quickly made their fortune and decided to buy a rundown cattle property called Cornish Downs, which fronted the Suttor River. The previous owners had been attacked several times by the local Aborigines and were keen to sell at any price. The Clancys were lambasted around Bowen for what was regarded as a foolhardy decision.

'Those Irish, not very smart, I'm afraid.'

'They'll be dead in a few weeks.'

'Blacks will spear them. No doubt about that.'

But the Clancys carried on regardless and settled on their new acquisition, setting up their meagre possessions in a slab hut near the Suttor. Patrick had been advised to shoot first if the 'blacks' came near the house but the Clancys had seen too many people, including close members of their families, die of starvation and disease to want to see wholesale death again.

It was one late afternoon when as a group of Aborigines, who had gathered around a fire roasting a newly killed kangaroo, were surprised by a nippy Irishman wearing a battered bowler hat approaching them and leading a horse bearing the hindquarter of a freshly slaughtered steer. The men raised their spears but soon understood, through Patrick's crude hand signals, that he would feed them and everyone could live in peaceful co-existence.

The co-existence flourished and the men helped Patrick muster and yard his stock, while the women delivered two of the five Clancy children and helped Bridget look after the expanding Clancy tribe. Tragedy struck a few years later when disease swept through the Aboriginal settlement, killing many. When the survivors were rounded up and exiled to the penal colony of Palm Island, Patrick and Bridget tried desperately to save them, but to no avail. They did manage to hide several survivors in the hills while the Native Police made their round-ups. But Patrick was broken by the trauma he had sustained here and in Ireland, and he died at the tender age of forty. He had begun the Clancy dynasty that survived fire, drought, flood and depression, and proudly claimed four hundred square miles of river country as its own. Patrick's legacy now rested firmly on the broad shoulders of Dick Clancy and in a decade or two, Peter would take the reins from his father.

The one thing Peter did know, however, was that he hated school that came via correspondence and was delivered by his mother or the occasional governess. Irene laboured hard to get any fragment of knowledge to enter Peter's the stubborn head, who appeared to take on the semblance of a statue whenever she asked him a question. He was only interested when she read stories to him. *Treasure Island* was a favourite. Peter's 'I don't know,' replies were enough one day. Irene snapped and grabbed Peter by the hair hitting his head repeatedly with her palms.

'You're so dumb,' she yelled repeatedly as she pounded.

Fortunately for Peter, Dick in the stockyards heard Irene's cries and Peter's wailing and rushed into the house just as Peter fell across the desk.

'You're killing the boy, Irene,' Dick roared as Irene was picking up a ruler ready to flay Peter's prostrate body. He pulled the ruler from her hand and threw it across the room.

'I can't take it. I can't take it,' Irene cried as she collapsed into Dick's arms. Dick pushed her aside and she stood rigid, clutching her hands to her face. Dick shook Peter who quickly came to. He held onto Dick tightly.

'Don't let mummy hurt me,' he begged as Irene ran from the room. From that day Dick would employ a governess until Peter could be sent to boarding school.

But employing a governess had created another dilemma for Dick and Irene. Peter didn't want to sit still and be bored at a desk learning sums and reading while he could be outside. He wanted to be a stockman like his father. Peter also knew that the governess would never hit him. Peter's first governess had left under a cloud after she was caught in bed with one of the stockmen. Peter's second governess, Kathy from Canada, was travelling around Australia when she had answered an advertisement Peter's mother had run in the paper. She was gentle and diligent and rarely raised her voice at Peter. He liked her but he still didn't want to be tied to a desk. It was worse when Dick went out on an overnight mustering trip. Irene had suggested that Peter be physically tied to the desk but Kathy thought that was cruel. So Kathy had learnt not to take her eyes off him.

One morning she made a mistake by going to her bedroom to collect an album of photographs of her home in Canada. She thought he would be interested enough to stay at his desk. Kathy was wrong. There was an empty desk on her return and a note scrawled: *Sorry Kathy, I'm a ringer. Dad needs me.*

Sam Saturday was cracking a whip over a breakaway steer when he spotted Peter emerging from a stand of trees and moving through the grass that he barely stood over. Sam galloped to Peter once he had settled the steer back in the mob.

'What are you doing out here young fella? You should be at school,' Sam said as he brought his horse to a halt.

'I don't want to, Sam. I want to be with dad and you,' Peter replied.

'You're too young little, mate,'

'Please, Sam,' Peter pleaded. Sam squinted at the boy.

'You've got two choices. You can stay with here and get a belting from your father who's down in the creek mustering or go home and get a belting from your mum.'

Peter thought deeply before replying. 'I guess Mum would be better. She doesn't hit as hard as Dad.'

'You better get out of here quick before your dad catches you. Otherwise you'll get two beltings.'

Peter took off back through the grass as fast as his skinny, scabby legs could carry him. He entered the kitchen in the late afternoon, hoping that he would be able to sneak food from the fridge and be able to scamper up to his bedroom without anyone noticing.

'Look at you. You look like a black boy,' Irene chastised as she pounced on him from behind a cupboard. Peter was dishevelled, wounded and shoeless, his shirt torn from a disagreement with a blackberry bush. He spun quickly and covered his head instinctively, as Irene rained blows on his head with the familiar wooden ruler.

'Where have you been? Kathy has been worried sick.'

'At the river with the dogs,' Peter cried between blows.

'You're going to drown or a wild pig will rip your guts out. Either way, I won't mourn for you.'

'I'll talk to him, Mrs Clancy,' Kathy interrupted in her soft Canadian drawl. Irene dropped the ruler and started to cry.

'I don't know what to do anymore. He's like a wild animal. I'll have to send him to boarding school. The Christian Brothers won't tolerate this kind of behaviour.' Peter stood motionless, looking at Kathy for help.

'I'll see what I can do, Mrs Clancy,' Kathy replied putting her arm around Peter.

'His father's too busy with the station. It's all left to me.'

Kathy put her other arm around Irene. 'It can't be easy living out here, having to do everything yourself.'

'If the town people only knew. And it's not helped by having a child that wants to live like a black.'

6

Clarkes Flat, 1965

Irene and Dick Clancy sat in the lounge of the Crown Hotel, comforted and relaxed by the cold beer and their long time friends, Ted Carrington, the local car dealer, Reg Sweeny, stock and station agent and John Tindall, owner of the saleyards. The Clancys had arrived at nine in the morning after driving for three hours from Cornish Downs over a dirt road laced with gullies and gates. Peter enjoyed opening the twenty gates and relished the time away from correspondence school. Peter always knew when they were getting closer to Clarkes Flat when Irene would remove a comb from her handbag and briskly comb his hair. She also checked that he was still wearing his shoes.

They had followed their usual circuitous route, picking up groceries and station supplies from Salmon's country store, then Alford's department store for clothing and manchester and then the Crown Hotel, the highpoint of their visit, for lunch and liquid diversion. Afternoons were free to catch up with friends and the news. Despite his constant bitter complaints, Peter had to be content with a visit to Boland's toy store with his father sometime after lunch. This depended on how much his father was distracted by the ambiance of the Crown Hotel and his drinking mates. Peter usually went to the store by himself.

Irene and Dick had not been into town for three months and by three in the afternoon were enjoying the company and endless drinks. As befitting their status in the area, the Clancys dressed as if they were attending a soiree at government house. Dick was wearing a long-sleeved shirt, tie and long pants. The tie had become looser as the day had worn on.

Today Irene was resplendent in a pillbox hat, pearl necklace and gloves that highlighted her soft olive skin, which she always kept well covered when she ventured out in the sun. Irene was an attractive woman with high cheekbones and fine features. Some people had unofficially judged her as the best looking woman in the district. She sipped slowly and quietly at her shandy with infrequent wry smiles on her face that were becoming more prolonged as the afternoon progressed. Irene wasn't from the country but had come from Brisbane where she had worked as a nurse. She had asked Dick when he had proposed whether he would he still want to marry her even though she hated horses, couldn't cook and had never been bush, not even to camp out. Dick had replied that he didn't want to marry a stockman or the station cook; he wanted her as she was, the most attractive woman in the room. Irene had slowly adapted to the bush, cooking for the stockmen and helping out in the yards, though she never ventured into the yards with the cattle.

The men smoked, drank and bellowed around her as she sat listening, dutifully aware by now that country men always held sway in conversations. Occasionally she would add a 'that's right' or a 'yes, that's true.' to the men's conversation in a soft voice. At another table, Peter had had enough and tossed the comic he had been reading for the past two hours on the floor. None of the adults noticed Peter's irritation. He got up from his chair and went to his father.

'Dad, when are we going to the toyshop?' Peter asked. 'You said you'd take me.'

Dick was too engrossed in conversation to notice Peter. Peter raised his voice.

'Dad. I want to go to the toyshop.' Dick spun around on his chair and placed his hand around Peter's neck.

'Don't interrupt. Can't you see I'm talking? Why don't you get your mother to take you.'

'I want you to take me. You promised.'

'I'm too busy. Here,' Dick reached into his pocket, pulled out some loose change and handed it to Peter. 'Buy yourself a toy car son,' Dick slurred, turning back to engage again in the conservation.

Peter walked hurriedly along Hocking Street past the dilapidated snooker hall, past the closed stock exchange with its collapsed roof, and the boarded-up Imperial Hotel, all faded reminders of a bygone age. The only shops that were still open were the department store, a fruit shop, the newsagents and Boland's toyshop. The street was largely deserted except for an elderly couple shuffling along the street, a stray dog and a drunken stockman passed out on a bench. Peter's pace accelerated as he drew near to the toyshop and by the time he entered the store he felt he was flying. He surveyed the collection of model airplanes, toy soldiers and miniature cars as if he had discovered a treasure trove. Mr Boland, an elderly man with a pronounced limp as a result of polio, approached Peter from behind the counter.

'Young Clancy. I haven't seen you for a few months. What car do you like today?'

'That one.' Peter pointed.

'Oh yes, the E-type Jaguar. A real beauty, she is.' Mr Boland opened the display case and removed the car. 'How are your parents?' Mr Boland asked, as he rang up the purchase on an ancient cash register.

'Good, Mr Boland.'

'Do you know your father used to come in here when he was waiting for your grandfather at the Crown? Your dad liked toy soldiers.'

Peter pressed his face hard up against the passenger door window, staring through the night's dark halo towards a stand of trees where he could faintly see cattle grazing. As the car swerved about the road, his mother's protestations became louder and his father's voice sounded more slurred. Peter imagined he could fly out through the car like Peter Pan, over the trees, along the river towards a magical land where no one drank and no one argued.

'Careful, Dick. Try and stay on the road, for heaven's sake,' Irene stiffened as the car drifted off the road.

'Don't get your knickers in a knot. I've got it under control,' Dick mumbled as he turned the car back towards the road, missing a gear change.

'Let me drive. I've had less than you,' Irene asked.

'I'm right. Stop your whinging,' Dick replied. The car continued its erratic path along the road. Irene tried to intervene and steer the car when Dick drifted off the road again.

'Get your hand off the bloody steering wheel. You'll cause an accident,' Dick shouted, smacking Irene's hands away.

'You'll kill us, Dick.'

'Shut up, woman. I'll drive like Jack Brabham if I want.' Dick sped up causing Irene to start crying. Peter joined in.

'Please don't, Dick,' Irene begged.

'Don't, Daddy, don't,' Peter added.

'Bugger the lot of you. All I ever hear is you complaining. It gets on a man's nerves.'

Dick failed to negotiate the sharp corner, causing the car to leave the road and carom towards a large tree. Irene leant across Dick, grabbed the steering wheel and pointed it away from a sure catastrophe, as the tree loomed closer. The car crashed into a clump of shrubs and stopped suddenly, causing Peter to be thrown to the floor of the car.

'You stupid bastard,' Irene yelled, punching Dick in the chest. Irene reached across and lifted the wailing Peter off the floor. She hugged him tightly, sobbing.

'You drive then, Irene. Obviously I can't.'

Irene looked up at Dick and shook her head.

Dick bought Irene a gift as an apology. It wasn't a piece of jewellery or a dress. Dick thought of a horse, but Irene didn't like horses, but he knew she had an interest in movies. It was one of her major criticisms about living in the bush: you couldn't go to the cinema every week. So it was an Eastman Kodak Super 8 camera and projector that he ordered via mail from the United States. Surprisingly, Irene had liked her gift and learnt to use and operate the camera with little difficulty. Her only concerns were that it couldn't record sound, and the film had to be sent away to Brisbane for processing. Soon the station became a movie set for Irene, where its tedious routine was recorded, from the yarding and mustering of cattle, swimming at the river, the always anxiously-awaited arrival of the mailman, all the way through to special events, such as Christmas, birthdays and visits from family.

Irene even went to the trouble of taking the camera to Clarkes Flat, to take footage of the annual show. As well as shooting horse events and the grand parade, Irene filmed Dick and Peter riding a dodgem car and a merry-go-round. For the first time in a long time, Dick noticed, Irene looked happy.

7

It was late afternoon when Peter and his little mate, Dave Tindall, drifted outside to a set of swings, away from the noise of the adults who were partying inside the house. Peter's parents were in town for the annual show and usually stayed for the week, spending a day at the show and then catching up with friends in the evening. Tonight they were enjoying drinks and a meal at the Tindall's, the Clancys' closest friends. Max Hillard had turned up unexpectedly for dinner in his uniform. He had taken the boys for a drive in a police car after dinner and had even let Dave turn on the siren, which scared Peter.

Peter sat on the swing holding his mother's Super 8 camera.

'What's that?' Dave asked, pointing at the camera. Dave was the same age as Peter but stood half a head taller and was more solid then Peter.

'It's my mum's movie camera,' Peter replied kicking off his shoes.

'Where did you get it?'

'Out of her bag,' Peter replied as he fiddled with it.

'You'll get in trouble.'

'I don't care. I want to take some pictures,' Peter stated confidentially.

'Do you know how?'

'Of course I do. I watch Mum.' Peter pointed the camera at Dave and turned it on. It made a whirring sound.

'Show me?' Dave asked. Peter zoomed in on Dave and told him to wave.

'Wow! Can I have a go?' Dave asked.

'Only if you don't drop it.' Peter handed the camera carefully to Dave. Peter gave him brief instructions and Dave pointed the camera at Peter as he swung back and forth.

'Slow down,' Dave said, 'I can't keep up,'

They both heard the sound of men's voices talking softly, coming from the house towards them. Peter stopped. Dave turned off the camera and quickly gave it back to Peter.

'I'm going,' Dave said anxiously.' I don't want to get in trouble.'

Dave ran back into the house, avoiding the men by ducking behind the old iron garage. Peter resisted the urge to escape, imagining himself a combat cameraman like he had seen on the news about Vietnam. He crouched near the swing as the two men walked past him to a set of trees at the back fence. He held up the camera and turned it on. Peter could see two men silhouetted in the trees but couldn't *recognise* them — maybe Mr Tindall or Mr Sweeney? He just couldn't tell, despite the outdoor light above the back door illuminating their silhouettes. Their voices grew louder when they reached the trees. Peter kept the camera going even though he could barely see them. One of the voices sounded nervous, the other sounded threatening. They fell quiet when a third man trotted out of the house. He joined the other two and, although Peter couldn't make out what they were saying, the three men seemed friendly enough. That was until they started to argue.

The film ran out and Peter dropped the camera. It made a clanging sound as it hit the seat of the swing. Looking around furtively, he picked up the camera and stowed it under his arm. The men stopped talking and strode as a group silently back to the house. Peter narrowed his eyes in an attempt to recognise them. He thought that maybe one of them was his father.

8

Clarkes Flat, December, 1968

Nipper Coleman's blobby body was quivering like jelly as he lay astride his favourite barmaid, Thelma, in one of the spare guest rooms at the Royal Hotel, fucking and panting like a thirsty dog. Thelma lay there nonchalantly blowing cigarette smoke from the corner of her mouth as Nipper struggled towards his orgasm.

'Come on, big fella,' Thelma said in her husky smoker's voice, 'you're on the vinegar stroke.'

'Shut up, Thel,' Nipper panted. 'I'll lose me concentration. I'm getting close.'

Suddenly there was a crashing sound and a series of raised voices and shouting coming from the public bar downstairs.

'What the hell is happening downstairs?' Nipper asked as he slowed his stride and listened.

'It's just another fight. Those bloody blacks.' Thelma glanced at her watch. 'You better finish. Isn't your Missus due home soon?' Thelma stubbed out the cigarette and reached for another one.

'Good one, Thelma, it's gone. Me fat's gone,' Nipper grumbled as he looked towards his groin. Nipper got off Thelma, wiped himself on the sheet and proceeded to dress himself in nothing but a faded Hawaiian shirt.

'Why did you have to mention the blacks and my wife in the same sentence?' Nipper complained. 'A bloody turn-off.'

'Where are you going?' Thelma asked dragging her emaciated frame out of the bed. 'You'll get it back with a little oral. We've got time.' Thelma lowered herself to her knees and started to lift Nipper's gut.

'Don't, Thel.' Nipper pulled away from Thelma when the noise grew louder. ' I better check out what going on.' Nipper found his trousers and started to put them on.

'You worry too much, Nipper.'

'They'd wreck the pub if I let them. What a way to make money! Should have stayed a car salesman,' Nipper said, exasperated as he headed out of the door.

The public bar was a cacophony of sound and frantic activity by the time Max arrived. He stood in the doorway and surveyed the scene before him. Activity began to slow as the crowd started to notice Max's presence. The hullabaloo emanating from the crying patrons on the footpath and the shouting police and ambulance officers quietened as Max walked through the bar, towards a body draped under a blood-soaked white sheet near the jukebox. The floor surrounding the body was slippery with blood. Max stood over the corpse and kicked at one of the shoeless feet that protruded. He leaned down and lifted the sheet, nodding as he inspected the body briefly, then casually dropped the sheet, leaving the top of the head visible. Looking around, Max threw a piercing stare at a fresh-faced constable standing in a state of inertia nearby. The constable drew to attention as Max stepped over the body and approached him.

'Don't just stand there like a stale bottle of piss, Constable,' Max bellowed into the constable's face. 'Get these coons off the footpath.'

'Yes, Sergeant,' the constable quavered. Max looked the constable up and down.

'Harden up, son. You might as well buy a bra now.'

'The man's wife is outside causing a scene. She wants to see the body,' another constable remarked as he approached Max.

'For God's sake. Are we recruiting wet nurses now?' Max roared at the constable. Shaking his head, he put his hand on the young man's shoulder.

'Arrest her! Disorderly conduct. Get it?' Max stated quietly, tapping the constable's face with an index finger.

'Where's Nipper? Max asked, looking at both constables. They looked at each other. 'You don't know where Nipper is?'

'Sorry, Sergeant. In the office over there,' the timid-voiced constable stammered, pointing to a door near the bar.

'Grow some balls, son, or join a bloody convent,' Max advised, slapping the constable on the cheek.

Nipper was in his office, flopped in a chair and attended by Thelma and his wife, Doreen, an overweight matron with lank hair and a flushed face. She was pouring him a drink from a whiskey bottle while Thelma glared jealously at her. Nipper attempted to get off the chair when Max entered the office but collapsed back into it, causing it to creak. Nipper started to cry as Max leant over him. Thelma reached into her jeans pocket, retrieved a handkerchief and handed it to Nipper who blew hard into it then dabbed his eyes. Doreen seethed and seized the glass from Nipper's hand.

'You can wait outside, Thelma,' Doreen ordered through pursed lips. 'You're no longer required.'

Thelma looked imploringly at Nipper who had now focused his attention on Max.

'I'll have a word with Nipper,' Max requested, looking at both women. 'Alone.'

'I'm his wife,' Doreen protested, throwing a withering gaze at Thelma.

'Alone!' Max repeated, slapping his hand on the desk for emphasis. Doreen looked for support from Nipper, which never came.

'Wait outside, alright? I'll be right,' Nipper blubbered and dabbed his eyes again.

'I'll be just outside, love,' Doreen clucked as she gave Nipper a peck on the cheek. Thelma spun on her heels and stormed out.

'Don't get too upset. You have to look after that heart of yours,' Doreen said as she stroked Nipper's hair.

'Doreen,' Nipper growled as he pushed her hand away, 'enough.'

'I'll be just outside,' Doreen said finally as she waddled out of the office. Max started to laugh.

'What's it like having two women fighting over a playboy like you?'

'Sincerely,' Nipper choked, 'it's fucked.' Nipper then broke into a torrent of sobs that were suddenly halted by Max slapping his face.

'What are you crying like a baby for?' Max roared.

'I've just killed a man,' Nipper cried. 'I just wanted to scare him, not kill him.'

'Having your chest blown out by a twelve gauge shotgun would scare anyone to death,' Max grinned. 'That would kill even a coon, although I have seen them survive having a knife put through their head.'

'Blackie Kennedy was always causing trouble here. I'd had enough,' Nipper admitted.

'You'll really be up the proverbial dung river, Nipper, if you say that in court.'

'What do I do then? You tell me! I don't know what to do,' Nipper cried.

'We'll get this sorted out at the station. Get our facts right.'

'What's going to happen to me? Look at me.' Nipper patted his belly that poured over the rim of the chair. 'I'm fat. I've got a crook heart. I'll die in jail. And who's going to run the pub? The missus couldn't run a pub raffle. And Thelma. I just fuck her.'

'You can stop whining for a start,' Max snapped. 'You killed a coon, Nipper. Big deal. If we have our facts right you shouldn't get any jail time.'

'Are you sure?'

'I'm as sure as the first piss in the morning, partner.'

'Partner?'

'Partner,' Max repeated with a soft grin. 'My wife is very entrepreneurial. She's always looking for business opportunities. I don't know how she finds the time. She wants to expand into the hospitality industry. '

'Of course.' Nipper sighed with the realisation that freedom came with a heavy price.

9

The three stockmen steered their horses at a trot through the early morning mist towards a gate in the distance. They displayed a singularity of purpose and manner but the stockier, ruddier one rode slightly ahead of the other two, indicating that he was the leader of the party. The leader halted his horse a short distance from the gate.

One of the followers rolled a cigarette and lit it, while the other hacked and then spat. He also rolled a cigarette. They were both lean and sinewed; their skin parched and cracked, except one had a recently broken nose after an altercation with an angry Brahman bull. The ruddier one spoke first, in a lazy, confident drawl.

'Clancy's got a hundred head of unbranded yearlings in this paddock. I checked the other day when I rode through here.' He leant over the pommel of his saddle to open the gate.

'Do you think Clancy's going to know?' The broken-nosed stockman asked.

'You can fuck off back to the homestead if you haven't got the guts,' the leader spat.

'Of course I've got the guts. I was just asking.'

'He won't notice fifty or so missing. He'll think they died in the bush,' his mate added.

'If you want to make money out here and you don't own a station this is the only way to do it. So are you in or out?' the leader asked.

'Sure. I'm in.'

'The boss and his family are in town for a while and I'm in charge. We'll have them branded and in the saleyards in a couple of days. Clancy has it coming anyway. He sacked me a few years ago for hitting one of his horses.'

The leader kicked his horse and it continued through the gateway. The other two soon followed.

The yearlings were gathered around the dam that was full to capacity. It had been a good season and the cattle looked fat and sleek. The three stockmen rode around the cattle and enveloped them in a pincer before they could decide to escape, then pushed the cattle away from the dam and towards the gateway. The leader stayed at the rear while the other two worked the cattle from the wings. The leader, not content with the slow pace of the cattle, cracked a whip to urge them forward.

Dick Clancy and his stockman, Sam Saturday, were riding the boundary fence checking for breaks when they heard the cracking whip through the morning air. They stopped the horses suddenly, as if hit by a solid force, and listened keenly. Sam spoke first.

'It's over by the dam,' Sam pointed towards the direction of the sound. Sam was a middle-aged Aboriginal man who radiated nobility, despite wearing a battered stockman's hat. His innate bush skills were renowned and bordered on the paranormal. Sam said that he only got guidance from his ancestors who had lived in this country for thousands of years. Every tree, rock formation and creek was woven into Sam's body like DNA. This was his home. One legendary story claimed that Sam once tracked a missing boy for two days through thick scrub and across a running creek. He found the boy semi-conscious under a tree, as two dingoes hovered, waiting for the boy to die. The story was the more fantastic for being true, of course.

'We better check it out,' Dick Clancy boomed and kicked his horse into a canter. Sam followed. Dick was also middle-aged and sat tall and solid in the saddle. He was heavy set and roughly hewn in the face with strong forearms, and the stamina, strength and determination of a man half his age. Dick was known for ability to judge and handle stock, whether cattle or horses. He was never cruel to an animal and had sacked a few stockmen for their cruelty to a horse or a cow. He was also known as a good boss and, if you were a willing to work hard, always fair and approachable.

Dick took the Marlin 30/30 from the saddle holster as he and Sam approached the dam. Sam's head shook with apprehension as Dick raised the rifle into the air and fired. The crack of the rifle scattered the cattle that the three stockmen were steering towards the gateway. One of the stockmen was now trying to control his terrified horse as it galloped towards the scrub.

Sam and Dick moved forward and approached the leader, who turned his horse defiantly towards them. The remaining stockman appeared to have vanished into thin air. Dick lowered the rifle as he approached the leader and pointed it squarely at his chest. The only reaction was a constant fidgeting of the reins.

'You won't be stealing any Clancy cattle today,' Dick snarled, lowering the Marlin.

'Keep your hat on. We were mustering strays.'

'I should shoot you just for lying.' He raised the rifle again.

'Don't, Dick!' Sam gasped.

'You don't want to go to jail, do you?' the leader retorted.

'I know you,' Dick said, studying him. 'You're Jack Perks. I sacked you a few years ago. A piece of shit no one would miss.'

'Are you finished?' Perks asked.

'If I ever see you on my place again I'll drill you without hesitation.'

'You're a big man with a gun, Clancy. You better make sure you always carry it with you. You don't know what can happen to you in the bush.'

Dick fired into the air again. Perks' horse leapt into the air, nearly dislodging him, and galloped madly away, Perks pawing frantically at the loose reins.

10

Clarkes Flat Saleyards, June, 1969

Billy Johnson was a Jack Russell of a man who stood tall at five feet two. He may have been diminutive in height but Billy's personality was larger then life; the jokey mate, the social charmer. Billy was known around Clarkes Flat as a bit of a ladies' man, sometimes running two or three fillies out of his stable at the same time, whether married or single. Billy was obliging to all women he cavorted with and a good mate to their unsuspecting partners. Despite his leisure pursuits, Billy still found time to be a hard worker. Always busy, always up and about early.

Before purchasing the saleyards with his mate, John Tindall, he had been a racing identity in the town, training the odd winner in Townsville and locally. He had had to give it away after been caught nobbling one of his horses. Always first at the saleyards, Billy was drafting cattle in preparation for today's sales. Wearing his customary porkpie hat and leather bomber jacket, he cajoled a mob into a yard with only his flailing arms and a high-pitched voice that could have shredded linoleum. Today was an important day at the saleyards. It was auction day. Tom Fry, the stock auctioneer arrived at seven to see cattle still milling around in the holding yard.

'I don't know what's bloody happened, Bess,' Tom remarked to his blue-heeler dog as he hobbled about on legs that had been broken too many times from falls off horses. Tom was a battle-hardened veteran of the bush; drover, crocodile shooter, station manager and now stock auctioneer. Add to that hero — he had won a DSO at Tobruk for taking out a German machinegun post single-handedly. Tom noticed that Bess was madly sniffing the ground. Bess looked up at Tom, awaiting the next direction.

'Is someone here? Where are they old girl? Get them off their fat arse,' Tom roared. Bess jumped with excitement and galloped towards a demountable hut that had taken on the important role of saleyards office.

'My God. That you Billy? ' Tom muttered when he sighted the body. He staggered backwards nearly losing his balance. Tom could only recognise Billy by his jacket. The pork-pie hat wasn't there nor was the back of his skull; a spongy grey mess covered by flies and black ants was the remnants of Billy's brain.

Billy lay spread-eagled and face down at the doorway of the office, his right hand still clutching a pistol. The torrent of blood that had exploded from Billy's shattered skull had seeped into a coagulated pond around Billy or had sprayed against the office wall. Brain tissue was splattered against the office wall in gelatinous splotches. The office door was open, swinging wildly. A torn pin-up on the back of the door flapped in the breeze. Tom looked up, distracted briefly as the pin-up was torn off the door and swept away in the breeze. Miss January. The door kept banging. Tom clutched his face and started to scream. The scene hurtled him back to his time in the army.

'Stay. Stay, for Christ sakes. The Germans are going to attack,' Tom roared at Bess as she crept forward trying to sniff the body. She sat dutifully, finding a spot in the dirt that wasn't covered in blood.

'Got to get back to our lines. Bloody hell. Bloody hell.' Tom leant down as painlessly as he could, trying to feel a pulse on Billy's wrist that he knew wouldn't be there. He gagged but managed to avoid vomiting by popping a lolly in his mouth that he always carried for Bess; he threw one to Bess.

'They did a good job on him, didn't they, Bess? Looks like he was hit with a dum-dum bullet. Fucking Hun bastards,' Tom speculated. He slowly stood upright, his knees creaking.

'Blew his head apart,' he added taking a long look at the pistol. 'That's a forty-five. They're going to attack. We have to save ourselves.' Tom shook his head and stepped carefully over the body. He staggered after taking several steps then collapsed. The town's rumour mill was in overproduction even before Billy's body had made the mortuary.

'Billy's wife screamed black and blue that he wouldn't kill himself.'

'She was under heavy sedation. A nurse told me.'

'The saleyard was in financial strife, you know.'

'Billy had girlfriends.'

'I haven't seen John or Lorna Tindall. Have you?'

'Poor Tom. He's had a breakdown. Shellshock came back. He's in hospital.'

When John Tindall was found shot dead in the kitchen of his house a day later, the rumour mill nearly exploded.

'Maybe he shot Billy.'

'Things like this don't happen here. What's happening to the place? Must have been done by outsiders. There were hippies hitch-hiking through here.'

'Have you seen Lorna Tindall? That poor boy of theirs. His father's shot himself. How's he going to live with the stigma?'

'I don't think they should have done a double funeral. I couldn't get near the church.'

'Did you see Lorna Tindall? She looked too calm.'

'Merle Johnson was so distraught I thought she'd collapse.'

'Merle's leaving town, I heard.'

And then, finally, 'Max says they were both suicides.'

11

Max was a block of seething anger as he threw the police car around a corner and headed back in the direction of the main street. Doctor Simon Renshaw wasn't in his usual haunts; certainly not at his practice. It was always closed on Fridays. He had tried the Crown Hotel; Renshaw wasn't passed out drunk at his spot at the end of the public bar as he would usually be at this time of day every Friday. Propping up the corner of the bar. Shouting drinks. Telling stories. The bar's inhabitants hadn't seen him.

'Doctor Renshaw's a good doctor when he's sober,' a bar denizen had joked.

'And that isn't very often,' another added.

Doctor Renshaw had arrived in Clarkes Flat as a welcome saviour — the town's first doctor in decades — and surrounded by mystery. The locals knew he had been a doctor in the British Army; he said he had served in Northern Ireland for two years and had come to Australia to set up private practice. No one knew why he drank so much or why a man in his forties didn't have a family. The doctor was a popular subject of the gossip- mongers; the latest was that he was having an affair with the widow, Merle Johnson. Max knew better.

Max kicked open the door of the miner's cottage and marched through the house until he was met by Joanne Taylor standing defiantly in the hallway, wearing a large T-shirt with the Foster's beer logo emblazoned on it that just covered her groin. Young Joanne was pretty in a neglected sort of way; she would have been a stunner if she washed her hair regularly and brushed her teeth.

'Where is he?' Max barked as he pushed past her and walked into a bedroom, kicking a path through the mounds of dirty clothes that lay on the floor.

'Don't know who you're talking about.' Joanne folded her arms.

Max looked at the bedside table that had an empty bottle of whiskey, two glasses and an empty condom wrapper on it. A tie and a pair of men's slacks lay over the foot of the bed. The bed and pillows appeared ruffled.

'Where's Renshaw?'

'Where's your search warrant?' she retorted, chewing sullenly on a piece of gum.

'I don't need one,' Max smirked, staring at the outline of Joanne's ample breasts. They shook when she spoke.

'I saw it on television. This is police brutality,' she argued. Before she could wait for a reply, Max had thrown her face first against the wall, pinning her arm behind her back. She yelped in pain as Max pulled it towards her neck.

'If you don't tell me where he is I'll be arresting you on drug possession. Get it, you smart arse slut?'

'I don't do drugs,' Joanne spluttered through the pain.

'And who's going to believe a little whore like you? Tell me,' Max growled pressing harder on her arm.

'Crashed on the toilet. I can't wake him up.'

'Good,' Max released her arm and ambled out the back towards a corrugated iron outhouse covered in choko vine.

'Renshaw. Come out,' Max tried to open the door but it wouldn't budge.

Max planted his boot at the wooden door. As the door broke and snapped open, a male voice could be heard muttering.

'Come out, Renshaw, or I'll drag you out by the fucking balls.' There was no reply. Max gingerly opened the broken door to find Renshaw propped up asleep against the wall of the toilet, naked except for a pair of white underpants at his knees. Max slapped Renshaw hard across the face. Renshaw came to with a jolt, punching at the air, his eyes still shut. A wild punch hit Max in the abdomen.

'I'm not going back to boarding school, Mother,' Renshaw mumbled through slitted eyes as he continued to flail at the air.

'Wake up, you pommy bastard. You're coming with me.' Max grabbed Renshaw by the arm, roughly dragging him to his feet.

'What? Who?' Renshaw clutched at his underpants as he was pulled forward. 'Sergeant Hillard?' Renshaw enquired as his eyes opened fully. 'What is the manner of this behaviour? I'll have you reported.' Max pulled him out of the toilet.

'I haven't finished my movement,' Renshaw protested as he slapped Max's hand away and attempted to stagger back to the sanctuary of the toilet. Max grasped Renshaw again, hooked him under the armpit and dragged him out by his arm, propelling him towards the house, underpants at half-mast. 'You've got all day to finish your shit. I need you to come to the mortuary. There are two bodies in there waiting for a doctor's visit.'

'I don't do post-mortems. They go to Townsville,' Renshaw protested, managing to finally hoist his underpants to his waist.

'The fridges are broken at the hospital and the bodies are going off. And you're it, Doc.' Max said as he pulled Renshaw up the back stairs. Joanne had disappeared.

'Make yourself presentable, Doc,' Max pushed Renshaw into the bedroom.

'I refuse to follow your directions, Sergeant Hillard. I'm a doctor. You don't treat a doctor like a common vagabond.' Renshaw sulked as he flopped on the bed and folded his arms firmly across his sunken chest.

'You have a choice, Doc,' Max cajoled, sitting beside Renshaw and putting a fatherly arm around his shoulders. 'Where do I start? Having sex with a minor.'

Renshaw looked aghast as Max continued: 'You must have known Joanne Taylor is barely sixteen. Oh, Doc. Don't you check your files before you have sex with your patients?'

'I didn't know,' Renshaw blubbered. 'I don't want to go to jail.'

'I know you don't, Doc,' Max consoled, patting Renshaw, 'Nearly been there before haven't you? Back in England. The medical board said that if you left England they wouldn't deregister you. Love the young fluff, don't you, Doc? That will get you in a lot of trouble. It's good to know you're using condoms this time.' Max threw a glance at the bedside table.

'How?'

'Don't assume that I'm some dumb flat-foot country cop.' Max slapped Renshaw hard on the back. Renshaw coughed.

'I can't do it,' Renshaw pleaded. 'I've been on a bender.'

'That's all right, Doc. I'll guide you through it.'

After three hours of Renshaw's sawing, cutting and endless requests for black coffee, the two autopsied bodies of Billy Johnson and John Tindall were returned to their respective morgue trays. The morgue's refrigerator had been finally repaired. Max Hillard had never seen two post-mortems back to back, and never seen a doctor turn green and suddenly vomit when he opened up Billy's abdominal cavity. Thankfully, it ended up on the floor of the mortuary and not the body.

It was also the most conclusive.

12

Dick Clancy wandered into the Clarkes Flat police station with an air of uncertainty about him. Dick never usually came to the police station except to renew his driver's license and his pistol licence that he was allowed to have to put down stock. Today was different. Dick was standing at an unattended counter when Max came out of an office and noticed him.

'Long time no see,' Max beamed, slapping Dick on the back. Standing side by side they could have been brothers; similar age, tall, broad-shouldered, prominent chins and chiselled faces. The most observable difference was that Dick's face was furrowed from years of sun exposure and worry. They shook hands vigorously and Max steered Dick into an office. Dick sat hesitantly in a chair that Max pointed to; Max grabbed a chair from the opposite side of the desk and pulled it in beside Dick. He slid himself into the chair then turned it towards Dick so they were nearly face-to-face. Dick appeared unsettled but didn't take his gaze off Max's.

'I haven't seen you since the funerals, must be three months,' Max reflected.

'Being busy with the muster,' Dick replied quietly. He paused to adjust a cuff that wasn't out of place, then continued.

'I wanted to stay out of the way. It was like a bloody circus when the funerals were on.'

'It's starting to settle back to normal now,' Max reassured. 'Clarkes Flat will be it's old self again soon.' Max noticed that Dick was constantly fidgeting with his shirt or his hair.

'Do you want a drink?' Max asked. 'We can talk down at the pub.'

'No. No. It's right,' Dick's eyes welled up. He reached for a handkerchief from a trouser pocket and wiped his eyes. 'You all right?' Max asked, putting his arm around Dick.

'I just can't believe that Billy and John would commit suicide. I'd seen them at the saleyards a few days before it happened and they looked fine. I had a beer with them at the office. They looked happy. I thought you'd look depressed if you were going to kill yourself. '

'Not always. They can appear to everyone as being happy on the surface. Sometimes they don't leave suicide notes. I think it's an easy way out. Fucking weakness. Only weak people do it.' Max cleared his throat as the anger started to gush through him. It settled. Dick nodded in the affirmative.

'Poor Lorna. And David and Merle. Have you heard the rumours? Some of them are bloody ridiculous.'

'Between you and me…' Max started to speak and then observed that the door was open. He quickly closed the door and returned to his seat. He leant closer into Dick.

'Between you, me and the gatepost, Billy and John had got themselves into a lot of trouble. I bet you didn't know that the saleyards were going broke and they were pinching cattle off Bert Canning's place.' Max stated in a low tone of voice.

'What?' Dick shook. his head. 'I can't believe it.'

Max touched his lips with his finger.

'I just can't believe it,' Dick repeated, this time in a softer voice.

'I was about to arrest them and they beat me by killing themselves.'

Dick fumbled with his handkerchief, drying his eyes.

'Sorry I had to tell you, Dick,' Max stated. 'I know they were good mates of yours.'

'I suppose you don't know everything about your friends. Stupid bastards.' Dick said bitterly. He screwed up the handkerchief, firmly pushing it into a trouser pocket.

'I was also about to arrest Sam Saturday, too.' Max added, 'He was finding the cattle.'

'Sam? He wouldn't do anything dishonest. We never brought him up like that.'

'Have you seen him? I know he left your place. Has he gone back?' Max questioned seriously, using his best police voice.

'I haven't seen him since we had the argument and he left,' Dick replied hesitantly. Dick's stare shifted from Max's face to the floor.

'Are you sure? Max demanded. 'He's not camped on your place somewhere?'

'I haven't seen him.' Dick exclaimed. 'I'd tell you if I had. If he's broken the law I'd tell you.'

'Of course you would,' Max said. 'Country people are honest to a fault.'

There was an awkward calm until Dick Clancy emitted a nervous cough.

'I was going to ask if you could do something for me,' Dick asked. 'I caught three ringers from next door a few weeks ago trying to pinch some of my cleanskins.'

'Do you know who they were?' Max asked, leaning forward.

'One was Jack Perks and I didn't see the others. They'd taken off.'

'Jack Perks. I know him. Chip on his shoulder. What did you do?'

'I warned them off but that won't stop them. They'll be back. I can't spend my entire life riding boundary fences looking for cattle duffers,' Dick replied.

'The law's not going to do anything,' Max fumed. 'Useless.'

'But don't you uphold the law?' Dick asked.

'I'm referring to what lawyers call the *law* You'll waste a lot of money trying to prosecute these pricks and they'll walk free, ready to do it again. The law that I uphold is bush law. Lawyers are a bunch of useless cunts. Out here it doesn't apply.'

'What can be done then?' Dick replied, perplexed.

'Leave it with me, Dick. I'll have a heart to heart talk with Jack Perks.'

'Talk?'

'Talk,' Max sniggered.

'All right,' Dick rose from the chair and adjusted his shirt collar then brushed his fringe back. Max stood slowly, surveying Dick's uneasy movements. Dick went to quickly shake Max's hand, who kept his arms by his side. Dick tightly folded his arms in response.

'Just one more thing,' Max asked.

'What's that, Max?' Dick replied uneasily.

'Fifty head of cleanskins wouldn't go astray. Send them in when you get back home. I'll take care of them.'

'Okay,' Dick faltered. 'No worries.'

'Good. Bush law.' Max now offered his hand. Dick slowly unfolded his arms to shake Max's.

13

Clarkes Flat Police Station, June, 1969

Doug had started hanging around the police station when he was ten. At first the officers told him to go home. He did at first but he always came back. Who could blame him? Doug's parents were always drunk and arguing. No food to eat at home except Vegemite sandwiches, if he was lucky.

The officers relented and Doug became a sort of station mascot. Max Hillard even bought Doug a little police cap. Doug never took it off, even at school. The kids teased Doug mercilessly but Doug was Junior Constable Clancy and he would tell Max if they didn't leave him alone.

To Doug, Max was a hero and parent all in the same package. Super Max. For a treat, Max would take Doug for a drive in the police car and even let him turn on the siren. And the biggest treat of all was when Max took Doug out to the lagoon on his birthday and let him shoot his pistol. But if Doug annoyed the officers, it was into the cells. When Doug started to cry, the officers would want to let him out but Max insisted that he stay for an hour. *It'll toughen the little bugger up.*

Doug was going to be like Max, no doubt about that. Sergeant Douglas Clancy, Special Investigations Branch. At first Max got Doug to do little errands for the station like going to the shops, then as Doug became a teenager, Max saw more potential for Doug. The kid was dumb as dog shit but as loyal as a sheep dog.

'Hit him harder,' Max demanded as he watched Doug gather up his arm and throw a punch into Jack Perks' bruised and swollen face. The punch connected with Perks' cheekbone and glanced off, barely rippling his parchment hide skin. To add insult to injury, Perks' head barely moved in the chair that he had been tied to in the old isolation cell under the police station. Doug clutched his hand with pain. Max grabbed Doug by the back of the neck and squeezed.

'I can't punch anymore. My hand hurts,' Doug pleaded, looking down at a cut in his knuckle.

'You're a sook. How old are you now? Twelve? You're hitting like a little girl.' Max inspected the cut on Doug's hand and sneered.

'For Christ's sake. Do you want me to kiss it better?' Max slapped Doug in the back of the head. Tears welled in Doug's eyes.

'You won't be a copper if you cry,' Max stated. 'Coppers don't cry.'

Doug wiped his eyes, stifling the sobs that threatened to rake his body.

'I'm sixteen and I want to be a copper,' Doug begged, looking up at Max 'I'll hit harder. Promise.'

'Using a kid to do your dirty work, you copper cunt,' Perks sneered. 'Who are you going to use next? Your fucking grandmother?' He gave a wry smile and spat a wad of blood from his mouth that spattered on the floor at their feet. Doug stepped back but Max grasped Doug by the wrist.

'Can't we let him go now?' Doug asked.

'Try again,' Max said in a fatherly voice, pushing Doug towards Perks. 'Hit him hard on the jaw and don't close your eyes. Tight fist. Like this.' Max closed his fists tight. Doug mimicked Max's instructions. 'Punch, don't slap. Alright?'

Doug nodded.

'Look him in the eye and get angry. Get angry,' Max growled. 'Really angry. Really angry.' Max slapped Doug hard on the back. Doug responded by taking deep breaths; deep, deliberate breaths. He clenched his jaw, staring into Perks' face. For the first time since the interrogation Perks looked uneasy.

'I won't pinch any more cattle. All right? I won't. I'll tell you who else was involved.' Perks confessed, gazing at Max, who ignored him as he continued to train Doug.

'That's it. Imagine Perks is raping your mother.' Doug looked baffled. 'All right. Imagine he's one of the bullies that been beating you up at school. Get ready,' Max added.

Doug screwed his fists into balls and went into a boxing stance.

'You're fucking sick, Hillard. Getting a kid to do this. Are you fucking him up the arse or something?' said Perks.

Perks' statement stopped Max with a jolt. His face turned crimson and he stiffened momentarily with rage. He took a deep breath and relaxed into an unsettling calmness. He raised his right hand that had become a fist, but let it fall open when he observed that Jack Perks had stiffened his body for the impending blow. Instead, he calmly laid his hand on Perks' shoulder and gazed into his face.

'Let me tell you both a story, Perks. When I was a young constable I once broke a coon's jaw with one punch. Snapped it in two. Give it a go, Doug. Show me what you can do.'

Max stood back as Doug leapt forward, throwing his fist hard into Jack Perks' jaw. Perks' head jerked backwards then fell forward.

'No more. Please,' Perks muttered in pain. 'I'm sorry I said that.' A trickle of blood ran from his mouth.

'Much better,' Max said, patting Doug on the back. Doug smiled with pride. He rubbed his hand then clenched it again. 'We'll try that again,' Max ordered, directing Doug's hands back up. 'Give him a one-two to the nose this time.'

Perks tried to move the chair with his body away from the wall as Doug threw his first punch into his nose. Max righted the chair as it started to topple.

'Harder!' Max shouted. Doug threw the second punch with all the weight he had behind him. An audible crack signalled that Perks' nose had broken. Blood spurted from his nose and seeped into his shirt.

'Very good, Acting Constable Clancy,' Max gave Doug a congratulatory pat on the head. Doug beamed as he rubbed his throbbing hand.

'You've busted my fucking nose, you cunts!' Perks protested through foaming blood. 'I want to go to hospital!'

'What do you think we should do with this man?' Max asked softly, ignoring Perks' pleas.

'I want to go to hospital!' Perks interjected. Max whipped his service revolver from its holster and held it to Perks' forehead.

'This cell is so insulated that no one can hear a gun go off down here,' Max said. 'Amazing what useless knowledge you accumulate.' Perks shuddered.

'Can't you see I'm trying to speak here?' Max growled. Perks' protests fell to a soft whimper. Max returned the pistol to the holster as he repeated, 'What are we going to do with this man?'

'Dunno. Tell him to behave himself and take him home?' Doug replied, shrugging his shoulders.

'You see, Doug, the first thing is that you have to be decisive and you've got to cover your tracks. Think.' Max concluded, tapping Doug on the head.

'We kill him?' Doug suggested.

Perks started to cry.

'Don't be rude,' Max barked at Perks, who immediately fell quiet.

'I'm the law around here,' Max remarked to Doug. 'That's what criminals do. Killing is against the law. You should know better.'

'Why don't we go for a drive out bush? Like the time we took that mad bloke?' Doug said excitedly.

'Where are you taking me?' Perks snivelled, 'I want to know.'

'Very good, Doug. You're learning.' Max gave Doug a fatherly hug.

The washed-out, disused bush track that led to the old mining camp was difficult enough during the day to negotiate to the uninitiated, and at night it was almost impassable. Denuded of most vegetation indigenous to those parts, the old mines were covered with rubber vines so thick that a man would need a machete to cut his way through them. The camp was riddled with deep, long-abandoned mineshafts, all unfenced and yawning up into the sky.

Max had used this track before and was aware of its particular idiosyncrasies; managing to dodge the potholes and soft sand that would have bogged the police vehicle, by taking advantage of Doug's extra pair of eyes. A large, solitary tamarind tree rising from the darkness alerted Max that they had arrived. He turned off the car engine, leaving the headlights on. Max got out first holding a large metal torch, leaving Doug trailing behind. A banging sound could be heard coming from the car boot.

'The natives are restless,' Max smiled as he went to the rear of the car. Doug followed. Max opened the boot to reveal Jack Perks lying on his back, his mouth covered in packing tape, his hands tied in front of him with light rope. Jack murmured loudly, his eyes wide with fear. He tried to lash out with his feet at Max but he stepped back deftly, leaving Perks kicking at the air. Max opened the rear door and retrieved a cattle prod, wired up to a battery pack, which he slung over his shoulder. Its operating light glowed as Max turned it on.

'It's just like handling stock,' Max instructed as he pushed the prongs into Jack's groin. Perks screamed and convulsed as jolts of electricity pulsed through his body. Max pulled the prod away.

'Get out of the car!' Max ordered. 'If you don't I'll give you another dose.'

Perks slowly lifted himself from the car boot and leaned unsteadily against the car.

'Now isn't that better than dragging him out of the car? You could get hurt,' Max said.

'I guess,' Doug replied, sounding a little shocked.

'Most human beings are like cattle,' Max philosophised as he pulled Perks away from the car towards the tamarind tree. Max gave Doug the torch as they walked. 'They have to be led. They have to be directed.'

Perks suddenly collapsed onto his knees, interlacing his fingers in a begging motion. After another shock into his buttocks from the prod, Perks was quickly back on his feet. Max kept leading Perks until they reached the tree.

'Stop!' Max roared at Doug as he was about to overtake them. Doug froze where he stood. After a nod from Max, he swung about and stepped back in Max's direction. Max cut the twine that bound Perks' wrists.

'There. You're free. Now get going before I change my mind.'

Perks crumpled into a sobbing heap at Max's feet. Doug itched to kick the blubbering man where he lay, but he took Max's lead and turned back in the direction of the car. As they walked away, they heard Perks scrambling to his feet followed by the rustle of the underbrush as he stumbled away in the opposite direction.

'People need to be careful when they walk through the bush around here,' Max remarked as he slid into the driver's seat and turned the key.

14

Dick and Irene were arguing again, as was their custom, during the preparation of dinner. Peter sat silently reading a book next to his father, at the dining room table. Dick was pouring rum and clumsily rolling a cigarette.

'No more, Dick, please. I'm getting dinner out,' Irene said, removing a roast from the oven.

'I've worked hard today. I deserve a drink,' Dick replied. Peter tried to catch Dick's attention.

'Dad. Can you help me with my model plane?'

'Not now, son. I want to relax and your mother's nagging is distracting me.

'Later then?' Peter begged.

'How about after dinner?' Dick replied, taking a deep swig of rum.

'Dick, I can't wait any longer.'

'Bloody hell. Is there no peace around here?' Dick roared, smashing his hand on the table. Peter started to cry.

'Why are you crying? Bloody sooky kid. How will you ever take over if anything happens to me?' Peter ran from the room, slamming the flyscreen door to the kitchen behind him. Irene left the roast on the bench and went to Dick.

'Just give me some peace is all I ask,' Dick implored. 'That's all I ask.'

'What's wrong, Dick?' Irene asked as she sat beside Dick and embraced him. He took hold of her arm and stroked it softly.

'It's been hard to take about John and Billy. They'd be the last people I thought would commit suicide.'

'That's what the official verdict is,' Irene remarked.

'I just don't get it.'

'What are you trying to say?' Irene asked. 'Don't tell me you're starting to believe the gossip going around town?'

'Of course not,' Dick snapped back. 'I think there's more to this. That's all I'm going to say.'

'I know it's difficult for you, Dick. People do commit suicide, even in the bush. You can't dwell on it. You've been like this for weeks.' Irene sounded irritated. She loosened her embrace and stood up.

'Okay.' Dick stood and embraced Irene tightly.

'What's that for?'

'I just realised I don't do this enough.'

'Oh God. Peter!' Irene cried, pulling away from Dick. 'We better find him. He doesn't usually run away at night.' Peter ran until he reached the riverbank then collapsed. He felt calmer when he put his legs into the warm, brown water and it swirled softly around them. The river and the bush were a haven. Peter couldn't comprehend how people could be afraid of the bush.

Peter kicked his legs up and down, wishing he could swim across the river and to the other side, away from his parents' arguments, to the dreamland. His father had promised to teach him to swim but that had been promised a long time ago. Maybe he could teach himself.

He felt the pull of the current as he walked into the river up to his knees. In an instant, it had pulled him off his feet and was dragging him sideways along the river's edge. Peter thrashed his arms, clawing at the bank in an effort to move his body forward. Suddenly his legs were in suspended animation as the river floor dropped away. He pumped his legs furiously, trying to co-ordinate them with his flailing arms, just as he had seen his father do when he swam. Peter's efforts proved fruitless, as the more powerful current took control of him. He tried to return on tiptoes to shallower water but the current pushed him deeper. He lost all contact with the river bottom and his feet paddled madly. Peter called for help and thrashed wildly, barely able to keep his head above water. But he was sinking downward and his thrashing strokes were futile. He choked as the muddy water entered his mouth. He was floating downward. Peter felt like he had entered a dream, as he abandoned all resistance and an eerie calmness came over him. He was suspended in a water cloud. Then all of a sudden, he was being jerked upwards. Peter was flying up and out of the water like Peter Pan. He vomited, the water spraying out of his mouth like a fountain. It was only then that he realised that his father had pulled him out of the water and he was dangling from Dick's huge arm.

'Are you all right son?' Dick cried, clutching Peter tightly.

'I wanted to swim the river at night just like you do,' Peter croaked.

'I'll teach you, son. I promise. I won't ignore you anymore.' Dick swept Peter up in his arms and carried him back to the homestead.

I'll be a good dad and husband from now on.

15

Dick Clancy lay unconscious on the dining room table, his broken head covered in a blood-soaked towel, his breathing laboured. Irene squeezed his hand tightly as his body convulsed. She knew from her nursing that it wasn't a good sign. The convulsions stopped and Dick's breathing became deeper and more laboured. Sam stood on the other side of the table holding Dick's arm.

'I looked around and Dick had been thrown. His horse had rolled over him, Missus. Old Tony never usually put a foot wrong. Never shied,' Sam recalled.

'I hope the Flying Doctors get here soon,' Irene cried. 'He should never have ridden Tony. He was too old. Dick should have retired him. I want you to shoot the horse.' Irene hung her head on Dick's chest and sobbed.

'I'll shoot it, Missus,' Sam replied painfully. 'If you want me to I'll shoot Old Tony.'

'Did he say anything to you, Sam?' Irene asked, looking up at Sam.

'Take care of Irene and the boy,' Sam replied in a faltering voice. 'He tried to say something after that but I didn't quite pick it up, Missus. It sounded like… I couldn't pick it up.'

'Don't die, Dick. You're a Clancy,' Irene howled. 'We can't live without you.'

The outside kitchen door tore open and Peter ran in.

'What's wrong with Dad?' Peter tried to touch Dick but Irene pushed him away.

'He shouldn't be here, Sam,' Irene howled. 'He can't see this.'

'Is Dad going to die?' Peter asked as Sam grabbed hold of Peter's hand.

'He came off his horse. He'll be right when the doctors fix him up,' Sam lied. Sam tried to lead Peter away but Peter pulled back and ran back to his father. He clutched an arm hanging off the table.

Don't die Dad. Please don't die. Don't die.

PART THREE

16

1970s

Irene tried to run Cornish Downs for a year after Dick died, but after Sam's sudden departure, she lost all motivation. Sam had disappeared one night without notice, leaving only a scrap of paper on his bed in the stockmen's quarters, saying he was going away and wouldn't be back for a long time. It had been an inconvenient time to resign, as Irene had wanted all hands on deck for the coming long weekend when Max Hillard and family would be coming to stay.

Irene had mentioned Sam's departure in passing conversation at dinner on the first night the Hillards had arrived. She thought it was particularly rude of Max to interrupt her and ask to use the phone while she was speaking. Max had already left the table before she could add that such behaviour needed to be tolerated, as Aborigines had always been and would always be nomadic people. She had hoped that the weekend would be an uplifting event, something to take her mind off Dick's death, but Max had spent the next day looking distracted, barely engaging in any of the activities she had planned for them. The next day, the Hillards left, a day earlier than expected. Max told her that he had urgent police business to attend to.

The station was sold and Irene decided to move to Clarkes Flat. Peter was barely twelve when they moved into town. He had hoped that they might move somewhere near the sea, but Irene was intent on purchasing Arkinholme, a house she had always loved and had often pestered Dick to buy. Clarkes Flat was now her home, and most of her friends where there. She would be able to live comfortably off the proceeds from the sale of the property for the rest of her life and fill in her days entertaining at her grand home and socialising. She felt reassured that wouldn't have to be isolated on a property any longer and be responsible for Peter's education. The Christian brothers would now be in charge and she didn't care how they brought Peter's substandard results up to scratch.

At first, Peter had felt like he had been imprisoned, the one-hectare grounds of Arkinholme too confined for Peter's nomadic nature. If his mother allowed him, he would wander down the road to a creek on the proviso that he didn't leave the road. Irene reminded him daily that Clarkes Flat was dotted with unfenced mine shafts, just waiting to swallow him whole. But the creek wasn't like the expansive river on Cornish Downs. Rather, it was a collection of puddles joined by strips of sand, and the bush that grew along the creek consisted mainly of thorny vines that threatened to bite into his feet, not the lush foliage of paperbark trees. The only wildlife he saw was an occasional darting wallaby escaping into the undergrowth, as well as the usual assortment of crows and magpies.

One day Peter grew tired of standing by the road, throwing pebbles at small fish as they scurried about in a pool below him. He decided to venture into the thorny foliage. Peter found a tunnelled pathway that the wallabies had created. He squeezed through the tunnel on all fours, a thorn occasionally catching his shirt, which he deftly prised away without tearing the cloth. He was only too well aware that there would be hell to pay if he returned with torn clothing.

He continued along the tunnel for about fifty metres until it opened up into a small clearing, devoid of all vegetation, including grass. Peter stood and carefully walked towards a semi-circular pile of gravel rocks that rose above his head at the other end of the clearing. The vines were slowly enveloping them but he could see a washed-out track coming through a break in the rocks. The ground near the gravel semi-circle was marked by deep erosion, probably from the water that washed off the rocks after rain. Tentacles of small gullies fanned away from the rocks then disappeared. Peter stopped when he realised what he had stumbled upon. He crept forward and peered into the mineshaft, a darkened chasm, even during the day. He threw in a rock. It made a plopping sound when it hit the water below. It was only then that he noticed a man's brown shoe lying near the edge of the mineshaft. It was withered and buckled from the exposure to the sun. He picked it up and examined it and imagined it might have belonged to a miner, although, he thought, it looked more like a shoe someone might wear when he dressed up. He considered tossing it into the mineshaft. He even thought of showing his mother but instead decided to take it home and hide it in the shed. He managed to crawl back through the tunnel with the shoe, and made it home unscathed.

He returned several more times to explore the old mine, finding a Chinese coin, an old rusted chisel, and finally some fresh car tracks. He wondered who had made the tracks. Could they have belonged to the car that he had heard from his bed one night, revving loudly as if it had been bogged?

He had heard the revving just the once, but it often returned in his nightmares. He dreamed repeatedly that he was being dragged towards the mineshaft. When he looked down at his feet, he could see that he was wearing the same shoes as the one he had found. In his dreams he felt himself being tossed like a rag doll into the mine and floating down an endless shaft, but he always woke up before hitting the bottom. He saw his father once as he dreamed he was tumbling down the mine. Dick was talking to Peter as if trying to tell him something important and waving his arms in frustration, but Peter couldn't make out his words. When Peter awoke he found himself out of his bed and poised as if he was about to step onto the ledge of the open window near his bed. He never went back to the old mine after that; the nightmares soon ceased and Peter forgot all about them.

Peter's transition from station life to town life was uneasy. He was held back in his class, as he was regarded as being behind the others. His classmates teased him and called him dumb. Peter could fight but he couldn't fight the whole class. The Christian Brothers strapped him unmercifully if he was unable to answer questions or didn't do his homework correctly. There was no reprieve or leniency from the Brothers in the classroom. He had hoped he would gain favour if he were good at sport, but he soon discovered that he wasn't good at sport either, so he soon became the outsider, the oddball, the weirdo.

Courtesy of the many committees she had joined, Irene was frequently out when he got home from school and she often went out at night, too. Her instructions were always marked on a blackboard in the kitchen. Don't do this, don't do that, and always concluding with *Don't leave the yard*. That was an easy one to obey, Peter had discovered. There was nowhere to go except the old mineshaft and he was too scared to go back there. He had no friends except Jimmy Hill who was always dishevelled, smelly and hungry. Jimmy had a nauseating habit of wiping his frequently runny nose on his shirtsleeves leaving them covered in a film of drying snot. Despite this, Peter felt some sympathy for him, sharing his lunch with Jimmy daily. Jimmy didn't say much except 'thanks' and a comment about how good the sandwich tasted as he wolfed it down. One day, Jimmy said his family were moving and next day he was gone. Peter later heard that his mother had died and Jimmy and his siblings had been sent to live with relatives.

When his mother went to a meeting at night Peter would be looked after by Maud Larsen, who lived next door. Dear old Maud could talk the paint off a post. The town humorists stated that the recent death of her husband, Perc, was caused by lock- jaw, as he had not been able to talk for twenty years. Maud even managed to hold a one-way conversation with Peter who uttered an irritated 'yes' and 'no' sporadically as he tried to watch television. The day he turned thirteen, Irene deemed that Maud wouldn't have to babysit Peter anymore. Peter's cheering was so loud and protracted that she immediately punished him by banning him from watching *The Brady Bunch*. As far as Peter was concerned, it was worth it.

Peter found solace in books, his favourites being general knowledge and adventure novels. In time, his grades began to improve, and he proved to be particularly gifted in English. Brother Reilly, an aging curmudgeon who hailed from County Limerick and who, it was said, could drain blood from a corpse with his withering stare, encouraged Peter. Through his encouragement he extracted the previously-dormant gift that Peter had for words. That year he came fourth in the class. Now he was teased for being a bookworm. He started to imagine a world beyond Clarkes Flat, living in a big city like London or New York where he could be part of a crowd, not an object of derision or sympathy.

In his final year of primary school, the class had to give a talk about what they wanted to do with their lives. Most boys had said they were going to own a cattle station or become a tradesman; Peter told them that he was going to live in London and be a writer like Jack London. The class howled with laughter, but not Brother Reilly. He strapped the entire class — two strokes on each hand, including Peter who had taken a swing at Donny Newton for calling him a poofter. Once again, the celebrating was still worth the punishment . At the end of the year, Brother Reilly gave him a book about the great Irish novelists. He had written in it, *To Peter Clancy, don't stop dreaming, that's how books are written*. From that day forward Peter knew exactly what he wanted to do with his life. He knew he couldn't wait to grow up, and leave Clarkes Flat. And his mother.

17

One event in particular caused Peter to loathe Clarkes Flat and to lose all respect for his mother. It coincided with becoming an adolescent during Grade Eight. Irene lost interest in CWA meetings and lamington drives after a few years, and started to be seen in the company of Noel Talford, who happened to be the Clarkes Flat's real estate agent. They were frequently spotted at race meetings or the Crown Hotel or Clarkes Flat's only restaurant, the Red Lantern. The town gossips wagged their tongues until they must have cramped, as they reported on the latest intrigue.

'I saw them kissing openly. On the mouth, for heaven's sake.'

'He's apparently separated from his wife. She lives in Townsville.'

'She's only been a widow for a few years.'

'No wonder that boy of hers looks so mixed up.'

'A disgrace to the good Clancy name.'

'I saw them drunk at the Crown. They were nearly falling over.'

Peter especially hated it when she started to bring Noel Talford home. While he sat watching television or stayed in his room, they drank, danced or smooched in the kitchen. Then Talford began to stay over. Peter didn't like Talford from their first meeting. Talford looked oily and sounded arrogant. He tried to engage him in conversation at first, even offering Peter a beer as a man-to-man gesture. But all Talford could elicit in response from Peter were monosyllabic grunts.

Peter managed to avoid Talford by staying in his room when he visited. If he had to venture out for sustenance, he would be met by Talford's teasing, usually about if he was still a virgin, or what he was doing in his room with Mrs Palmer and her five daughters.

Talford's teasing was supported by Irene's inane giggling. Peter wanted to escape. He wanted to run away from this crap hole. *Why did you have to die, Dad?* Peter's room wasn't totally insulated from what was happening outside. When the lights were turned off in the house, he knew they would start. Peter would hear their love talk and lovemaking, even though they had the radio turned up in Irene's bedroom. Peter knew exactly what they were doing although Irene had not yet given Peter the birds-and-bees talk. That task had been left to Brother Ryan, who had shown a film during class about where babies came from, without showing how they were conceived. That part was filled in by one of the boys during lunch break, who said he had found his father's Penthouse magazine showing couples shagging in missionary, doggie style and sundry other positions. Another boy had boasted that he had fingered a girl at the pictures and he was going to get his older brother to buy a packet of frenchies so they could go all the way. Peter's imagination was left to fill in the gaps.

Peter covered his ears with his pillow and wrapped it tightly around his head and thought the same distracting thoughts over and over: *London, writer, books*. He felt nauseated whenever he heard Talford and Irene. When he could no longer endure their noise, Peter would go out into the yard and look up at the sky for hours or fall asleep in the garage. *Fucking hate this place. Fucking hate Talford. Fucking hate Mum.* Then he'd feel guilty for expressing that level of antipathy for Irene. Peter decided that disliking his mother intensely sounded more appropriate.

One night he lay in bed, listening to them. Talford and Irene were arguing in the bedroom. It was a pleasant change. Peter smiled. It sounded like they were arguing about nothing important, like he didn't think much of what she wore. It was too revealing or something. The arguing steadily became more heated, Talford's voice more contorted with anger, Irene's more submissive until it was just loud sobbing. There was the sound of crashing, like someone falling on the floor. Then a scream. Peter sat bolt upright then froze. He heard the sound of bare feet running along the hallway followed by the steady fall of heavy boots. All of the footsteps drew closer to Peter's room. The door to his room burst over and Irene rushed in, her nightdress torn to shreds, her face bleeding.

'Peter,' Irene begged as she fell into bed beside Peter, 'don't let him hurt me.' She clutched Peter tightly, her nails digging into his arms.

Peter was just beginning to respond when Talford lumbered into the room.

'I haven't finished with you yet,' Talford slurred drunkenly.

'Help me, Peter,' Irene cried.

'What's your pansy son going to do?'

'Leave my mother alone,' Peter demanded as he extricated himself from his mother's grip. Peter hopped off the bed, hoveringly protectively near his Irene.

'Sounds like you've had too much time with Mrs Palmer,' Talford laughed as he pretended to masturbate. He came towards them. He pushed Peter away and reached out to grab Irene's arm. She screamed, covering her body with her arms. Before Talford could take hold of her, Peter unleashed a punch, a punch that had been bottled up by years of anger and frustration. It caught Talford on the jaw and he fell with a heavy thump on the floor. Talford lay unconscious.

'What have you done?' Irene yelled as she hoped off the bed. 'You've killed him.'

Irene shook Talford but still no response. She put a pillow under Talford's head.

'What am I going to do?'

'Get an ambulance. You did this, you stupid bitch,' Peter cried as he fled from the room.

Peter was able to stay away for two days. He wanted to stay away forever but hunger and curiosity brought him back. He expected the police to be waiting for him when he crept into the house but there was silence. He went to his room and sat on his bed. Irene appeared in the doorway.

'He's all right. We won't be seeing him anymore. I told the school you were sick. Dinner will be ready soon,' Irene said before leaving the room.

The incident was never mentioned again. Talford was soon seen around town with another woman. After that, Irene and Peter's fragile relationship deteriorated into a war of attrition where neither would be the victor. It only got worse when Peter developed an interest in rock music.

Peter didn't see his mother rush into the lounge room as he mimed to the record with a battered, unplugged electric guitar slung around his shoulders. The record ground to a halt as Irene turned down the volume and then shut off the record player without first lifting the stylus.

'Why did you do that?' Peter shouted, removing the guitar and going to inspect the record. He looked it over. 'You've scratched it!'

'I could hear that noise from the driveway. Thank God I came home early. That noise will send you deaf,' Irene said.

'It's my music. I should have a right to play it on the stereo. That record player of mine is crap,' Peter protested.

'How dare you speak to me like that? If your father was here you wouldn't be saying that.'

'Well, he's dead, isn't he? And don't you remember he didn't care about me anyway?'

'You little mongrel!' Irene raised her hand to slap Peter.

'Do it and you'll never see me again,' Peter spat as if he was almost welcoming it. Irene dropped her hand and fled crying from the room.

Then Peter met Sally Enright. What a breath of fresh air.

Peter and Sally walked out of the theatre engrossed in conversation, their bodies touching occasionally. Sally was Peter's first date, unless you counted Peter meeting a girl at a school dance the previous year and her dancing with the school captain for most of the night. Peter had been relieved when Sally had agreed to go to the pictures with him and was even more relieved that she hadn't found him boring. They went to a dance at the state high school where they danced two dances together and then, for the rest of the night, talked about music, books and what they were going to do when they left Clarkes Flat. They both agreed that couldn't come quickly enough. Sally was going to be a journalist like Peter and work for *Rolling Stone* magazine. They both debated why *Rolling Stone* didn't like heavy rock music.

Sally had a pretty innocence and an infectious laugh. After a moment, Peter noticed that he had stopped looking at the small eruption of acne on her chin, to see only her beaming smile. Peter imagined she wouldn't be afraid to live her dream, wherever she wanted. He wished he had that confidence. At last, Peter felt he had met someone with a common soul.

'That movie didn't scare you too much?' Peter asked.

'I think vampires are a joke. They're not scary.'

'How come I saw you close your eyes when the priest put the stake into the vampire's heart?' Peter teased.

'I was just blinking. How come you had to go to the toilet when the witch was been burned?' Sally replied.

'I was busting. Really busting.' They both laughed and Sally took Peter's hand.

'You're funny,' Sally said.

'You are too.'

They arrived at the front gate of Sally's house. Loud music, interspersed with a male and a female arguing could be heard emanating from her house.

'Are your parents having a party?' Peter asked.

'No. They're just getting drunk.'

'Do they always do that?'

'Only when Dad gets paid. The shire council paid him last night.'

'I liked going out tonight. Can I see you again?'

'I liked tonight, too, Peter Clancy. Where would you like to go? We have a big choice. There's the pictures and if you know someone with a car, you can go out to the lagoon and get drunk around a campfire.'

'I'm getting a car next week. I saved for one.' Peter beamed.

'Sounds great. We could go to the drive-in in Townsville.'

'You could come around my place and listen to my records. My Mum has an old stereo. I've got the latest Led Zeppelin record. You like them, don't you?'

'Of course I do,' Sally replied, suddenly looking sad. 'I hate it here. No one likes what we like, Peter. We're outsiders here. I can't wait to get out of Clarkes Flat. I'll be on the bus as soon as school finishes. Where to? Anywhere as long as it's near the sea and has a population of more then a million.'

'Don't catch a bus. I've got a car, remember,'

Sally quickly kissed Peter on the cheek and ran inside.

18

Peter, Danny 'Chong' Butler and Noel 'Gibbo' Gibson sat around the campfire taking turns drinking from a large bottle of Bundy rum. They had driven out to the river in Peter's car, an unassuming second-hand cream Datsun 120Y, that he had just bought on his seventeenth birthday and his final year of school. Peter had saved hard for the car, working at the local paper during the school holidays. He loved the car for three reasons: the freedom to go anywhere, another stepping stone away from his disapproving Mother and the new friends he had acquired. The sort of friends he always wanted.

Danny Butler and Noel Gibson were the Jack-the-Lads you had to know if you wanted to have a good time. Danny was a well-built Aboriginal boy from a broken family. His father had left the family when Danny was a toddler and his mother had raised him and his three siblings alone. Mrs Butler worked hard as a cleaner and had ambitions for all of her children to succeed. She was proud when Danny's eldest brother had scored an apprenticeship at a factory in Townsville.

Danny had a hearty laugh, dry humour and a quick temper, and had ambitions of playing rugby league professionally.

Noel had a mop of red hair, a face full of freckles and a street-savvy attitude. He wasn't from a broken home. On the contrary, his father was serving as Clarkes Flat mayor. He and Danny were the blokes who were quick to fight, quick to have a drink, quick with the women, occasionally in trouble with the police and always ready for anything. They were state high school boys, only attending classes sporadically, choosing instead to spend more time at the local pool hall.

Peter had managed to make a few friends in secondary school. He had always been categorised as a bookworm and so he mixed with bookworms. Bookworms, as a rule, spent most of their time studying, hanging out in the library and picking at their pimples. One of the bookworms once had a birthday party to which Peter was invited. Apart from the boy's parents, the guests comprised only other bookworms, dressed in their best old man's clothes and sporting their best acne. Following a barbecue dinner, the night culminated in playing board games and listening to folk music, though at some time during the proceedings, there was a heated discussion between two bookworms about which was the best university, Brisbane or Sydney.

Peter's mind had gone numb by then and hadn't bothered to find out the answer. He revived himself instead with a glass of cordial and went outside to look at the sky.

Another reason to get the hell out of Clarkes Flat: meet exciting friends.

Soon after he bought the 120Y, Peter met Chong and Gibbo. It was to Peter like entering the inner sanctum of the Rolling Stones. Peter had decided to live dangerously. He audaciously went to the pool hall instead of going to a bookworm's place to study. The pool hall was where all the 'no-hoper boys', as Irene had tagged them, mixed with other no-hopers, drank alcohol, got into trouble and made girls pregnant. Irene had strongly warned Peter that he was forbidden to go there. Now Peter had a car. He felt he could do what he wanted.

Next stop London.

Peter entered the pool hall and immediately felt like a fish out of water. The boys were nonchalantly playing pool, smoking and swearing. One of them was canoodling with a girl in the corner. They looked messy, shirts hanging out, hair uncombed. A juke-box was playing a Creedence Clearwater song. Peter quickly tried to pull out his shirt and mess his hair but the pool boys had already targeted him.

'Get lost mate?'

'You're from the cattle tick school?' Two of the larger boys left their table — Gibbo with his wild mop of red hair, and the other a well-built Aboriginal boy, Chong. They encircled him. Peter thought of leaving, but a third boy blocked the doorway.

'I'm Peter Clancy,' Peter replied hesitantly. 'I've come to hang out.'

The boys broke into laughter. One of the boys punched Peter playfully in the arm. Peter smiled slowly.

'That your car out there?' one of the boys asked as he glanced out the door.

'That's mine,' Peter said proudly.

'It's not your mum's is it? You look like a mummy's boy,' the Aboriginal boy said as he shoved his face closer to Peter's. Peter flinched, which made the boy laugh.

'Gammon.'

'Leave him alone, Chong, you black cunt,' the red haired boy pushed Chong away. They playfully shaped up, threw wild punches at each other and then slapped each other.

'Call me Gibbo,' the red-haired boy said, 'and this idiot is Chong.'

'I'm Peter.'

'Don't you have a nickname?' Chong enquired, 'Everyone should have a nickname.'

'Just Peter.'

'I know,' Chong joked, 'what about "Pervie"?'

'Sounds fucked to me,' Gibbo replied. 'Let's go for a drive in Peter's car. You right with that?

'Fine. It's only a small car. I can't take everyone.'

'Not everyone's going, Pete. Just Chong and me. We have first say in what happens around here. We'd like a friend with a car. None of us has got licences.'

'Where do you want to go?' Peter asked. Chong and Gibbo looked at each other and smiled wryly.

'Let's get some booze and head out to the lagoon. Let's get to know each other,' Gibbo remarked.

That night, Peter returned home well after midnight, drunk and with the side of the car covered in his vomit. Irene was waiting for him. They had had a blazing row and Irene threatened to take the Datsun off him. Peter told her to piss off because it was his car. He was leaving at the end of the year, going to university and never coming back. He'd use his father's inheritance to support himself, so she could piss off and leave him alone. Irene complied and retreated further into herself and the brandy bottle. Now Peter went out whenever he wanted. Gibbo and Chong were the best friends he had ever had. Peter had finally won the war of attrition against his mother. He was wrong.

One night, Gibbo brought his father's gun with them to the lagoon. They headed out after consuming a large bottle of rum between them, intent on shooting a kangaroo. The three boys prowled along the creek, Peter holding a large torch, Chong carrying a butcher's knife and Gibbo with the rifle. Peter spotted a single doe grazing near a stand of trees. Peter shone the torch on the kangaroo, the light blinding her. Gibbo held up his rifle firing two quick shots into the doe's head. The kangaroo fell wounded, twitching and crying with pain. The boys rushed forward. Chong was there first. He hacked and sliced wildly at the kangaroo as it tried to kick him, initially only making shallow cuts into the kangaroo's torso. At first the blood trickled slowly from the first frenzied nicks Chong had made, and then it poured freely, as Chong became more deliberate in his cuts.

'I'll skin you alive,' Chong yelled as he slashed.

The kangaroo fought hard for its life, kicking and scratching with its front paws, making a tortured cry as the knife sank deep into her. Peter wavered with the torch.

'I can't see,' Chong shouted. Peter held the torch on the kangaroo again, trying not to look. Gibbo noticed Peter and smiled.

' It's only a roo, Petie. Toughen up, you fucking girl.'

' Die, you slut,' Chong screamed at the kangaroo as it affronted him by continuing to live. He kicked the kangaroo hard in the head, leaving it stunned. He then reached into its pouch and pulled out a joey by the tail, pink and harmless. It struggled as he swung it round several times about his head, before dashing its head against a tree and flinging it away. It was the moment Gibbo raced toward the kangaroo, pushing Chong aside.

'I want to kill the fucking bitch,' Gibbo demanded impatiently as he placed the gun against the kangaroo's head. He fired, shattering its skull. He fired until the magazine was empty, laughing maniacally.

Chong caught his breath and called to Peter. Peter came forward tentatively choosing not to stand too close to the carnage.

'What are you afraid of? This is what blokes do. Don't be such a girl,' he said as he wiped the knife's bloody blade on the kangaroo's fur. He pressed the blade softly against Peter's face.

'I'm gammon, you cunt,' Chong smiled when Peter flinched.

'You should enjoy it,' Gibbo added. 'Killing roos is good. Fucking vermin.'

19

'I want a root,' Gibbo declared loudly one night as he staggered drunkenly to his feet. He went to a nearby tree to relieve himself. Peter and Gibbo were sharing a bottle of rum near the campfire they had built at the lagoon.

'It's been two fucking weeks,' Gibbo continued, spraying wildly against the tree.

'Well, you're not rooting me,' Chong replied, snatching the bottle from an unprotesting Peter and taking a long drink. 'I thought you were going steady with Rhonda Kelly?'

'I dropped her. She was getting too serious. And her cunt stinks like dead fish.' Gibbo did up his fly and staggered back to the campfire. He snatched the bottle off Chong and handed it to Peter who was sitting quietly.

'Don't let him push you around. He's a black fella,' Gibbo joked.

'I'm trying to toughen him up,' Chong laughed. 'He's been with his mother for too long. Haven't you, Petie?' Chong punched Peter playfully in the arm.

'I guess you're right.'

'Do you want to root my ex, Chong?' Gibbo asked.

'Fuck that. She's ugly as a hatful of arseholes. Besides I don't want to go where your cock's gone before.'

'So who are you giving it to? I hope you're not rooting your cousin anymore. You'll end up with inbred kids,' Gibbo said.

'She's left town. Just good old Mrs Palmer at the moment.'

'What about you, Pete. Didn't you go out with Sally Enright? She looks pretty hot,' Gibbo asked.

'We went to the pictures last week,' Peter replied softly.

'We went to the pictures,' Chong mocked in an effeminate voice. 'But did you root her?'

'Yeah. Of course,' Peter replied, 'Down at the park.'

'How was she? She looks like a goer,' Gibbo asked.

'I'd root her. She's got big tits,' Chong smirked, pretending to stroke his groin.

'I couldn't stop her,' Peter added, sounding more confident.

'Why don't we go back into town, get some more grog and pick up some girls. We'll bring them back here for a party. I'll drive, Pete. You've had too much to drink.'

'You don't have a licence,' Peter replied.

'Party. Fuck yeah!' Chong jumped up with excitement and reached into his pocket, pulled out a handful of .22 bullets and threw them on the fire.

'You stupid black cunt!' Gibbo yelled. 'Get down!'

The bullets exploded, sending fragments of metal buzzing through the air as the three boys hurriedly crouched behind a fallen log.

'Party!' Chong yelled as the explosions died down. 'Let's fucking party!'

20

Sally sat in the back seat of the 120Y with Peter, looking undecided, while Gibbo and Chong sat in front.

'I'm not too sure,' Sally said.

'We're meeting people out at the lagoon,' Gibbo replied.

'Is that true, Peter?' Sally asked.

'Yeah. Of course.'

'Don't trust us, love?' Chong enquired.

'I trust Peter,' Sally replied. Gibbo and Chong laughed.

'That's funny,' Gibbo laughed. He turned around and handed Peter a bottle of rum. Peter took a tentative swig before giving it to Sally. She gave it immediately back to Gibbo.

'No thanks,' Sally replied with conviction.

'We're harmless,' Chong said,' Peter wouldn't be friends with us if we weren't.' Sally was sitting close to Peter at the campfire as Chong and Gibbo sat drinking watching them.

'Aren't you going to do anything, Pete?' Gibbo asked.

'I want to go. I'm not comfortable here. Can you take me home, Peter?' Sally asked nervously.

'You've only just arrived, slut,' Chong said.

'I'm not a slut,' Sally replied.

'Pete reckons you love it.' Gibbo stood up and sat on the other side of Sally.

'Peter's lying,' Sally replied.

'I didn't say that,' Peter spoke out.

Gibbo tried to put his arm around Sally. She brushed it away.

'If Pete isn't going to give it to you, I will,' Gibbo lunged forward, grabbing Sally's breast.

'She doesn't want to,' Peter said nervously.

'You go home to your mummy and we'll take care of her, won't we, Gibbo?' Chong jumped up and moved beside Peter. Sally tried to stand but Gibbo pushed her back down. She attempted to scream but he had already covered her mouth. Peter tried to grab hold of Gibbo but Chong punched him in the back of the head. Peter fell to the ground and struggled to stand. He heard Sally screaming as Chong and Gibbo swarmed on her like wolves pulling down prey.

'Help me, Peter,' Sally screamed as they tore at her dress. Peter staggered to his feet and tried to pull Gibbo off but another punch from Chong sent Peter crashing head first to the ground, hitting his head on a log.

Peter woke to the sound of guttural noises and muffled crying behind him. He stood slowly and felt a sharp pain in the back of his head. Peter swayed towards the commotion, at first recognising that the fire had gone cold. Chong lay on top of Sally next to the fire, thrusting into her limp body. Her clothes had been ripped off her like bark off a tree. They lay bloodied about her. Sally's mouth had been gagged with a pair of underpants, her face covered in cuts and welts.

'Hurry up. I want another go,' Gibbo complained as he took off his pants. He looked up when he saw Peter.

'Come to join the party, Petie,' Gibbo smirked. 'We're having a great time here. You'll have to wait until I've had my go.'

Peter didn't reply but looked impassively at them. Sally looked at Peter imploringly and tried to move but Gibbo slapped her across the face. 'Lay still, bitch'

Peter reached into his pocket for his car keys then realised that Gibbo had them.

'What are you going to do, Petie Pervert?' Gibbo asked, 'Just stand there? Have a wank at least.'

Peter seemed agitated and staggered towards them, then stopped abruptly. He wanted to face up to them, but his feet wouldn't move. He looked at Sally again and saw fear in her eyes. He wanted to scream. Peter wanted to hit Chong and Gibbo but he felt an emptiness envelop him, exactly as when he was a child.

I have to escape.

Peter turned around and ran. He ran until he got to the highway, where he collapsed on the soft shoulder. After drawing deep breaths into his lungs, he stood up and kept running. He ran until he got home, a distance of six kilometres. Irene stormed into his room in the early hours of the morning after she had noticed the car missing from the driveway. Peter lay fully clothed in bed, asleep, screwed tightly into a foetal position on top of the sheets. He woke with a start when she shook him.

'Where's the car?' she demanded.

'I didn't do it. I didn't do it,' Peter sobbed. He reached out to hold Irene, something he had not allowed himself to do since childhood.

'What have you done now?' Irene insisted, pushing Peter's hands away as they touched her. He collapsed back on the bed, crying into a pillow.

'Bloody no-hoper. That's all you are.'

21

Peter sat impassively, head down, at the desk as his mother cried beside him.

'I'm glad your father's not alive to see this. I told you those boys would get you in trouble. They're no-hopers.'

'They're my mates.'

'They just used you. But you're too stupid to see that. You'll never amount to anything. A disgrace to the Clancy name.'

'Shut up, Mum. I'm sick of the Clancy name. It doesn't mean anything,' Peter retaliated, getting out of the chair.

Max Hillard overheard the commotion and thundered into the office. He placed his hand firmly around Peter's neck and squeezed. Peter winced.

'I don't care what you do with him. He needs a good flogging with a stockwhip,' Irene said as she watched Max push Peter back into his chair. Max sat down on the other side of the desk. Peter sat rigidly, avoiding Max's gaze.

'Don't speak to your mother like that, son. You should never speak to your mother like that. ' Max warned. ' I don't tolerate that behaviour in my station.'

'I can't do anything with him. He needed a man to knock him into line. And now it's too late.'

Max leant across the desk and gently touched Irene's arm.

'Don't worry Irene. I'll sort out this mess. Nothing will happen to the boy. He's Dick Clancy's son. You wait outside while I talk to him.'

'Thank you, Max. He doesn't deserve to be helped but thank you.' Irene turned to Peter and shouted at him.

'You don't deserve anything. You're a bigger no-hoper than your stupid cousin.'

'Neck sore?' Max asked.

'A little,' Peter replied without looking up.

'Good.' Max crossed his feet on the desk and linked his hands behind his head. 'What do you want to do with your life son?' he asked. 'Look at me when I'm talking to you!' Peter's head shot up.

'A journalist in London, Max,' Peter whimpered.

'Sergeant Hillard to you,' Max shot back.

'Yes, Sergeant,' Peter said clearing his throat.

'A bloody journalist!' Max laughed, 'Bloody parasites of society. I thought you'd want to end up in the bush like your dad.'

'I don't like the bush,' Peter replied.

'You're a bit of a disappointment all round, aren't you, son?' Max said removing a notepad from the drawer of the desk and pushing it towards Peter.

'I guess,' Peter said.

'You're not a poofter are you, son? You sound like a poofter to me. Thank God Dick's not alive to see his son a poofter.'

'I'm not a poofter,' Peter replied as tears ran down his cheeks.

'Why didn't you rape the girl then?'

'It wasn't right.'

'You pissed off like a dog and let your so-called mates have their way with that poor girl. Why didn't you come to the police?'

'I was scared.'

'You should be scared now. I could charge you with being an accessory.

'If I charge you tonight, you can forget about being a journalist or anything else not involving manual labour. You could go to jail, son.'

'I saw them doing it. I tried to stop them. They bashed me,' Peter shouted, saliva spraying from his mouth.

'Someone has to go to be charged for this. I've seen rapes before and this is the worst I seen. Those boys nearly killed her. Ripped her insides out. The doctor reckons she'll never have children. Scum.' Max shook his head as he recalled what he had seen.

'I don't want to go to jail,' Peter howled.

'Pick up the pen. I want you to write a statement. As I tell you, all right? I've already got a statement from your mate, Noel Gibson. He says that your coon mate did all the raping. That's what I want you to write. Gibson and you went into town and while you were away, Butler raped Sally Enright. Maybe I should be a journalist,' Max chuckled. 'Creative ain't I?'

'Gibson didn't come with me?' Peter lowered the pen.

'Are you saying that the mayor's son is lying? You'll write what I bloody say, you little bastard,' Max banged his fist down hard, startling Peter so much that he dropped the pen.

'Butler is going to jail. One less coon on the street.' Max sighed contentedly as he leaned back in the chair, placing his feet back on the desk.

'I want to go to the toilet,' Peter said

'After you've written the statement. You and Gibson should consider yourselves very lucky. Don't you little shits forget it? All right? I won't. Remember I may call in the favour one day,' Max warned. 'You never know.'

PART FOUR

22

Clarkes Flat, 1987, Wednesday

Peter sat in the front pew of Saint Anthony's Church with his mother's casket and Douglas Clancy and his wife for company. Peter had not been into a church for many years; the Christian Brothers had beaten that out of him. Peter took a look at his cousin and if it hadn't been for the surroundings, would have laughed out loud. Doug looked his finest: oily bouffant and Elvis sideburns, wearing a bone-coloured safari suit. Doug had introduced his wife as Gloria, his Filipino bride, whom he had met when he was there on 'holidays'. By the look of her rouged lips, low-cut dress and towering high heels, Doug obviously liked her to dress according to his sexual fantasies.

Douglas and Peter were cousins but never friends. In fact, the last time Peter had seen Doug they had nearly come to blows. They had inherited their respective fathers' dislike for each other, which began when Doug's father, Frank, had squandered his inheritance on fast American cars, slow race horses and easy women, nearly sending Cornish Downs broke. Dick had agreed to pay Frank's debts as long as he was given total ownership of Cornish Downs and Frank never graced his door again.

Frank moved into Clarkes Flat and became known as the no-hoper Clancy. He got a job at the meat works, married a barmaid named Beverley, had Douglas who was regarded as 'slow', and died in his forties from the effects of alcohol.

Peter looked around the church noting the small gathering of unfamiliar people. By contrast, Dick Clancy's funeral had been one of the biggest ever held in Clarkes Flat. He remembered mourners spilling onto the footpath, the funeral officiated by the bishop, and his mother collapsing with grief at the gravesite. The priest's statement today that

Irene Clancy's funeral was the end of an era was made all the more poignant by the absence of mourners.

At the burial, Peter stood apart from the other mourners trying not to look at the casket as it was lowered. His mother place was in the Clancy plot, next to his father. As he glanced away, Peter noticed a familiar face, one he hadn't seen at the church. Max Hillard, even in his fifties, stood imposingly ramrod-straight, towering over the other mourners. He was even more imposing in his full police uniform. Max saluted as the coffin was lowered.

Irene was interred next to Dick and the other Clancys. *She's the last Clancy that'll be buried here*, Peter thought as he surveyed the headstones. Three generations in the cemetery and still a stranger here.

In total, there were six Clancys spanning three generations buried in the family plot. Each headstone was proudly inscribed with, *Of Cornish Downs*. All of the Clancys were buried here, except Doug's parents. After the burial, the crowd slowly dispersed; some offered their condolences, others drifted away. Doug made a bee-line for Peter as he moved from the grave, leaving Gloria behind.

'I've organised a wake at the RSL Your mother wanted it. She wanted you to pay for it,' Doug blurted when he approached Peter.

'How do you know?' Peter replied with surprise. Irene always kept a vast distance from Doug's family. *She must have softened over the years,* Peter thought.

'I used to visit her. I kept an eye on her. More than you ever did.'

'Can we manage to get out of the cemetery without having a fight?'

'I'm not here to fight, mate. I'm just telling you.'

'All right. I'll pay for the wake.'

Max interrupted the two men.

'The last of the Clancy family,' he proclaimed, draping his large arms around the cousins, pulling the pair closer to him and scrutinizing them. 'It's a sad day indeed. Dick and Irene will be up there having a good old chin-wag.' Max released his arm from around Doug and gave him a curt look.

'You go ahead, Douglas. I want to talk to Peter.' Douglas took the statement to be an order and left quickly.

'Sorry to hear about your mother. She was a good woman. Nearly all the old station people are gone.'

'Thanks, Max,' Peter replied softly.

'I haven't seen you for a while. Must be ten years.'

'About that.'

'I guess you have your reasons.'

'Too busy chasing a career, Max.'

'I guess so. I'm glad we sorted you out, son. It must have been hard on your mum without Dick. She can rest a lot easier now knowing that you've turned out fine.'

'Are you coming for a drink at the RSL?' Peter said in an effort to change the conversation.

'I'm on duty, son. But we'll catch up,' Max slapped Peter on the back leaving Peter looking back at the men already shovelling soil into his mother's grave.

Peter sat with a group of mourners at the public bar while Doug and Gloria sat nearby at a table. While Peter's mood grew happier with each drink, Doug's grew more sullen as he downed each free beer in rapid succession, glaring at Peter frequently, as if annoyed by Peter's cheerfulness. Gloria's attempt to soothe him was ignored.

'Your mum used to enjoy coming out here in the taxi. It was a big day out for her,' a male mourner stated to Peter.

'Was a lovely old dear, she was,' a female mourner added.

'She was always talking about you at *The Age* in Melbourne. She was so proud.'

'Funny she never told me,' Peter replied sadly as if struck by the statement. 'But mum was a stoic person.' There was an awkward silence that was interrupted by Doug staggering to the bar. He pushed Peter in the back.

'Looks like the free drinks have taken their toll, Cuz,' Peter jibed.

'Look at you,' Doug slurred as he continued to jab Peter with his finger. 'Think you're the big man from the city. Sitting up telling everyone how good you are. Bloody show-off.'

'I don't how you do it, Doug,' Peter replied, pushing Doug's hand away, 'but that chip on your shoulder must be incurable.'

'Don't use your fucking fancy words on me.' Doug shook his arm at Peter, losing balance momentarily before righting himself against the bar.

'This is a wake for your aunt,' a female mourner stated indignantly, 'Show some respect.'

'Talk about respect. He never ever respected his mother. Never saw her. Never helped her. Uncle Dick would be ashamed if he was still alive. A disgrace to the Clancy name.'

'You can talk,' Peter fumed. 'Your father was a drunk and you're so dumb that you don't even understand what dumb means.' Doug was raising his fist when Gloria interrupted.

'Dougy. You get too uptight. You need to relax,' she cooed massaging his shoulders.

'Gloria. Go and sit down,' Doug pulled away from her.

'Let's go home. I'll massage you all over with oil,' Gloria winked. Doug softened while he contemplated what Gloria had said.

'Sounds nice, love,' Doug replied, patting Gloria on the bottom. 'Sounds really sexy. I love your magic hands and especially what you do with your mouth. Let's get out of here,' Doug said as he steered Gloria towards the door.

'I bet you're jealous, Cuz,' Doug grinned before walking out of the door. 'She wants it all the time.'

'Poor girl. She's got her work cut out for her,' a male mourner said after Doug and Gloria had left.

'Things must be crook in the Philippines to want to marry Douglas Clancy. No one else would have him.'

'No disrespect to your family, Peter,' a male mourner whispered. 'But your cousin, Dumbo, I mean Doug, was never quite right. He spies on people, you know.'

'That's silly talk, Ces,' A female mourner said. 'Max would never allow that to happen.'

'Douglas and I were always close. Always close to killing each other.' The mourners laughed awkwardly.

'Another round!' Peter called to the barmaid. The day wore on and Peter found himself alone at the bar struggling over a beer that had gone warm. He fished into his pocket and pulled out a wad of money before calling the barmaid.

'Cold carton to take away, thanks.'

A tall, muscled man in his thirties with cropped hair walked into the bar and came straight up to Peter.

'Peter Clancy?' the man asked. Peter eyed the man up and down before replying.

'Maybe I am. What have I done?' Peter laughed.

'You don't recognise me do you?'

'I haven't got a bloody clue who you are,' Peter replied.

'Dave Tindall, John's son. We used to play together in primary school.'

'That's right. We used to go fishing at Eden's Lagoon,' Peter recalled. 'It looks like you've grown into a muscle builder,' Peter added as he looked Dave over.

'I like to stay fit.'

'Can I buy you a drink?' Peter asked.

'Sorry. I can't stay. I'm in a bit of a hurry. But can we catch up? You're not going home yet?'

'I'm here for a few more days.'

'That's good,' Dave replied sounding relieved, 'Meet me tomorrow at ten in the café on the main street.'

Dave left hurriedly, leaving Peter puzzled.

23

Peter was walking by old Mr Alford, who stood watch outside his department store, greeting passers-by as had been his custom for forty years. He had acquired an affected accent during his education at a private grammar school in Brisbane many decades earlier.

'Peter Clancy,' he said, raising his sweat-stained pork pie hat. 'Many condolences to you and the family.'

'Thanks, Mr Alford.' Peter remembered with gratitude how Mr Alford opened the store specifically for his mother one Sunday morning, just because they were returning to the station that day.

'The passing of an era,' he lamented before another passer-by caught his attention.

The Wintergarden Picture Theatre was next door to the store, its once grand Athenian façade crumbling, its heavy oak doors boarded over, the brass fixtures removed. A faded poster hung in tatters from the billboard. Peter lifted it and read the title of the theatre's last picture — the 1980's remake of *Flash Gordon*.

A sad end to a picture theatre that showed all the classic films.

'You got a smoke mate?' an Aboriginal man staggered up to Peter from the opposite direction. The man was barefooted, dishevelled and obviously drunk. He carried an opened bottle of wine in his hand.

'Don't smoke,' Peter replied, briefly stopping to talk to the man.

'You got any money? I need a feed, Bro.' Peter looked in his wallet, removed a five-dollar note and handed it to the man.

A woman walking behind Peter interrupted, sniffing the air as she walked by.

'Don't give them any money. They'll just spend it on alcohol.'

'I won't. Honest, missus,' the Aboriginal man replied.

'Get yourself something to eat,' Peter said.

'Thanks, Brother.' The Aboriginal man grabbed Peter's hand and shook it African-American style, before staggering on. Peter watched with sadness as shoppers coming along the street either gave the man a wide berth or crossed the road to avoid him. A police car driving by screeched to a halt near the Aboriginal man. Peter observed the man freeze to the spot as two burly policemen grabbed him; one snatched the bottle from him and poured it into the gutter. Then they pushed the Aboriginal man into the back seat of the police car and drove off.

'Get them off the streets!' an old man covered in skin cancers remarked to Peter. 'Should have shot them all when we had the chance.'

'Piss off, you stupid old redneck,' Peter replied angrily, leaving the old man open-mouthed.

Dave was already seated in the Palms Café when Peter walked in. The interior of the café was country-and-western themed; a mélange of whips and saddles surrounded a bull's head, mounted to the wall as a centrepiece. Country music playing on an ancient juke-box enhanced the ambiance. Peter surveyed the surroundings with disdain before seating himself in a booth.

'I didn't think you were coming,' Dave said gruffly.

'I was just watching the police in action. It's good to know that the Aborigines are still well treated.'

'I don't get you,' Dave replied.

'It's all right,' Peter, replied, 'I shouldn't have expected anything to change.' A young waitress with stringy hair and cigarette breath approached them.

'What are you having?'

'Pot of tea for me,' Dave requested.

'Cappuccino please,' Peter asked brusquely.

'Hey?' the waitress appeared confused.

'Sounds like you don't have that,' Peter said. 'What about a flat white?'

'We've got Nescafé or International Roast.'

'Give me a white Nescafé,' Peter laughed and shook his head.

'You've been away for a while,' Dave observed after she left with the orders.

'Thank God. What are you doing with yourself now?

'I'm a copper. Day off today,' Dave replied quietly. Peter noted that Dave was dressed in long pants and business shirt, sleeves buttoned at the cuffs, as if he were going to an important meeting.

'I thought you would have taken over the family business.'

'Mum sold up the saleyards after Dad died.'

'A Queensland copper. That must be fun in Joh's police state.'

'There's talk of an enquiry into police corruption ever since that *Four Corners* programme went to air,' Dave remarked.

'I bet that goes nowhere. Joh may sound like a mumbling idiot with dementia, but he's as cunning as a shithouse rat,' Peter stated. 'Are you worried if there is an enquiry?'

'No. The dishonest cops might be.'

The waitress returned with the order.

'Are you having anything else?' she asked, rolling her eyes.

'If we want anything we'll let you know,' Peter teased. 'We'll call you when you're needed.'

Dave spoke again after the waitress had left.

'Do you do any of that investigative reporting?' Dave asked quietly.

'Yes, if you call finding out who's fucking who investigative,' Peter took a sip of his coffee and pushed it away. 'What is that?' He complained loudly.

Dave looked around the coffee shop before speaking.

'We used to be good friends for a while, right? Didn't we? Our parents were friends remember,' Dave continued nervously.

'I guess we were, a long time ago. We haven't exactly sent Christmas cards to each other every year,' Peter replied.

'Do you remember the day when my father died?' Dave asked.

'Not exactly. I was only a kid.' Peter noticed Dave's hand shaking as he held the cup of tea.

'I've been working on something.'

'What do you know, Dave?'

'I know...' Dave abruptly stopped speaking when he saw a policeman enter the café and approach the counter. He stood up, knocking the table.

'Another time, Peter,' he added, before leaving Peter contemplating his coffee.

Peter was opening the door of the car when a barefooted, unkempt woman in a wraparound skirt and tank top approached him on the footpath. Without the crevices criss-crossing her face and the limp greying hair, she might have been of a similar age to Peter.

'Don't recognise me do you?' the woman spat through a gap of missing teeth. She leaned against his car for support.

'Sorry. I don't,' Peter replied. 'Should I?'

The woman reached into her pocket, took out a small bottle of spirits and took a swig.

'You should,' the woman coughed as she swallowed the raw spirit.

'You're not going to tell me?' Peter asked.

'Think it over. You'll find out soon enough,' the woman sneered before walking away unsteadily.

Later that day, Peter found a Super 8 projector, a box with canisters of film and a camera stored together in a box beside bundles of what appeared to be every greeting and condolence card Irene had ever received, neatly packaged according to type.

Peter had the unenviable task of cleaning up a lifetime's worth of household detritus. Thankfully, Peter finally concluded, he would take all personal effects to the dump and give the rest to charity. Anything of worth he'd keep and he'd just purged that down to six photo albums and his mother's jewellery. Then the house would be sold as soon as he could arrange it. After that, all connections with Clarkes Flat would finally be severed.

Never have to come back here. Done. Finished.

He remembered his mother using the camera when they lived on the station. He recalled the film nights when she had shown each film on a screen set up in the dining room, to an audience usually consisting of his father, the governess, Sam and himself. He got smacked during one film night for using the camera without permission at the Tindall's place. As he recollected, Irene never used it again. She had said it never worked properly again. Peter's memory was assisted by the fact that Irene liked to retell the incident periodically over the years, usually when she could humiliate Peter the most, in the company of friends when Peter was present. The sting-in-the-tail to her sad story was that the camera had given her her greatest joy. Until he broke it, that was.

Peter set up the projector in the lounge and took out a film canister marked *Stockyard 1968*. He pulled the curtains shut. The screen had disappeared over time, so Peter had to be content with projecting the film against the lounge wall. He removed the film from the canister, carefully wound it onto the projector and turned it on. It jammed. After readjusting the film, he tried again. The projector flickered into life and as he focussed the grainy images onto the wall, he was suddenly transported back to Cornish Downs.

Peter watched Sam and his father drafting cattle on foot in the dusty stockyards. Because of her fear of livestock, Irene filmed from outside the yard. Sam and his father waved and laughed through the dust in the direction of the lens from time to time. Peter approached the wall to study his father — how he walked, how he shook his head, how he laughed. Details about his father that he'd forgotten. Then the film came to an abrupt end when a cow ran towards the camera. Peter turned off the projector and sorted through the box. All of the canisters were neatly marked with the events, as Irene had filmed them. He wrestled with consigning the camera and its paraphernalia to the dump, but seeing his father alive on screen changed Peter's mind. Courtesy of Irene's camera, a man once dead and almost forgotten had been brought back to life.

Peter watched the news from the discomfort of the threadbare, sagging couch, beer in hand and Bindy, who lay on the floor, for company. The news was saturated with stories of Queensland police corruption and brutality, politicians with their heads in the trough, brown paper bags full of money. Peter watched with an air of cynicism.

You have to give him credit. Joh is a survivor. You may hate him but you have to admire him for being a tough old bastard.

He soon grew bored with the television and got off the couch to turn it off. The old stereo in the corner and the adjacent wooden cabinet containing records caught his eye. Peter had never been allowed access to it, except when his mother went shopping, and then clandestinely. His mother abhorred his taste in music so much that she thought that it would damage the stereo if he ever played his rock albums on it. Jerry Vale and Marty Robbins were more suitable for her stereo. His music was confined to a cheap mono record player with a torn speaker in his room. The music was barely audible and always accompanied by crackles.

Peter turned on the stereo, slipped on a record and turned it to full volume. The music blasted out, causing Bindy to scamper from the room. He sat on the couch, feeling liberated and ignoring the occasional jumps of the record.

Deep Purple's *Made in Japan*. A fucking classic.

Peter heard a loud knock on the front door as track number three came to an end. He got off the couch to turn down the volume.

'Bloody wowsers,' he fumed as he went to the front door.

An elderly Aboriginal man wearing a battered stockman's hat, moleskins and a T-shirt with *Blondie* emblazoned on it stood on the doorstep.

'Sorry about that,' Peter apologised.

'You may not remember me. I'm Sam Saturday. I used to work with your father.'

'Sam. Of course I remember you,' Peter said excitedly. 'I haven't seen you since I was a kid. The last time I saw you was not long after dad's funeral. That is, if you don't count seeing you in Mum's films.' Peter shook Sam's hand vigorously. 'I didn't see you at Mum's funeral. Didn't you know about it?'

'No. Couldn't make it. Sorry about that.' Sam's voice started to trail off then regathered momentum. 'It's been a while. You're grown up, young fella. What are you doing with yourself?'

'I'm a journalist in Melbourne.'

'Melbourne? Never been there. That's where they have the Melbourne Cup? Any black fellas there?'

'Not many,' Peter replied.

'I thought you would have gone back out bush. Never known any Clancy ever live in the big smoke,' Sam said sadly. 'Thought you'd end up on a station.'

'Do you want to come in? Peter asked, 'Have a cup of tea?'

'I need you to come with me. It's very important.'

'I don't really want to go anywhere tonight. I'm buggered,' Peter replied.

'It's very important. Come with me now,' Sam insisted, raising his voice. 'I need you to come with me now.'

'All right. All right. I don't want you to have a stroke at my front door.'

Peter helped Sam to buckle the seat belt in his car.

'Where do you want me to take you?' Peter asked as he completed the task and started the car.

'Brookland,' Sam replied.

'What part of town is that? I haven't been here for ten years.'

'Brookland Park. The station. Have you forgotten? The city must have fucked your brain up,' Sam smiled.

'That's sixty frigging miles away from here and it's dark. There'll be roos and cattle all over the road. Is it that important?' Peter asked.

'Fucking oath it is. You've got lights,' Sam replied.

'I don't want the car wrecked, it's a hire car.'

'I'll keep an eye out. No worries,' Sam assured Peter as he pulled his hat over his face, slumped down in the seat and went to sleep.

Peter drove along the highway and left the outskirts of town with only Sam's snores for company. When he thought Sam was in a deep sleep, Peter slowed down and began to turn back towards Clarkes Flat. Sam awoke with a jolt.

'What are you doing? We're going to Brookland Park,' Sam said curtly.

'You're supposed to be asleep,' Peter replied.

'I sleep with one eye open,' Sam laughed. 'Keep driving. I'll let you know when we get close.'

Peter continued on with the original route, Sam's snoring filling the cabin once more as the car sped on. Peter glanced occasionally at the shadowy bush as a distraction from Sam's snoring. He felt strangely calm, mesmerised by the hum of the road.

He screeched the car to a stop as a large buck kangaroo suddenly darted across the road in front of him. Peter shook Sam.

'Hey! You were supposed to let me know if there are roos on the road!' he complained.

'Only ones that might actually hit the car,' Sam replied smugly as he shook himself fully awake and looked around.

'There's the turn-off,' Sam pointed to his left to a track off the highway.

'Where? It's fucking dark,' Peter peered through the window.

'Just there. Why can't you white fellas see in the dark?' Sam pointed again.

Peter turned the car down a rough track that meandered through the open grassland.

'I can barely see the track, Sam,' Peter said looking keenly for any traces of road. The car pitched as a wheel went over a large rock, and then it fell suddenly, its chassis scraping against the rock.

'I'd really like to be able to return this car in one piece, Sam.'

'White fellas — always worrying about what you own.'

'That's the trouble. I don't own this car.'

'Shut up,' Sam ordered. 'I'm losing concentration. I'll tell you where to go. This is my mob's home country. I know everything about this country,'

'Well how come you didn't know that big fucking roo that nearly hit the car?'

'He must be here on holidays. He's not from here,' Sam laughed.

'You're a bloody old rogue, Sam Saturday.'

After another ten kilometres and one hour of traversing the rough track, the sun peering above the bush canopy was a welcome relief.

'Here. Stop!' Sam shouted. Peter stopped the car and followed Sam, who was walking briskly towards a clearing in the dense bush. Peter chose this to be a good time to relieve himself.

'Hurry up!'

'I'm having a piss. A man's allowed to have a piss,' Peter replied. Annoyed, he continued urinating for what felt like an eternity then slowly did up his fly. He walked unhurriedly to where Sam had stopped. He was now looking back at Peter, shaking his head.

A set of six broken, white-anted yard posts stood like bent fingers in the clearing. Sam touched one and pushed it over with ease. It fractured into shards of splintered wood and dust when Sam stood on it. Multitudes of angry white ants frantically swarmed without purpose about the broken post, unsure how to defend or direct themselves. Sam watched them briefly then walked on again.

'This is where it happened,' Sam recalled, looking about. He reached down and picked up a broken horseshoe and rubbed it softly then threw it away.

'If you're going to tell a boring old bush yarn about yarding up cattle and chasing wild brumbies after I've driven sixty fucking miles, I'll…'

'Shut up, young fella. You're not in the city now. Respect your elders.'

'Sorry,' Peter apologised, startled at Sam's brusqueness.

'This is where we brought the clean skins to put on the truck.'

'Sam, I'm tired. I need a coffee.' Peter sat on the ground and rubbed his face. 'What are you going to say to that? "The trouble with you white fellas is you like coffee too much"?'

'Will you stop your whining? You sound like a fucking kid. Listen. You know what cattle duffing is?'

'Of course I do,' replied Peter. 'I know the story when dad caught the ringers from next door and fired the gun over their heads.'

'I've never seen a man and a horse both shit themselves,' Sam grinned as he recalled the incident. He crouched down beside Peter, surveying the bush.

Sam told Peter how he did some work for Bert Canning for a little while, how he and Peter's father had an argument and Sam left in a huff. Bert Canning had been drunk most of the time and let the place run down over the years. Sam became a caretaker of sorts, when Bert was put in hospital to dry out.

'Bert had unbranded cattle everywhere. Some people thought they could make a lot of money. They offered me money if I would help them find the cattle. They said I could set myself up for life.'

'You brought them here?' Peter asked, feigning interest.

'We made a set of yards here so no one would see us. We mustered the cattle here, then loaded them on a truck and put them through the saleyards. Easy. Three thousand head all up. Took about three months on and off. That's good money except I didn't see much of it. They said I'd be able to buy a house but all I got was a hundred dollars.' Sam pinched the skin on his forearm. 'Might be due to the colour of this, I guess.'

'Probably,' Peter nodded.

'I was going to ask for more money but then some bad things started to happen. I left Bert's and went back to your dad's. Then your dad died. I couldn't take anymore so I took off up the Gulf for twenty years. I only came back recently.'

'What scared you off?' Peter asked, getting off his backside to sit on his haunches.

'Things went crook,' Sam replied quietly as his face fell. He took off his hat and brushed a hand through his thick greying hair. There was a long silence. He finally heard himself utter the words he had clung tightly to himself all those years. 'People started to die,' he whispered as he lifted his eyes and looked at Peter.

'Who died, Sam? Can you tell me?' Peter asked, noticing that Sam's hands were trembling.

'Two blokes. Two blokes who shouldn't have died,' Sam sobbed. Peter leaned across and put his arm around him.

'Who were they, Sam?' Peter asked softly, 'You can tell me.'

They fell silent when they heard rustling in the nearby bush.

'What's that?' Peter asked nervously.

Before Sam could answer, they heard, 'It's me,' as Dave emerged tattered and disoriented from the weedy undergrowth. He lumbered towards them, carrying a pistol.

Peter leapt to his feet. 'What the fuck are you doing, Dave?' he shouted, as Sam followed suit.

'Why weren't you interested before?' Dave asked, inching slowly towards them and waving the pistol about. Peter started to back away. Sam didn't move.

'Put the gun down, Dave,' Peter pleaded. 'I didn't mean to upset you the other day. We can talk about this. Don't shoot. Remember how we used to play together? We were good friends. Weren't we? You wouldn't shoot a friend. Dave?'

Dave's attention turned to the pistol clutched in his right hand.

'Settle down. I'm only carrying this 'cause I thought I might come across a wild pig,' he chuckled as he put the pistol back in its holster.

'Dave. You white fellas. Always scared of the bush,' Sam chastised. He then looked at Peter. 'You've seen too many *Dirty Harry* movies.'

'I thought you were meeting us here before sunup?' Sam continued.

'I got bloody lost didn't I?' Dave replied sheepishly.

'What the fuck is going on, you two? Obviously you know each other.' Peter was fuming.

Sam glanced at Dave and nodded.

'Unfortunately, Billy and my father were part of the cattle duffing ring. Sam was helping them. That's what I was trying to tell you the other day.' Dave blurted out.

'So what? I'm sure half of Clarkes Flat has been involved in cattle duffing at one time or another.'

'But Billy and my father died one day apart, supposedly both suicides,' Dave continued.

'Have you ever thought that they couldn't handle the guilt? Maybe they argued over the money. Who knows? These things happen,' Peter spat back. 'Maybe you have unresolved grief issues.'

'Stop being a smartarse and listen,' Sam said angrily, walking up to Peter and punching the words straight into his face.

'I'm telling you. It wasn't suicide,' Dave implored.

'Okay. Are you trying to say they were murdered?' Peter asked, softening his voice.

'They were murdered,' Dave replied, looking at Sam for support, 'Weren't they Sam?'

'I reckon they didn't kill themselves. They didn't look like they would kill themselves,' Sam replied.

'No disrespect, Sam, but you can't usually tell when someone is going to commit suicide. I've interviewed people who seemed happy when I spoke to them. Next day they're found gassed in their car,' Peter said.

'Let me finish,' Dave persisted.

'There's more,' Sam added.

'I've heard enough.' Peter turned around and headed in the direction of his car.

'Listen, Peter,' Dave called after him.

Peter stopped and spun around. 'You know why I don't want to hear any more? I hate this place. I hate this place so much that I want to spew when I think about it. I came to bury my mother. That's done. So let me get the fuck out of here.'

'We need your help,' Dave begged. Sam came up to Dave and patted him on the shoulder.

'And, Sam, get a lift back with your mate,' Peter said as he jumped into the car. Sam and Dave watched as Peter's car sped up the bush track, leaving a plume of dust in its wake.

24

Friday

Don't die. Don't die. Don't, Dad. Daddy, Daddy.

Peter awoke from his sleep just before midday, crying and covered in sweat, the sheets pulled clean off the mattress. Courtesy of his overnight adventure, half the day was already gone. He stared at the ceiling until the urge for a coffee got the better of him.

I can't bear it, another day of fucking cleaning. Another day of fucking Clarkes Flat. Should burn this fucking place down and piss off.

He plodded around the house in his underwear, throwing his mother's trinkets and treasures into boxes destined for the charity shop, scrubbing the bathroom and the kitchen and pretty much everything in sight. It reminded him of his mother's annual spring-cleaning ritual, which always took place out-of-season, just before the New Year. At the end of the day he would put on another film. Today it would be *The Mailman, 1968*.

It was a big event at the station when the mailman arrived. He came every week, not just with letters and parcels, but with essential supplies such as groceries, medicines and newspapers. Peter watched as George Christy, the mailman, arrived in his heavily-laden Bedford truck, got out, and, noticing Irene pointing the camera at him, jokingly jumped back in. He then watched himself as a boy running up as George, who kept looking awkwardly at the camera, handed him a much-awaited comic book. Old Peter cringed as Young Peter jumped up and down with excitement, the comic book flapping in his hands. Was he really that scrawny?

What a great life for a kid. Then Dad died.

Peter was deep in thought when he threw the stick far out into the lagoon for Bindy. This was the first time he had returned to the lagoon since that night, the night of the rape. Peter had always thought he would never be able to return here, but he was drawn back without reason. The lagoon was calming; its water still, except for ducks landing, feeding and taking off it; waterlilies in full bloom; paperbark trees branches hanging heavily in the water. Peter sat on the bank drinking his third beer and pondered the events of the previous day, the past, all of it swirling in his head like a whirlpool. He only noticed that Bindy had returned when she dropped the stick in his lap and barked incessantly into his face. He threw the stick out into the lagoon again. Bindy dived into the water and swam frantically to retrieve it, scattering a group of ducks as she paddled through them.

He looked up when he heard a car with a broken exhaust come to a stop in the car park, rev loudly several times and turn off its ignition. As he climbed up the embankment, he saw the same unkempt woman from the street, leaning against a battered old Ford Cortina with multi-coloured panelling. It was the same car he had noticed following him when he had turned off the highway to the lagoon. It had followed him for ten kilometres before disappearing into the thick dust churned up by the wheels of his car.

'Remember me?' the woman asked as she swigged from a bottle of wine.

'You were in the street the other day,' Peter replied.

'Funny bastard,' the woman replied as she approached. She glared into Peter's face. 'It's Sally. The girl you left to be raped when you ran away.'

'Sally? Peter replied sounding shocked, 'I didn't recognise you.'

'The years haven't been to kind to me. Thanks to you and your mates.'

'Mum told me you'd committed suicide five years ago.'

'I nearly did but that the fucking doctor revived me. Bastard.' Sally continued after a swig from the wine bottle. 'I had nothing to run away from, besides, my parents have taken good care of me.'

'That's good,' Peter said inanely.

'Do you ever think about that night? Sally questioned.

'I've put it behind me,' Peter said abruptly. 'I don't believe in living in the past.'

'Why did you come here today then?'

'Give the dog a swim,' Peter threw back. Peter looked at his car as he noticed Bindy jumping in through the driver's open window to settle on the driver's seat. She shook herself, spraying her wet fur around the car interior. Happy and content, Bindy nonchalantly peered out of the window. Peter rolled his eyes.

'Good for you,' Sally replied. 'Couldn't remember anything? That's a gift.'

'I can't help you, Sally,' Peter replied forcefully, as he hopped from foot to foot. 'Excuse me but I have to go.'

Sally stood closer to him. Her wine breath stung his eyes and made Peter blink.

'You always sounded so sincere, Peter Clancy, the nice, quiet boy. But I've seen what's underneath that façade. You would have raped me if you could have. You would have loved to. Wouldn't you?' Sally ranted at Peter as he gazed past her, looking for a way of escape.

'Why don't you get therapy, alright?' Peter spat out as he pushed past her and made a beeline for his car. Sally raced ahead, blocking his path again.

'Is that what you think I need?' Sally yelled into his face, 'You know what I need? I want revenge.' Sally shook her fist under Peter's nose. He pulled back and tried to move around her but, again, she blocked his path. He felt himself growing nervous.

'Do you know Butler and Gibson are dead?'

'No. I never heard.'

'Butler hung himself in jail. Gibson died during a domestic a few years ago. Ironic isn't it? I should have felt happy they died, but, you see, not everyone has been punished yet.' Sally reached into a pocket

'Fuck. She's going for a knife. Push her out of the way. Run like shit to the car. Crazy woman with a knife. Like the time...like the time the Saint Kilda madam chased me around her establishment with a meat cleaver!

'Revenge doesn't solve anything. Hurting me isn't going to…' Peter stammered as he moved backwards. He tripped on a rock, almost falling and quickly righting himself. Sally kept creeping towards him.

'Do you think I'm going to hurt you? Sally cackled in a laugh that was the by-product of too much alcohol. 'I want you to help me, you idiot.' Peter stopped moving backwards. Sally threw the bottle aside, pulled out a tissue and blew her nose.

'How could I do that? I can't do anything to change what happened,' Peter was puzzled. He felt the sudden urge to urinate.

'You could go to the police and say you were coerced into giving a false statement. I know what Max Hillard did. Gibson got off 'cause he was the mayor's son. Butler? Just happened to be black. Now I want Max.'

'It's the past, Sally. Be happy you're alive,' Peter advised.

'You're pathetic. Being dead would have been a better option a lot of times. You know what it's liked to be raped? It's like your guts have been pulled out. You wish you were dead. I would have killed myself years ago but I wanted people to pay,' Sally cried then swung a wild punch at

Peter that missed. She collapsed to the ground and lay face down before tucking herself into a foetal position, sobbing and beating the ground with her hands. Peter watched motionless and helpless. Of course, he had seen grief. Parents who had lost children were the worst. *Guttural grief*, he called it. He'd learnt how to deal with it by building a wall around him.

Peter looked about; the lagoon, his car, Sally. He knelt beside her and made motion to put his arm around her back but stopped as when he felt her blouse. He was paralysed. Her pain was paralysing. He remembered that pain. The wall. Sally suddenly stopped crying and stood unsteadily. Peter tried to take her arm but she rejected it. Sally continued walking briskly to her car.

'Are you all right?' Peter asked as he followed her. Sally didn't answer. She didn't look at him. Once she got to her car, Sally robotically turned over the ignition, revved the Cortina so loudly that it sounded like the worn-out exhaust pipe would shatter, and sped off without giving Peter any further recognition.

Peter arrived home from the lagoon just on dusk to see a green 1975 Ford Fairlane parked out front. Peter knew it would be Doug's. Who else would have a large Elvis sticker emblazoned across the rear window, a confederate flag hanging from the antenna and a personalised number plate that said, DUG NO1? Bindy growled as Peter parked beside it.

'What's wrong old girl?' Peter said patting Bindy, 'Don't like visitors?'

Peter found Doug rummaging through the toolshed at the back of the house. Doug seemed startled when he saw Peter and Bindy. Bindy took one look at Doug and began barking furiously. With that, he slammed the toolshed door shut and darted towards Peter.

'Get that fucking dog away from me!' Doug yelled. 'I hate dogs!'

'She won't bite,' Peter reassured. 'She's being protective.'

Doug lashed out at Bindy when she drew near him. His kick missed. Bindy drew in closer, baring her teeth.

'I'll kill the fucking thing!' Doug threatened.

'Come on, Bindy,' Peter called softly then whistled. Bindy stopped and trotted back to Peter with a satisfied look on her face. Peter took hold of her collar as a precaution. She continued to snarl at Doug every time he spoke.

'What are you doing here?' Peter questioned.

'I was looking for a shovel I left here. I used to look after your mother's yard.'

'Doesn't look like you did a very good job,' Peter remarked looking at the overgrown garden and dead grass.

'At least I was helping your mother,' Doug replied. 'Better than you ever did.'

'What are you really doing here?'

'You need to relax, Cuz,' Doug concluded, as he strutted away. 'You're not in the big smoke now. This town isn't full of druggies and crims. We're decent people here.' That night Peter watched another one of his mother's films, marked, *At the River*. He watched Dick wearing swimming trunks, sitting on the riverbank, drinking a beer and surveying Young Peter as he swam with a dog. The dog swam over to Peter and began to scratch him. He hit out at the dog and paddled closer to the riverbank. Dick continued to watch Peter. He called out. Peter emerged from the water, crying, wearing an inflatable vest. The dog emerged, shook itself and ran over to Dick. Peter noticed how fit his father looked, certainly a lot fitter than him.

25

Saturday

Peter entered the office of the *Golden Miner*, Clarkes Flat's newspaper for a hundred years, with a feeling of nostalgia. The dusty, cob-webbed office had seen its heyday a long time ago, but a heavy oak counter still stood proudly in the entrance as a reminder that this paper had once been the miner's voice, a mouthpiece for the common man. Peter stood at the counter and banged on a rusted bell several times. A camp bed tucked behind a desk caught his eye.

'Jack. Are you there?'

'Yes, yes. I'm coming.'

Jack Gooley, the *Miner's* long serving owner, editor, typesetter and journalist, entered the office via a creaking side door and limped to the counter. He peered through a pair of taped glasses at Peter without recognising him.

'Still writing your own letters to the editor, Jack?' Peter asked.

'Peter Clancy! I didn't recognise you,' Jack replied finally, shaking Peter's hand. 'Sorry to hear about your mother. What a loss. I'm doing her obituary at the moment. Anything you want to add?'

'No. I think you know the story,' Peter replied.

'Your mother said you work at the Melbourne *Age*. That's a great paper.'

'I hate to tell you this, Jack, but I work for *The Truth*,' Peter replied in a secretive voice.

'But your mother said…'

'I think Mum was a little embarrassed.'

'I've never read it,' Jack returned.

'Are you sleeping here?' Peter's eyes settled on the camp bed.

'Ever since the wife died. Didn't want to live in the house. Too many reminders, you know,' Jack admitted sadly. 'I have to look after this old girl. No one else is. When I'm gone there'll be no more *Golden Miner*.' He added with a sly grin, 'Not interested are you?'

'I don't think Clarkes Flat would like my style of journalism.'

'You know, I remember a pimply-faced kid coming here for work experience, saying he was going to win a Walkley Award and work in Fleet Street. You better hurry. I'm not getting any younger.'

'I've been nominated but just haven't found the winning story yet.'

'You've got it in you, the fighting Clancys. I know...' Jack chuckled.

'I wanted to ask if you could help me with something,' Peter interrupted.

'Yeah,' Jack said slowly. 'What might that be?'

'Do you still keep back issues of the *Miner*?' Peter asked.

'Every issue since 1895. How far back do you want to go?'

'I'm interested in the year 1968,' Peter answered.

'Follow me to the library. Let's see. That was the year Col Joye and the Joyeboys came to town. That was an eventful year what I remember. And there was something else?' Jack scratched his head as he tried to recall.

Peter and Jack squeezed into a dingy storeroom that had most of its floor space covered by stacks of yellowing newspapers.

'Library?' Peter questioned, as he managed to force himself between two stacks.

Some of the stacks reached to the ceiling. Jack pulled at one of the smaller stacks, blowing off years of collected dust to read a card.1965. He continued to scrounge around the stacks like an inquisitive rodent before finding what he was looking for.

'The year 1968,' Jack said, as he pulled at the string tying the newspapers. The string snapped and the pile of papers fell towards him, billowing dust all over the storeroom. Jack and Peter coughed loudly. Jack nearly tripped as he stepped back to avoid the small avalanche bearing down on him

'Have you ever thought of storing them properly? They're going either to kill you or fall apart,' Peter said, coughing out the years of accumulated dust that was now consolidating in his lungs.

'I know where everything is,' Jack replied, as he picked up a newspaper that lay at his feet. He brushed away the dirt as he skimmed the front page.

'That's it. How could I forget,' Jack recalled. 'That was the year of Clarkes Flat's last murder.' He handed the paper to Peter to read then took it before Peter had read past page two.

'Don't hold it too long. It could fall apart,' Jack remarked as he tucked it under his arm.

'The publican shot an Aboriginal man in the bar,' Peter replied. 'I vaguely remember that.'

'Nipper Coleman. What a character. The black was drunk and came at Nipper with a knife. Nipper shot him in self-defence.'

'Where did the gun come from? I didn't think publicans could walk around with guns,' Peter questioned.

'He was allowed to. The bloody blacks would have wrecked the place otherwise.'

'How long did he get?'

'No sentence. Got good behaviour.'

'Interesting verdict,' Peter replied. 'Nothing to do with the colour of the deceased?'

'It was a fair trial,' Jack said tersely. 'Is that what you wanted to know?'

'Do you have any stories about John Tindall and Billy Johnson? That was in 1968 too, wasn't it?'

'It was 1969. But there won't be any stories about John and Billy, just funeral notices.'

'Why's that?'

'Suicide is a sensitive issue in a small town. I didn't want to distress the families any more,' Jack replied.

'Let's go outside,' Peter suggested. 'I'd like to be able to breathe clean air again.' The pair emerged from the storeroom, both blinking as the sun hit their faces. Peter inhaled a deep breath of air as Jack locked the storeroom door.

'Why do you reckon they committed suicide?' Peter continued.

'I heard the saleyards were in financial trouble. John and Billy started stealing cattle and putting them through the saleyards. Apparently Max was about to arrest the both of them when they shot themselves,' Jack replied quietly.

'Was it just Billy and John involved?' Peter asked.

'I think Sam Saturday was, but he took off to the Gulf before he got caught. There were a lot of rumours going around,' Jack recalled. 'The best one I heard was that Billy was having an affair with Lorna Tindall. John caught them in the act, shot Billy and later shot himself. She still lives in the town. Lost her mind after the deaths. Became very religious. Still has to be taken away for treatment every now and again. Her son, Dave, is a copper here. It must have been hard for her bringing up a child without a father.'

'What do you think happened, Jack?'

'Two good men died, Peter. That's all I'm going to say. Why all the interest in history?' Jack looked uneasy.

'I ran into Dave Tindall the other day and he was talking about his father and how he died. My father died tragically too, but I've put it far behind me.'

'You're not doing any thing further are you? Jack asked brusquely. 'There's no story in their deaths.'

'No. No,' Peter said. 'Fortunately and unfortunately, I've got a journalist's view of the world. Just interested. I've got too many scandals to write about in Melbourne. There's always a scandal happening down there.'

'Good. People around here don't like people prying into their business, that's what I've learnt,' Jack replied looking distracted. 'You came from here. You'd know what they're like.'

'Could have sold a lot of papers otherwise,' Peter replied semi-seriously.

Jack fidgeted uneasily with his walking stick.

'Excuse me, Peter. I better check the front desk. Those bloody blacks will wander in and steal everything if I'm not there.' Jack limped away towards the front office.

A torn piece of one of the newspapers was lying on the ground near the storeroom door. Peter picked it up and read it: *Tragic accident at Cornish Downs. Dick Clancy dies after throw from horse*. Peter slipped the paper in his pocket and walked towards the front office.

Peter was just leaving the *Golden Miner* office when he nearly collided with Max who was walking up the street.

'Look out,' Max grinned, as he ducked away from Peter, 'Nearly knocked me over.'

'Sorry, Max,' Peter apologised as he sidestepped.

'In a hurry to get away from Jack? He'd bore the tits off a cow, wouldn't he?'

'I came to say hello. This is where I did work experience when I was at school. I guess this is where my career started.'

'A walk down memory lane. How nice,' Max smirked. ' Who would have thought Dick Clancy's son would have become a journalist,' Max wrapped his arm around Peter and gave him a hard slap on the back. 'You were supposed to chase cattle, not stories,' he added, slowly drawing away his arm.

'It's a hard life. Look at Dad — died too soon because of the bush,' Peter replied.

'You shouldn't blame the bush. Your father was doing what he loved. If you'd spent more time here you'd have grown to love it.'

'I'm afraid I like my conveniences too much.' Peter pretended to look at the watch on his hand. 'I'd better go. I want to clean Mum's house up before I go.'

'Just one thing I have to ask you, son. Have you been talking to Sally Enright?' Max pushed his face close to Peter's. Peter stepped backwards.

Fuck. The old bastard can still unsettle me. What's wrong with you? Harden up.

'Sally made a point of running into me,' Peter responded. 'I didn't think she'd be still alive.'

'She's nothing but a pain in the arse. That girl's either going mad or getting drunk. God knows how many times we've had to take her to the psych ward,' Max positioned his hand around the nape of Peter's neck. Peter stiffened. 'What did the stupid girl have to say for herself?'

'She said that Butler and Gibson were dead.'

'Anything else?' Max inquired, staring so intensely into Peter's face that Peter felt compelled to look away.

Why did I do that? Makes me look weak or like I'm lying.

Peter shook his head. Max moved his hand.

'She came into the police station saying that you were going to do an exposé on me. She was fucking drunk of course.'

'What a load of crap!' Peter exclaimed. 'I didn't promise her anything. I don't know where she got that idea.'

'Maybe it was the voices in her head telling her all this. Let's hope so. I guess there are people who want to live in the past. What about you? Have you moved on?'

'I've barely given it a thought,' Peter replied. 'I was a kid.'

'Good. Very good.' Max sounded relieved. 'I don't like bringing up the past. I like to leave the past dead and buried.'

'Dead and buried,' Peter mimicked.

Fuck. He looks uncomfortable. That's a turn-up.

'Do you want Doug to clean up so you can go back earlier?' Max asked.

'No, I'll be right. There's not much more to do,' Peter responded.

'All right. If you need help, let me know,' Max said as he gave Peter a parting slap on the back. 'Everyone helps each other in this town, you might remember.'

Peter watched Max as he strode away. He stopped to talk to an elderly couple then continued down the street, passersby saying hello as he marched along. Paying homage.

Max owns this town. The Godfather of Clarkes Flat.

Peter knocked so hard on the door of the ramshackle miner's cottage that he felt the whole structure shaking. He could hear a television blaring inside. When he had knocked several times Peter decided to open the unlocked door and enter.

'Sally. Are you there?'

Peter looked around the filthy lounge room. An assortment of dirty clothes, empty bottles of alcohol and plates of uneaten food was strewn about the room. All of the walls had holes punched in them. The only items of furniture were a torn beanbag and a couch with a broken leg that had been replaced by a house brick.

Peter tentatively searched through the house until he found Sally sprawled out on her back on a stained foam mattress in a bedroom. An empty bottle of spirits lay beside her. Peter shook her.

'Wake up, Sally,' he called. She didn't stir. Peter shook her again, harder this time.

'What the fuck?' Sally woke up with a start, throwing punches blindly. 'Don't fucking touch me.'

One of her fists nearly caught Peter in the side of the head. She cackled when she saw Peter.

'What are you doing here?' Sally said as she reached for the bottle and took a swig. Realising it was empty, she threw it on the floor. 'Go to the pub and get me more grog. I want breakfast,' she demanded.

'I don't know why you went to Max. It was fucking stupid. I never said anything about helping you,' Peter snapped.

'I want him to know I'm on to him. Copper bastard.' Sally sank into the mattress.

'Do you think that's wise?'

'I want Max. You fucking owe me.' She pulled herself onto her elbows and made a feeble attempt to sit up.

'It's over ten years ago. The rapists are dead. Isn't that enough. Just put it behind you,' Peter implored. 'Try and forget about it.'

'Well it's just yesterday to me,' she cried.

'Just get some therapy,' Peter retorted flippantly.

'I want justice, not therapy,' Sally fumed, finally staggering to her feet. 'Get out of here before I do something I regret! Gutless bastard.'

'It's over,' Peter replied. 'Put it to bed.'

'Don't you get it?' Sally yelled into Peter's face. 'It's not over. Not yet.'

Doug's Fairlane was parked behind Peter's car when he came out of Sally's house. *Love me Tender* was playing loudly on the car radio. Doug sat up and turned the volume down as Peter approached.

Doug, don't you see you're a fucking cliché?

'What are you doing here?' Peter queried as he leant in Doug's window. 'Are you following me?'

'I was in the area, Cuz, 'Doug said with his customary smirk. 'I wanted to say hello.'

'Sure you did,' Peter replied. 'I've seen enough of you recently to last a lifetime.' Peter tapped the metal roof several times and turned towards his car.

'How's she now?' Doug asked as he leant out of his window. Peter stopped and spun around.

'What do you mean?'

'She'd be a dull fuck now, wouldn't she?' Doug sniggered. 'Does she just lie on her back? Better be careful,' Doug laughed, 'she's probably full of crabs and the clap.' Peter slowly walked back to Doug's car, clenching his fists. .

'Fuck off,' he spat as he drew closer, 'before you regret it.'

'That's right,' Doug sneered as he started the Fairlane, 'you didn't get the chance to poke her when she got raped. Shouldn't have run off. Gibson and Butler had all the fun, didn't they?' Doug quickly wound up his window.

Peter clasped Doug's door handle but before he could open it, Doug sped away showering Peter with gravel. The only injury he was able to inflict was a graze to his own knuckles as he punched the car door. Doug stopped a short distance and got out, arms akimbo.

'Be careful, Cuz,' Doug laughed. 'I don't want you to get hurt.' It was early evening by the time Peter arrived home. He had aimlessly gone for a drive and found himself parked at Lookout Hill. The hill overlooked the town and the surrounding countryside. There were no distinguishing landmarks, just open bushland for a distance of thirty kilometres. Clarkes Flat was the only sign of human habitation as far as the eye could see. The hill had been one of his favourite adolescent drinking haunts and it was where he had lost his virginity with a girl called Robyn in the back seat of the 120Y. He couldn't remember what she looked like, only that he thought she had a pretty face and their lovemaking had been a fumbled mess of nervous hands and fingers, illuminated by an interior light; pulling at pants and bra, bodies cramped into unusual positions in a small space, culminating in Peter entering her, her whimpering and Peter coming soon after. It had all happened so quickly and so clumsily. The longest part of it had been the application and removal of the condom. He never dated Robyn again. He had been too embarrassed and as for Robyn, he could only assume she felt the same.

He drank a stubby and stared at the countryside as the setting sun draped it in shadow, only deciding to leave when a couple in a panel van parked beside him.

Peter was opening the front gate when Bindy barked from the backyard. She stopped when he called to her. He knew that she would meet him at the front stairs. He was walking through the yard and had just passed the dead palm tree when he felt a sharp blow and then excruciating pain to the back of his head. Peter knew he had been hit. It had happened before. *Fucking intruder*, Peter thought as the pain overwhelmed him. He fell, still conscious, trying to turn his head to identify his assailant, but all he could see was someone wearing jeans. A kick connected to his head and he felt his face drop heavily into the ground. He tasted dead grass and blood in his mouth. He tried to mouth words. Then a kick in the back of the head. Peter heard Bindy growling, a primeval growl rushing towards him, then the guttural snarling as she tore at his attacker. He heard the attacker swear, cry out, then disappear. A male's voice? Young? Who? Then a car speeding away. Bindy's wet tongue licking his face. Then nothing. Peter lay on a trolley grimacing in pain as a weary-looking doctor put the final stitches into the wound in the back of his head.

'Shit, that hurts, Doc.'

'Try not to move, Mr Clancy. I must have you lying completely still,' the doctor replied.

'My skull isn't fractured is it? It's only that I don't have a lot of the grey matter to go around,' Peter asked jokingly.

'Only six stitches,' the doctor replied flatly, as he removed his gloves. 'You don't have any brain damage. You'll just have a headache for a day or so.' The doctor made a final inspection of his handiwork and nodded with satisfaction.

'You're lucky this time. I think there could have been some serious damage done if your dog hadn't fought off the attacker,' Max said, as he pulled over the curtain that surrounded the trolley. 'You're lucky, son,' he continued as he inspected the wound. 'Must have a hard head like your dad.'

'Have you caught anyone?' Peter asked, raising his hand to feel his wound.

'Don't touch your stitches,' the doctor warned.

'We caught a young Abo kid nearby. He confessed that he was trying to break into the house,' Max replied.

'That was quick.'

'Well, the bastards aren't that bright. He was walking around in a torn shirt, covered in blood when we caught him,' Max replied as he patted Peter's back. 'And don't worry about giving a statement tonight. Come down to the station when you're better.'

'Sounds good.' Peter hopped off the trolley and stood unsteadily. He became aware of the pulsating throb in his head. Max took hold of him.

'Careful!' He held onto Peter's arm until he felt satisfied that Peter was okay. 'Do you want a lift?'

'No,' Peter replied, 'I'll get a taxi.' Peter was still waiting for the taxi at the front of the hospital when Dave approached him from the shadows, wearing civilian clothes.

'Want a lift?'

'I'm right,' Peter eyed Dave with suspicion.

'How's the head?' Dave asked.

'Worse than the worst hangover I've ever had. At least I won't have to feed Bindy tonight. She took a chunk out of the bastard,' Peter replied rubbing his head. He winced when he accidentally touched the stitches. 'What are you doing here when you're off duty?'

'I heard about the attack from someone on duty.'

'Cops never sleep.' Peter rolled his eyes. 'Or is it curiosity?' He looked up and down the street, hoping the taxi would arrive soon.

'Funny. I saw the bloke they caught. He didn't have any bite marks on him.'

'What do you mean? Maybe Bindy has no teeth. I'll have to check,' Peter said cynically.

'Someone doesn't want you here,' Dave continued. 'It's a hint.'

'Hint?' Peter replied, 'I thought it was an intruder — or don't you have them in the perfect world of Clarkes Flat?

'You've been watched since you arrived. You just have to ask questions to attract attention around here. People in Clarkes Flat don't trust outsiders,' Dave stated looking around.

'This isn't fucking East Berlin, Dave. I was brought up here. There's three generations of Clancys in the cemetery.'

'You don't belong here anymore. You left. You're seen as a traitor.'

'You talk shit, Dave.'

'You know where we are,' Dave said as he melted back into the darkness. Peter had wanted to snappily reply with, *Yeah? Who do you work for? KGB or CIA?* but the taxi had stopped and the impatient driver was asking for his address.

26

Peter's rambling thoughts sometimes kept him awake at night. It was how he did his research, how he made sense of it all. Michelle once suggested he keep a notepad and pen by the bed, but he never took up her suggestion. And now added to an accumulation of random thoughts he had a throbbing headache.

Despite using time-honoured sleep strategies Peter lay awake for most of the night. The two paracetamol tablets and two beers he had taken before bed to alleviate the headache (for medicinal purposes only) hadn't helped. When his mind was overloaded, as it was now, he often found comfort in visualising himself as a kid swimming in the river at Cornish Downs. Not tonight. Next strategy. Peter would have watched late night television, as he did in Melbourne when he couldn't sleep, but the local channel had already signed off for the night. The next step: Toss and turn, punch the pillow until it happened. It was five o'clock in the morning before he managed to finally fall asleep. He was dreaming that someone was standing over him. Watching him. Peering at his face. Peter woke with a jolt. Sam Saturday? Sam was seated on a chair beside him.

What the fuck?

'What the fuck are you doing here? How did you get in? How did you get past Bindy? Useless dog,' Peter rattled off, shaking himself awake.

'You don't know the secret ways,' Sam whispered light-heartedly, as he rose from the chair to sit at the foot of the bed.

'What's this about?'

Peter jumped out of bed wearing only a pair of underpants. He searched through a pile of dirty clothes and decided that the T-shirt and pair of shorts were the least offensive.

'I wanted to tell you the other day but you were too fucking angry,' Sam replied.

'You told me about a cattle duffing ring you were involved in.' Peter slipped into the clothes, quickly glanced at his reflection in the mirror and ran his hand through his hair. He was alert enough to be aware of the stitches. 'Billy and John Tindall killed themselves. I know. You told me.' He felt the bump on his head and rubbed it gently with his fingers, avoiding the sharp stitches. He felt pain in his back.

Look like shit. Feel like shit.

'If you feel that guilty, talk to the police. It's history as far as I'm concerned,' Peter continued.

'Looks like you've been in a fight,' Sam commented.

'It wasn't a fight.' Peter turned to Sam who was now lying sideways on the bed with his head propped on his hand. 'Are you right? Make yourself at home.'

'Good bed,' Sam replied patting the bed. 'Better then a swag.' He hopped off and threw a last admiring glance at the bed. 'I might buy one of those beds one day.'

'It wasn't a fight, as I was going to say,' Peter continued. 'More a bashing.'

He adjusted his shirt and walked down the corridor towards the kitchen with Sam in his wake.

'I didn't know how to tell you the other day,' Sam paused, 'who I thought killed John Tindall and Billy Johnson.' Peter stopped and turned to face Sam.

'Sam. They committed suicide,' he snapped. 'I checked the old newspapers.'

'A day apart?' Sam asked.

'Happens all the time in Melbourne. Husband and wives stuff.'

'You believe what they put in the newspaper? You should know. Don't you just write bullshit in that Melbourne paper?' Sam shot back.

'Good one, Sam. Clever,' Peter said. He tried to turn his head but it started to throb.

'It was Doug, your cousin,' Sam uttered suddenly. 'That's what I was trying to tell you the other day.'

'Doug?' Peter chuckled, aware of the headache that threatened to return. 'That dickhead? He needs assistance to piss. Doug's the village idiot. Dumbo Clancy? Isn't that what the town calls him? He'd have trouble killing an ant.'

He walked into the kitchen to be greeted by Dave sitting calmly at the kitchen table drinking a cup of coffee.

'The jug's just boiled,' said Dave with a wry grin. 'I would have made you one too but I didn't know when you'd wake up.'

'Is the entire town here?' Peter asked. 'Is the mayor here too? I'm going to sack Bindy.'

'Sam has his ways,' Dave grinned.

Sam entered the kitchen and sat beside Dave. Peter turned on the kettle and stood at the bench pushing two paracetamols from a blister pack.

'Anyone for a hot breakfast? Looks like I've just opened a café.' He poured a coffee, took a mouthful and swallowed the tablets.

'Stop your crap. Sit down,' Sam ordered. 'This is serious.'

Peter took another sip of his coffee, sauntered over to the table and sat down.

'What about me?' asked Sam. 'I'm all right, Jack.'

'What do you want? Tea or coffee?' Peter left the table and returned to the jug.

'Coffee. Black with a big one. Like me.'

'Okay. I'm putting on my journalist's hat. Let's look at the details,' he said as returned to the table with Sam's coffee. 'You say Doug murdered both men?'

Sam nodded.

'You believe that too, Dave?'

Dave also nodded.

'Was he in the cattle duffing ring?'

Sam shook his head as he tasted the coffee.

'Did you see anything? Maybe him killing them?' Peter paused. 'Doug would only have been about sixteen years old at the time.'

'Will you stop being a smartarse and listen,' Sam said angrily, thumping the table. He took a deep breath. 'Billy told me a story not long before he died. Him and Johnny gave Dumbo a job at the saleyards. I don't know why. They must have felt sorry for him. As we know, Doug's not the full quid.'

Peter and Dave nodded furiously in agreement as Sam continued.

'Apparently, Doug was useless. The final straw was when he left the main gate open and all the cattle got out onto the highway. Doug got sacked, just as he should have been.' Sam paused to gather his thoughts. 'One day he turns up at the saleyards waving a gun around.'

'A gun? This true?' Peter looked at Dave for confirmation.

'Do you think I'm spinning a yarn around the campfire?' Sam fumed.

'No. No,' Peter reassured him. 'Can't imagine it. Thought he'd shoot himself first. Go on.' Peter leaned in towards Sam.

'Are you interested yet?' Sam asked.

'Maybe,' Peter replied.

'Anyway,' Sam continued, speaking slower as he recalled the story, 'he threatens to kill them.'

'What happened?'

'They get the gun off him. Apparently Johnny gave Doug a thrashing with a stockwhip,' Sam replied.

'Did they tell the police?' Peter enquired.

'Don't know,' he replied vaguely.' Maybe they thought he'd get locked up in an institution for the rest of his life.'

'It was probably the best place for him,' said Peter.

'He must have come back again,' Sam's voice trailed off. He dropped his head and sighed. 'Poor buggers.'

'Does Max know the story?' Peter asked.

'He must,' Dave spoke up. 'Max knows everything that happens in Clarkes Flat.'

'I don't know why Max would protect him,' Peter wondered as he drummed his fingers on the table.

'He protected you,' Dave retorted coldly, 'didn't he?'

'What do you mean?' Peter shot back.

'I know about the rape,' he replied quietly. Peter looked awkwardly at Dave.

'I was a stupid kid in the wrong place at the wrong time, with the wrong friends. All right?' Peter took a deep breath and stared at the fridge. 'I don't want to talk about it.'

He rose from his chair and went over to the fridge. He took out a can of VB, ripped off the tab and swallowed quickly. After a couple of gulps, he wiped his mouth and returned to the table.

'Early for beer, isn't it?' Sam asked.

'I'm having breakfast.'

'I didn't mean to upset you,' Dave apologised. 'I know how our parents were all good friends with Max and his wife. Max looked after people he was close to.'

'But Doug's parents weren't part of that social group,' Peter interrupted. 'His dad and my dad hadn't spoken to each other for years.' Peter crunched the can after draining the last of its contents. 'His parents were the town drunks, if you remember.'

'Maybe it looked bad for Max if Doug was charged with two murders,' Peter surmised. 'So he kept it on the quiet.'

'Could be,' Sam stated.

'Maybe Max is rooting Doug,' Peter stated coldly. 'It happens.' Sam and Dave screwed up their faces.

'That's crook,' Sam squirmed. 'That only happens in big cities.'

'Sure it does,' Peter shook his head. 'Homosexuality doesn't exist in the country?

'You know Doug's the town spy, don't you?' Sam interrupted.

'How's that?' Peter said in disbelief.

'He comes to the station dobbing on people all the time,' Dave continued. 'Always minor stuff. I always thought it was strange that the other cops always gave him the time of day.' He stopped to gather his thoughts. 'One day he complained to me about a neighbour playing their music too loud. I was really busy and I told him to bugger off. Doug starts telling me how powerful he is in the town. Next minute I'm in Max's office getting hauled over the coals for ignoring a complaint from the public.'

'Doug is probably the town busybody. Every small town has one,' Peter stated.

'It's more then that,' Sam cut in.

'It gets better. I was called to his house one night after receiving complaints from his neighbours about a domestic. I get there to find his Filipino wife unconscious on the floor. I arrested Doug and he starts going on about how powerful he is again, blah, blah. What do you think happened?' Dave asked.

'He doesn't get charged'.

'Precisely. I'm in the office having to explain why I shouldn't be transferred to the back of Bedourie.'

'But why?' Peter was getting more interested.

'Max looks after Doug for some reason,' Dave said. 'We haven't worked that out yet.'

'Could be just a father-son relationship,' Peter commented. 'Max more or less adopted Doug.'

'The station mascot,' Dave added. 'Remember how Doug used to hang around the station when he was a kid?'

'He had nothing to go home to,' Peter remarked. 'And mum wouldn't have taken him in.'

'I thought you didn't like Doug,' Sam retorted.

'I don't. Maybe I was luckier than him. Who knows?' He dropped his head in thought. It shot up again when Dave spoke.

'We need your help. This is too powerful for us,' Dave looked at Sam who was nodding in agreement.

'Me? How can I help? I'm not in the police force.'

'I'm not game to go to anyone in the police,' Dave said. 'Max has friends everywhere. I know for a fact that he's good friends with the commissioner. Apparently they went through the academy together.' He leaned forward, clenching his hands tightly.

'Sam wants to give evidence but he doesn't want to be charged for the cattle duffing. That's why he's hiding out,' he continued.

'That Dumbo, he's no Clancy. No Clancy. I want to put him in jail,' Sam fumed. 'Fucking Max. He should stay out of it.'

'But what do you want me to do?' Peter asked.

'When we knew you were in town, we thought, it's the same thing that's happening with the government. Expose Doug for the murders and Max covering him up,' Dave said.

'You want me to do a newspaper exposé on this?'

'I hear that's what you're good at,' Dave smiled.

'Turn bullshit into chocolate, 'Sam sniggered. Peter responded with a faint smile.

Peter got up from the table and went to the open window in the kitchen. He stared out of the window for an eternity before closing it.

'I can't do it. I don't want to be caught up in this. I don't want to stay here any longer then I have to. Even if I wanted to, there's not enough of a story to warrant me busting my balls over it.' Peter went to the fridge to retrieve another beer. He ripped off the tab and threw the tab in the sink. 'I'm sure there's a local journalist looking for a story like this. Sorry.' He returned to the table.

'Jack Gooley?' Dave cried. 'He couldn't do it. The *Miner's* not that kind of paper.'

'I mean,' Peter sounded irritated, 'go to the *Townsville Bulletin*. I'm sure there's someone there looking for a story that doesn't involve potholes in the road, car accidents and store openings.'

'But we want you to do it,' Dave argued. 'You know the players and your mum said you were good at this.'

'Mum,' Peter replied looking upwards. 'Thanks, Mum.'

'Are you going to help us?' Dave asked, barely restraining his anger.

'No,' Peter said brusquely. 'I'm not.'

'Are you protecting Doug too?' Dave asked. 'You make out that you don't get on with Doug but he's still your cousin.'

'Fuck,' Peter swore, nearly knocking over his can of beer. 'I don't give a shit about Doug. He's not a cousin. He's a fucking liability. And I'm not protecting Doug. In fact I barely know him. You should both know that.'

'We're wasting our fucking time here,' Sam said, angrily grabbing his hat. 'I've helped your family since I was a kid and when I ask you for help — nothing.'

'That's it, then,' Dave finished off.

'Look at you. You were always running away when you were a kid and now look at you. Still doing it,' Sam's disappointment cut Peter to the quick.

'I'm sorry,' he apologised, hanging his head. He took a sip from the can and pushed it away. 'I just can't help you.'

'Come on, Sam. We're wasting our time here,' Dave tapped Sam on the shoulder as he got up from the table.

'You're not like your father. Not even half your father. Dick never ran away from a fight,' Sam said as he put on his battered stockman's hat.

'Where did that get Dad, Sam?' Peter asked. 'Killed him.'

'Dick died because he cared. He cared about the station, you and your mum. Me even. A black fella.' Sam dabbed his eyes with his fingers. 'That was his fault. He cared.' He and Dave walked to the doorway of the kitchen where Sam stopped and spoke, keeping his back to Peter. 'Stop running, young fella. Or you'll be running for the rest of your life.' Then Sam and Dave were gone.

'Anything else?' Peter yelled sadly at the now empty kitchen. He slumped down in a chair and started to doze, the can of beer still cradled in his hand.

The ringing phone woke Peter with a start, causing him to drop the beer can still clutched in his palm. Beer spilled over the table and onto the floor in thin amber rivulets. He got up from the table to get a dishcloth while the phone kept ringing. As he sopped up the beer, he wondered momentarily who might be ringing him. He decided he really didn't care.

Not answering any calls today.

He hadn't exactly been inundated with calls since he'd arrived in Clarkes Flat. One had been from a life insurance company and another from an old friend of his mother's from Brisbane who kept saying, 'I can't hear you. Can you speak up?' The last was a wrong number wanting to order a pizza. Peter jokingly took the order. He threw the cloth in the direction of the sink but it missed, ending up on the floor. The phone kept ringing.

Fuck. Shut up.

After a second round of rings, he finally relented and grabbed the phone off the receiver.

'Who is it?' Peter said in his best offhand phone voice. There was a familiar cackling laugh at the other end. Bob Connolly.

Shit. Should have rung him.

'You sound like crap,' Bob rasped. 'Must be hard, living off the land.' He broke into a gale of laughter that culminated in a spasm of coughing. Peter held the phone away from his ear, only returning it when the coughing subsided.

'I had a bad night,' Peter replied. 'Can't sleep here. No traffic noises.'

'Did you turn your clock back twenty years at the border?'

'Clock? They use sundials here,' Peter shared the joke as Bob chuckled.

'Have you forgotten about your job back here?' Bob said, suddenly turning serious. 'Or you going to stay up there and go native?'

'No fucking way,' Peter replied. 'I was meaning to ring you. Sorry, Bob. Got caught up sorting out Mum's house. It's a frigging mess.'

'We need you back here, mate.' Bob sounded close to pleading. Funny, Bob had never called him mate. He felt honoured.

'I don't know what you do to get a story. Frankly I don't want to know. But the juices have dried up down here like a nun's cunt. These journos here don't have the mongrel in them like you do,' Bob complained between coughs. 'Did you hear anything about Christine McGuiness up in the bush?'

'No. All we get here is Queensland news. Fucking pathetic,' Peter grumbled. 'Why?'

'She nearly cut her wog ex's cock off with a pair of scissors,' he continued salaciously.

'Really?' Peter wished he were back in Melbourne. 'Great story.'

'When are you coming back?' Bob asked through a throat hack.

'Two days. I'll have this sorted in two days.'

'Excellent. We'll see you then. I'll pick you up from Tulla myself.' Bob was about to hang up.

'Bob,' Peter asked vaguely, 'what if I found a story up here?

'Where are you again? Crap Flat? It would have to be good. I don't usually look for stories outside Victoria. What have you found?'

'Well,' Peter replied hesitantly, 'I'm not sure yet. It's probably nothing. Probably just small town gossip.'

'Don't stay any longer then you have to. We need you here.'

Peter thought of going back to bed but there was still some more cleaning up to do. He'd already determined that today he'd attack the garage. The garage was, just as he had envisaged, full of rubbish. There were stacks of magazines piled high. Jack and Irene made a good couple,

Peter thought, as he threw the rubbish into a trailer he had hired, both of them being such inveterate hoarders. He returned to the garage; an old mower, boxes of clothes, a black and white television, garden tools were all consigned to the trailer. He shifted his father's saddle and a bridle to the 'Keep' pile.

Tucked under an old box buried in a corner of the garage, Peter found a perished brown shoe. He turned it around in his hands, examining it, remembering that he had picked it up at the old gold mine when he was a kid. He felt its rough texture. It peeled open when he bent it. He turned it over and tried to decipher the label but it had long become illegible. He tossed the old shoe on the trailer, hooked it up to the car, and threw Bindy into the car for the drive to the dump.

He was unloading the trailer at the dump when the shoe came into view again. He picked it up and examined it again. He had always wondered who owned the shoe, who had driven to the mine shaft that night. Criminals disposing of a body, Peter had imagined as a child. As an adult he thought it far more likely that it was just locals looking for a different place to get drunk. He threw the shoe on the heap of rubbish.

On the way home he stopped at the old creek and went for a walk with Bindy following. The area had changed since he last visited it as a child. A couple of houses had been built along the creek where once there was nothing but a canopy of vines. The mineshaft, Peter surmised, would now be located in the backyard of one of the houses. He guessed it was now all safely filled in. Peter returned to the car, called Bindy and left, wondering why he had bothered to visit.

It was early afternoon when Peter got back, made himself a sandwich and turned on the film projector. He examined the canister titled *Show 1968*. The last film left to watch. Bindy saw it as an opportunity to hop on the couch. She lay there looking sheepish.

'Okay. You're the hero,' Peter joked as he flopped himself in a recliner chair, allowing Bindy to have the whole couch to herself. She stretched herself out and went to sleep. The film flickered into life; the first image was of Young Peter and Dick riding on the dodgem car. They both laughed as they crashed into the other cars. Next image showed a show competitor horse jumping in the arena. The camera swung to Dick standing with John Tindall and Lorna, Max Hillard and his wife, then back to the horse jumping.

The film suddenly jumped to a completely new image. It showed Young Peter playing on the swing. The camera initially tried to capture him going up and down on the swing but it couldn't keep pace. The film became a blur.

He recalled that was the shameful night he took his mother's camera to the swings at Dave's house and got belted for it.

The film drifted across the yard to a set of shrubs. Two men walked into view. The camera then swung back to Young Peter as he slowed down. The swing picked up pace, the camera unable to track the swing's momentum. The camera was rolling all over the place.

Peter remembered how Dave had gotten frightened and handed the camera to him. The camera returned to focus on the men.

Peter got off his chair and stood close to the wall, peering at the images. The film had been taken at night and was grainy, making it exceptionally difficult to identify the men. By the look of their arm movements and their posture, the men appeared to be arguing. One man seemed more aggressive and moved closer to the other, his arm pointing at him. The other man stepped back, raising his hands in a defensive stance as the aggressive man pushed him in the chest. As he stumbled backwards, the film cleared briefly, the men suddenly illuminated by light from a source other than the back door. Peter gasped and took a step back when he realised who the men were, brushing against the projector. He righted it before it fell, still stunned by what he had seen. *Max Hillard was pushing John Tindall.* Max stopped as soon as a third man wandered into view. Although Peter couldn't distinguish the man's face, he recognised the familiar striding walk, the swinging arms. The third man carried a large torch in his hand, utterly unaware of what had been happening between Max and John Tindall.

No doubt about it, that's Dad.

It seemed to take an eternity from when Peter rang Dave until his arrival at Arkinholme. Peter was pacing the front veranda with a can of beer in his hand, oblivious to the rotten floorboards. He was standing at the top of the stairs as Dave tentatively negotiated his way up.

'Be careful of the stairs. The only thing holding them together is the white ant shit,' Peter warned.

'What's this all about? You want to show me a film that you and I took as kids?' Dave asked when he reached the top of the stairs. Peter didn't reply but beckoned for Dave to follow him.

'I can't remember,' Dave continued in the lounge room, 'I honestly can't.'

'Quiet,' Peter snapped as he turned on the projector. 'Watch the film carefully.'

He stopped the film when he arrived at the argument between John Tindall and Max.

'Recognise anyone?' Peter asked.

'That's Max and Dad,' Dave replied. 'I'm sure of it.'

'What do you think they're doing?'

'By the look of it they're having a heated discussion.'

'That's what I thought. I'll show you the rest. There's not much more.' Peter switched on the projector again. They watched the film until it finished.

'That's Dad at the end,' Peter said as he turned off the projector.

'What are they up to?' Dave asked in a puzzled voice. 'What do you think?'

'They're having an argument. Max is obviously the aggressor.' Peter said as he sat in the recliner. Dave sat on the couch, pushing away a ragged ball that Bindy had deposited there.

'Max had found out about the cattle duffing,' Dave replied.

'It looks like he's telling your father what to do,' Peter thought. 'A stuff up.'

'Then what's your dad doing there?'

'Don't know. Maybe he was wondering where they were?'

'They seem to stop when he approaches them,' Dave remarked.

'Is this anything important?' Dave sighed. 'Will it alter what we already know?'

'It could be nothing,' Peter sat forward in the recliner, 'but it could be a dot in a series of dots. If they could be joined...'

'Are you saying there's substance in what Sam and I have been saying?'

'I don't know. This film is interesting,' Peter said evasively.

'Okay. What's the point?' Dave said with annoyance.

'Let me talk to your mother.' Peter seemed genuinely enthusiastic at last.

'Mum won't know anything. She's mentally ill. She's never talked about what happened.'

'One thing I've learnt in my game. Never judge people at face value. I've gotten a lot of leads from people who are regarded as on the fringes of society. That's how *The Truth* operates.'

'Mum lives in another world. She finds that more comforting. I doubt if you'll get anything out of her,' Dave replied with bemusement. 'The psychiatrists have never got anything out of her. How are you going to?

'I can get an afterlife story from a corpse,' Peter boasted.

Lorna Tindall sat in a chair clutching rosary beads, ashen face looked upwards at a crucifix that was mounted on the wall, her wizened body perched on the edge of the chair.

'Mum,' Dave said, 'someone wants to talk to you. You remember Peter Clancy?' Dave crouched beside her and held her hand. She patted his hand and continued to pray. 'Mum. It's important.'

She stopped praying, her eyes shifting from Dave to Peter.

'I know you,' she croaked in a dry voice as Peter sat beside her. 'David and you used to ride your bikes to the lagoon to fish. That was before John went away.' Lorna pulled at the rosary beads.

'You have a good memory, Lorna,' Peter replied.

'I know a lot of things but I occasionally have difficulty remembering them. Does that make sense?' Lorna smiled enigmatically. Her mood suddenly changed and she looked around frantically. 'You know they drive past here in their big cars, looking in,' she continued.

Peter and Dave exchanged glances and Dave who raised his hands as if to say, 'I don't know'.

'Sometimes they come into the yard,' Lorna said anxiously.

'I've never seen anyone, Mum.'

'Why don't you believe me? You must believe me, Peter?' Lorna asked.

'I believe you, Lorna,' Peter said, looking at Dave and shrugging his shoulders. His eyes drifted around the room. It was entirely adorned with religious icons and statues, except for a solitary portrait of John Tindall in a suit, hung beside a freshly pressed suit suspended from the door. He took another look at the portrait and then the suit. It was the same suit he wore in the photograph. Lorna caught sight of him looking at them.

'That's John the day we were married,' Lorna sighed. 'What a handsome man he was. He loves that suit. I have it dry cleaned every week.'

'Mum,' Dave said sounding annoyed. 'Dad's died. He's being dead for twenty years. I wish that psychiatrist could get through to you.'

When Lorna wasn't watching, Peter looked at Dave, put his finger against his lips and shook his head gently.

'My David gets cross with me,' Lorna laughed, 'but I see John all the time. He talks to me when David isn't here.'

'What does he tell you?' Peter asked. Dave got up shaking his head and signalled that he was going outside. 'What do you talk about?'

Lorna began threading the rosary beads slowly between her fingers.

'Everything. We have a great chinwag,' she smiled.

'What? About the past?' Peter asked.

She started to move the beads faster through her hands.

'He likes talking about the saleyards and Billy. He always sounds sad when he talks about Billy.'

'Why's that?

'Billy was such a larrikin. Made John laugh. He could get so serious sometimes, especially towards…' Lorna's voice trailed off.

'Towards what?' Peter asked anxiously. He noticed that Lorna had stopped moving the rosary beads.

'When Billy died,' Lorna cried, tugging at the beads. 'Poor Billy. John wanted to leave town. He didn't want us to live here anymore.'

'Did you leave?' Peter asked.

'John told me to go on holidays with David and he'd meet me. They came for John that day when I wasn't here.' She pulled so hard that the rosary beads snapped and scattered noisily over the floor. Peter reached down to pick them up.

'Don't touch it! Please don't touch it,' she wailed as she knelt on the floor to retrieve the broken rosary beads. 'Only John wants me to touch the rosary.' She gathered the beads towards her and remained in a kneeling position.

'I wasn't there. They wouldn't have taken him if I was there,' she continued, taking a deep breath.

'Are you comfortable like that, Lorna?' Peter asked.

'I kneel for hours.'

Dave came back into the room. 'Is everything all right?'

Peter signalled for him to come no further.

'Lorna, do you remember who took John?' Peter asked.

'His friends wanted him to go away. They didn't want to be his friends any longer.'

'They're not very good friends,' Peter commented.

'John always said his best friend was Max.'

'Max?' Peter repeated in a whisper as Dave came closer.

'Max was always coming here and John was always going somewhere with Max. Never told me anything. Men's business. I hope you're not like that?' Lorna asked.

'I confess that I could do with some training,' Peter winked.

'You're a funny man. You make John laugh too. When John went away, I thought I wouldn't see his friends anymore.'

'And? Have you? Seen them again, I mean,' Peter asked.

'Max wanted to see where John left from.'

'Left from?' Peter glanced at Dave, who pointed in the direction of the bedroom.

'He said he had to be alone and closed the door behind him,' Lorna replied clutching her hands in prayer. She looked at John's picture as she spoke.

'What happened then?' Peter asked.

'He was in there for a while. I got curious and opened the door quietly. Max was picking up something from the floor. He turned around when he heard me.'

Dave began to move towards his mother but Peter waved at him to stop.

'And what happened after that?'

'Max got angry. He shook me hard and said that I have to forget what I've seen. He said I could go mad if I didn't forget what I'd seen and who'd look after David then?' Peter looked up at Dave, who was sobbing.

'Maybe if I'd kept remembering what I'd seen I may have been alright.'

'Why do you think he was so angry?'

'I'm not sure. He was protecting me?' Lorna replied vaguely. 'It was still messy in the kitchen. Friends cleaned it up later.'

'Yeah, sure he was protecting you,' Dave cried as he punched the wall.

'My poor David.' She slowly stood up, went over to him and cradled him in her arms while he sobbed.

'My poor David. My poor, poor boy,' Lorna soothed.

Dave and Peter were sitting in deep silence on the porch, sipping coffee.

'You all right?' Peter asked finally.

'If my mother wasn't here I wouldn't have ever asked for a transfer to Clarkes Flat. It's just that she needs more help as she gets older. I want her to move to a retirement village in the city. She won't, though. Doesn't want to leave dad,' he answered sadly.

'What was it like after your father died?'

'You mean when he was murdered? Let's stop beating around the bush and call it like it is.' Peter nodded in agreement. 'People started avoiding us. You know the rumours, don't you?' he asked.

'I heard,' Peter replied softly.

'People would call Mum a slut to her face and I got teased at school. Kids used to pretend to shoot themselves in the head,' Dave's voice trailed off. 'Pricks.'

'Small towns,' Peter responded.

'Now Mum's just called the madwoman of Tindall Lane. What Mum has had to endure...' He took a large mouthful of coffee. 'She's been really affected by your mum's death.'

'How's that?'

'Your mum was one of the few people that always stuck by Mum, no matter what anyone said. She was a good friend.'

'Is it going to make your mother worse if we go any further with this?' Peter asked.

'You've seen her. She couldn't get any worse,' Dave replied. 'I'm hoping she'll have closure one day. She deserves that.' He took a final sip of his coffee and placed the mug on the table next to him. 'It sounds like you've had a change of heart? I thought you were keen to get out of here.'

'Yeah, I was, but maybe it was seeing Dad that changed my mind. Did he know something? Or maybe it's the injustice of it. I hate people like Max who think they can do anything they want and get away with it. Maybe it's just that it's got the makings of a good story. Could be any one or all of these. There's only one way to find out.'

'How's that?'

'We start digging.'

'For information?' Dave sounded relieved. 'You're really going to help?'

'I'll give it a go,' Peter responded with a grin after draining his cup of coffee.

'We're going to have to move fast,' Dave warned.

'I know. I've only got another two days before I have to go back to Melbourne. I could extend that if I could sweeten the boss.'

'It's not that. I'm getting transferred to Brisbane in a couple of days. Of all the times for this to happen! Mum's taking it hard and Sam's pissed off. Reckoned I'm running out on him.'

'So why don't you resign?' Peter enquired.

'Being a cop has helped me make some headway.'

'That throws a baby in the blender,' Peter sighed. 'I can't do this all myself.'

'The transfer's nothing to do with me. I suspect that Max wants me out of here. I'm John Tindall's son, remember?' Dave paused. 'And when Sam came to me and told me the story about the cattle duffing, I didn't think I needed to be discreet, so I started to ask questions around town. Nothing serious,' he chastised himself, 'but I should have been more careful. It must have got back to Max.'

'What did you find out anyway?' Peter asked as he sat down.

'The locals didn't tell me much, but I expected that. They worship Max like he was a god. He's the Joh of Clarkes Flat.'

'But the yokels must have said something. Any information is better then none. We're trying to join dots here,' Peter insisted. 'You're the cop.'

'Let me think.' Dave collected his thoughts. 'I tracked down Billy's widow, Merle Nolan, in Darwin.'

'That's good work, constable.' Peter remarked happily. 'I'm impressed. Ever thought of going into business for yourself?'

Dave ignored Peter's comment and continued. 'Merle told me that Billy never killed himself. She was really strong about that. She said that no one ever listened to her suspicions. She's never stopped thinking about it.'

'Okay,' Peter questioned impatiently. 'What else?'

'Merle said that Billy looked like he had something on his mind around that time. All he would say was that he's wished he'd stuck to training horses. And the other thing…'

'Yeah?'

'Merle said that it was strange Billy shot himself even though he hated guns.'

'That's a dot.' Peter patted Dave on the back.

'Should I believe this stuff?' Dave asked. 'I'm trained not to believe people.'

'In my job you believe everything. In this case, guilty until proven otherwise. What else?'

'And I found the orderly, a bloke called Bannerman, who was working at the hospital the night Billy and Dad had their autopsies.' He wiped his eyes with a handkerchief and struggled to continue.

'He reckons that a local doctor named Renshaw did the PMs because the morgue fridge was broken. Usually the non-routine stuff would be done in Townsville. Said that Max was worried that the bodies would go off.' Dave ended by inching forward and hanging his head in his hands.

'You all right?'

'Right as I'll ever be,' he rested back in the chair. 'The orderly said the post mortems were a mess. It was like the bodies had been butchered. Renshaw was pissed. Bannerman said he had to leave the morgue frequently to keep getting coffee for the doctor. He said Max looked like he was in a hurry.'

'Have you been able to speak to Dr Renshaw?'

'He was killed in a car accident in Tasmania in 1982,' Dave paused momentarily before resuming. 'He had a record for having sex with a minor in England before he came to Australia.'

'It just gets better,' Peter remarked.

'That's all I've got, I'm afraid.' Dave bit his bottom lip.

Peter stood and began pacing backwards and forwards as he spoke.

'Lots of floating dots. Where they connect, we don't know yet,' he reflected as he waved his hands in the air.

'Dots? It all looks like dead ends to me.'

'We need to talk to Sam,' Peter said rapidly. 'Is he around?'

'He's living in a deserted homestead twenty miles from town. I take him supplies every week.'

'Can you get hold of the forensic reports? I'd love to have a look at those,' Peter said excitedly. 'That will tell us whether it was suicide or murder.'

'I reckon they'd be locked in the dungeon at the station,' Dave answered.

'Dungeon? Peter laughed. 'Sounds medieval.'

'That's what we call it. It's an old cell underneath the station. Max has got the keys.' Dave raised his eyebrows. 'Only Max.'

'Hmm. I'll need to think about that. That's a real obstacle. Shit.'

'We'll have to be careful. Doug will be keeping an eye on us,' Dave warned.

'Don't use the phone. In case it's bugged,' Peter added quickly.

'Bugged? You're joking.' Dave guffawed.

'No. It's happened to me before. Crooked cops stuff,' Peter stated, feeling tension rising in his neck. 'We are going to have to be careful. I have a feeling we're dealing with something sinister,' he added.

Sam was nowhere to be found when they arrived in Peter's car at the old McDonald homestead. The McDonald family had arrived from Scotland with ambitions of building a vast cattle empire in the early twentieth century. Their first mistake had been building Cessnock, a rambling double story sandstone edifice. It was only partially finished when a drought sent the McDonalds bankrupt and they had had to abandon Cessnock to a slow death from the elements and the local authorities taking the sandstone blocks for building the town hall and post office. Now only a vine covered wall and a weathered, broken gravestone nearby remained of the Cessnock empire. For Sam it was a good place to hide as it offered isolation and the river was nearby. Sam's weather-beaten Kingswood was parked under a large Burdekin plum tree.

'Sam. Are you there?' Dave called out while Peter checked inside the car. The back seat was full of tins of food.

'He might be at the river,' Dave suggested as they walked along. 'He could be having a swim.'

'You boys are just too easy to sneak up on!' Sam joked as he emerged silently from a thicket of vines hanging over the wall and stood behind them. Dave and Peter spun around.

'Are you sleeping in there?' Peter asked. 'You're like an old boar pig.'

'It'll be hard to find me in there. I've built a house in there, you know. I've got a kitchen and a bedroom. I just need a television,' he laughed. 'What are you doing here with the young fella?' He looked at Peter and walked over to a tree a short distance from the car with Dave and Peter in tow.

'He wants to talk with you,' Dave replied.

'So you finally got interested in what we've been trying to tell you, hey?'

In the shade beside the tree was a dormant campfire. Sam sat on a partially burnt log, Dave rested on his haunches and Peter remained standing.

'I would have cooked corn beef if I'd known visitors were coming,' Sam remarked ruefully.

'It's fine. We won't stay long. It's probably risky coming here during the day anyway,' Dave countered.

'I've got beer. Not cold though.' Sam reached into a torn carry bag and retrieved a stubby of beer. He opened the bottle, which immediately spurted a stream of frothy foam. Sam licked the froth from the mouth of the bottle before taking a sip. He offered one to Dave who declined. Peter licked his lips with anticipation.

I could go one of those. I don't care if it's warm as your armpit, Sam.

Sam took one look at Peter's face, gave a sly smile, dug into the bag and handed Peter a beer. Peter opened it with trembling hands and placed his mouth over the throat of the bottle as it frothed, spilling some of it on his shirt. He threw back his head and had drunk half of it before he decided to stop.

'You'll end up a bloody alco,' Sam counselled. 'Don't want to end up like your grandfather. Your dad liked a drink but he cut back as he got older.'

'I needed that!' Peter drained the last drop before adding. 'I know. I know. I'll cut back. Promise.' He placed his hand over his heart.

'You ever been in the horrors, young fella?' Sam asked.

'Never. I just require at least twelve beers a day to maintain my health.'

'Don't drink so much, young fella. I've seen too many good men, white and black, die from the grog. I'm telling you,' Sam's voice rose, 'I'll put the kurdaitcha man on you.'

'For you, Sam,' Peter smiled, 'anything.'

Sam smirked and ignored Peter. 'So what did you want to ask me?' he asked Dave.

'We've got evidence that Max could be involved in John's and Billy's deaths. Peter and I both suspect that Max may have told his loyal follower, Doug, to do the killings. Max could have been a silent partner in the cattle duffing ring. He may have wanted to cover his tracks.'

'Murder. Like I said,' Sam said, excitedly slapping his hand on his leg.

'What I want to know,' Peter replied, emphasising each word, 'did Dad know anything?'

'Was he involved?' Sam shook his head. 'Fuck no. Dick was the most honest man I knew.'

'You told me that you and Dad caught three ringers flogging our cattle one morning.'

'Jack Perks and two other blokes. Don't know who they were.'

'Did you know Jack Perks?'

'I knew of him. He was a bad bloke, you know. Been in jail a few times.'

'What happened to him?' Peter sat next to Sam on the log. Dave came up closer.

'Don't know. Your dad must have scared him out of the place. Not long…' Sam's voice faltered. He coughed and then continued, 'not long before your dad died he told me. Excuse me.' Sam rubbed his chest.

'You right. Sam?' Peter asked.

'Heart jumps around like a buckjumper sometimes. It's worn out from too much swag, not enough sleep,' Sam grinned and went on. 'Your dad told me he had gone to Max to see if he could stop the cattle duffers.'

'What did Max do?' Dave questioned.

'Dick told me that Max said he would take care of it himself. No need to go to court.'

'Anything else? Think Sam, think,' Peter asked impatiently.

'Slow down, young fella. I'm an old bloke.' Sam took a moment to gather his thoughts. 'Dick said he had to give cattle to Max so it could be taken care of on the quiet.'

'Shit,' Peter exclaimed loudly. 'That's it. Max didn't like anyone on his turf.'

'Why didn't you tell me this before, Sam?' Dave asked sternly.

'You never fucking asked, did you.'

'Did Dad tell you anything else?'

'That's it.'

'We'll never know what happened to Jack Perks or the other blokes,' Peter remarked as he scratched his head.

'I remember Dick looked worried about something before he died. He wasn't himself, you know. John and Billy dying really threw him and I think what happened with Max did also.'

'None of this can be proved.' Dave kicked an empty food can and walked away.

'That's why I reckon your dad got killed. He was worried too much. He wasn't doing things properly that day. Too worried. Old Tony was a good horse, never put a foot wrong. Dick just wasn't concentrating.' Sam put his arm around Peter. 'Sorry I had to tell you that, young fella.'

'Dad died when I was so young but it still hurts. It still hurts.' Peter sniffed and briefly looked at the bag containing the beer then turned his attention back to Sam.

'Your dad wants you to be strong. He's looking after you but he can't do all the work. He reckons you given him a few close calls.'

'Sorry, Dad!' Peter yelled, looking upwards. 'Wherever you are.'

'Dick wants you to be a Clancy. Stop the grog. Stop fucking around with your life. Be proud,' Sam counselled as he rubbed Peter's back.

'I know you believe what you just told me is true,' Peter said, 'but I don't know if I can yet.'

'I believe my ancestors talk to me all the time.' Sam paused and smiled as if he could hear them. 'If white fellas listened to their ancestors they mightn't be so fucked up.'

'You're right, Sam, you old bastard.' He smiled as he dabbed at the tears in the corner of his eyes with his thumbnail. 'You always have been.'

Peter and Dave didn't speak until they'd reached the outskirts of Clarkes Flat. Dave spoke first.

'Is this going to get us anywhere?' He looked at Peter. 'Or are we just pissing in the wind?'

Peter didn't rely.

'Peter?' Dave repeated.

'Sorry. I was thinking,' he responded vaguely. 'What was that again?'

'Are we wasting our time?' Dave sighed. 'It's all circumstantial. Max is a very clever operator. You can bet he would have done all this without getting his hands dirty.'

'I need to look at those forensic reports. No matter how bad the autopsies were.' Peter punched the steering wheel with annoyance.

'What if we talk to Doug?' Dave pondered. 'He may crack.'

'Doug won't talk,' Peter laughed. 'He worships Max.'

'Then we're wasting our time,' Dave said bitterly.

'I have an idea. It could be a fucked idea but who knows.' Peter slowed the car, stopping in a quiet suburban street. He switched off the ignition and turned to Dave.

'Can you get into the dungeon? Is that feasible?'

'Max has the keys. I've never seen them hanging with the other keys,' Dave replied. Peter watched a cat cross the road as he thought. The cat jumped onto the sill of an open window and entered the house.

'Is there anyway of breaking into the dungeon?'

'You're fucking joking!' Dave replied, surveying Peter's face for any hint of a smile.

'No, I'm not.'

'You can't break into a police station,' Dave shook his head. 'That's lunacy.'

'It has been known for a *Truth* journo to enter an establishment that's locked. I may have had to do it once or twice myself,' Peter confessed. 'I once broke into a union office after my source there had disappeared. It was a big story and I had a deadline.'

'You're a crook,' Dave joked.

'No. I'm a journalist at *The Melbourne Truth*.' Peter considered for a second whether there was a difference before continuing his questioning. 'How many doors to the dungeon are there?'

'One. It's a like an old bank safe door. Solid metal.'

'Can it be jimmied?' Peter asked.

'Only an oxy cutter or explosives would get that door open. It's solid.'

That's not going to work, Peter thought. 'Does it have a window. It must have ventilation.'

'You can't do this,' Dave protested. 'What if we get caught? And you can't write a story saying you broke into a police station to get evidence. And no prosecutor will touch it after you've had your hands on it!'

'It's called sources — "sources within the police force have informed me". Get it?' Peter responded with irritation. 'Do you really want to sort this or not, Dave? Do you really want to undo Max?'

Dave snapped, grabbing Peter by the collar with both hands.

'I want Max to pay,' Dave growled. 'I want him jailed.'

'Good. Now you can let go.'

'Sorry,' Dave said sheepishly as he loosened his grip. They didn't speak for several minutes. Then Dave piped up.

'We won't be able to get Max charged. Why should we bother?'

'A story will generate an enquiry. The enquiry will look deeper into Max's dealings.'

'I guess so. I suppose that sounds all right,' Dave remarked, gradually warming to the idea. 'Sounds good.'

'Are all Queensland coppers as thick as you?' Peter teased.

'Watch it,' Dave retorted good-humouredly.

'So where were we?' Peter continued. 'A window?'

'As you know the station is nearly all built of wood but the back wall of the station is brick. I have noticed a small window with bars at ground level. I don't know if it leads to the dungeon.'

'We'll have to chance it. Can a person squeeze in?'

'I know I couldn't,' Dave patted his abdomen, 'but I reckon you could. You're built like a greyhound.'

'Weaken the bars for me and we have a deal,' Peter stated. They shook hands.

'Let's see,' Dave reflected. 'I'm doing a night shift at eleven. I'll take a hacksaw to work. It'll give me something to do. Usually we go for drives or we sleep.'

'Good. Tomorrow night it's on,' Peter stated.

'Are you worried?' Dave asked.

'Not really,' he replied nonchalantly as he turned on the ignition, 'but Max should be.'

27

Sunday evening

Peter found Sally's note stuck on his front door when he arrived home after dropping off Dave in the early evening. Peter read the note: *I came to say goodbye, Peter. I wish you could have helped me. You should have helped me.*

Peter screwed up the paper and threw it in the garden. He wanted to ignore it.

I'm tired. I'm pissed off. I have to break into a police station. And this? Leave me the fuck alone.

How many times had he seen suicide notes like this? Argument with a lover. A suicide note and a bottle of valium. Stomach pumped out. A night in hospital. Home next day after psych review. Jilted lover. Wrists cut. Never deep. A night in hospital. Home next day after psych review. Sally. What about Sally? An attention-seeking cry for help. Was it for real this time?

Why would you want to live when that happened to you? Sally Enright, once a shining star now a fucking mess. Raped like she wasn't human. Just flesh to be ripped apart. And he had done nothing. *Stop running. Be strong. Be a Clancy.* Peter flew back down the front steps calling to Bindy.

'Time to make amends,' Peter said as he raced to his car, Bindy just behind him.

Peter tore along the dirt road that led to the lagoon. It was his first choice. Where else would you want to die in Clarkes Flat? At least there was scenery. At least it would be tranquil as you drifted away to the other side.

He pushed the car hard, finally giving up on the fact that he'd be returning an undamaged hire car. *That's what insurance is for*, he told himself. A sharp corner loomed without warning, one he hadn't anticipated. He spun the steering wheel a little too quickly, overcorrecting the car and rotating in a circle. Bindy was thrown from the back seat into the passenger seat. The car stalled in the graded guttering that ran adjacent the road. Peter started the car, its wheels spinning momentarily as he pushed the accelerator down. It shot out of the guttering and was in danger of spinning again as Peter quickly corrected the steering. He continued in the direction of the lagoon, pushing hard, the car screaming as he missed gears going from third to first.

Push the car to its limits. Nearly there.

He was hoping that Sally was just attention seeking. What would he say? Be angry or happy? *What's if she's already dead? Leave her there? Take her into town?*

Peter found Sally's car at the car park but Sally was nowhere to be seen. He switched on the torch. It flickered dimly. He was barely able to see two metres in front of him. What a time for the torch to have a low battery. He called Bindy, who seemed to have disappeared. He had to move quickly. Unable to see clearly, Peter stumbled down the bank, slipping several times and ultimately coming to rest at the water's edge.

A half-moon cast just enough light across the lagoon for Peter to conclude he didn't require the torch any longer and he threw it away angrily. It must have landed in the lagoon judging from the splash, amplified in the still night. *Where is Bindy?* He called again. No response. Finally he heard a stirring sound near a large paperbark tree on the bank of the lagoon, about twenty metres to his right. He rushed towards the tree, hoping that he hadn't disturbed a wild pig that had tusks as sharp as razors. The moonlight wasn't nearly as bright as he had first thought and he tripped on something, possibly a rock. He came to rest on his left knee, swearing as pain seared his foot. He looked back and in the dim light he recognised Bindy busily licking Sally's face. He could make out enough to see she wasn't responding. *Sally!*

Sally was sitting propped upright against the paperbark tree, head drooped forward and arms hanging limply by her side. One hand hung in the water. She looked like she had fallen into a deep sleep. Peter shook her furiously.

'Sally! Sally wake the fuck up!' Peter felt a strong pulse on her left wrist but he also a wet sensation on his fingers. He knew exactly what she had done. He held up her left arm for closer observation, sighing with relief. Sally had cut her left wrist, but only superficially and in a horizontal direction. *A few stitches and she'll be fine.* It was like the last time when he had found the faded pop queen unconscious with slashed wrists on the banks of the Yarra. The Queen of Pop. He pulled a handkerchief from his pocket and tied it tightly around Sally's wrist. Then he set about trying to wake her up. She finally stirred after Peter had pinched her face several times.

'Urrgh,' she groaned. 'Why did I have to see your face? Let me die, you bastard.'

'I guess you were expecting to see a different Peter, huh? Sorry, but you left a note at my house, remember? It was fairly obvious what you were going to do.'

'Alright, alright, so I wanted attention. I wanted help and I wasn't getting any.' Sally reached out her right hand. 'Have you got a drink?'

'No I haven't,' Peter stated. 'A drink would just make the bleeding worse. Besides which I should take you to a hospital.'

'No fucking way. They'll put me in the psych ward again and pump me full of drugs.'

'Wouldn't that be a good thing?'

'I'll end up like Lorna Tindall if I go back.'

'Here's the deal,' Peter negotiated. 'Get those cuts attended to and I'll make sure you don't end up in the psych ward.'

'Yeah, sure you will. Why should I trust you now? I trusted you once before and look what happened.'

'Because you have to. I believe I can bring you closure on Max.'

'You're joking? Sally chuckled. 'You'll run away again. Chickenshit.'

'I've done a lot of wrongs, Sally Enright. If I had to explain every one of them now, the rest of your blood will have drained out,' Peter declared. 'This time I'm going to right a wrong.'

'So you're going to Max and retracting your statement?'

'That won't get us anywhere,' Peter replied. 'His mates in the police force will make sure it doesn't go anywhere and he'll just make life hard for you.'

'You said you were going to help?' she said drowsily, trying to stand. Her legs gave out from beneath her. Peter caught her as she slumped.

'Here, you'd better lean on me. I got you, we can do this together.' Peter momentarily thought he caught her lips curve into a smile, but she had already drifted into unconsciousness and he had to carry her to his car.

Sally woke up as the doctor put in the first stitch in her wrist laceration. She wanted to hit the fresh-faced doctor as he dug in the needle but Peter was holding her other hand tightly. She had to resort to swearing instead.

'What the fuck?' Sally squirmed with pain. 'Are you trying to push the fucking needle out the other side or something?'

'Now hush. Calm down, dear,' Peter said gently. 'Allow the doctor to do his good work.'

Sally looked at Peter with amazement.

'What? Dear?' she stuttered. 'What…'

Peter interrupted Sally before she could continue.

'You see, Doctor, she's quite clumsy, my wife. She was cutting up food when the knife slipped.'

The doctor looked at Peter incredulously. 'The cut looks like your wife has tried to self-harm. I'll have to call the psychiatrist in Townsville. She'll have to be admitted to the psychiatric ward at the General.'

'Now, there's really no need for that, Doctor,' Peter sermonised. 'As a man of faith I can declare to you that she did not self-harm.'

'Man of faith?' the young doctor replied as he continued stitching, a snigger in his voice. Peter winked at Sally, who winked back, finally up to speed with what Peter was doing.

'Yes. I'm Pastor Nathan Goodwill and this is my wife Temperance Goodwill of the Society of Friends,' Peter produced an identity card, flashing it in the doctor's face. 'I'm a practising pastor from the domination that is known to you as the Quakers. I can vouch for my wife,' he continued in his best booming voice.

'But your wife just swore. Do Quakers say the F word?'

'A mere lapse, good doctor. Under the circumstances, you understand. After all, we are human. My wife and I will now pray. Pray for repentance.' Peter nodded at Sally then crossed himself. She imitated Peter. He recited the Lord's Prayer with Sally trying to mimic him. They were on the third recitation of the prayer when the doctor completed his stitching and allowed them to go.

'Perhaps you should do all the chopping in future,' he said to Peter, shaking his head as he watched them scurry away.

Sally and Peter were seated in his car in the hospital car park before Sally felt secure enough to break into laughter.

'What the fuck was that all about? Pastor Goodwill?' Isn't that blasphemy?' she asked through spasms of laughter.

'I don't know if it's blasphemy. I've never been near a church or a priest to find out. It's one of my little tricks I use to get information from the untrusting, Mrs Goodwill. This is between you and me,' Peter lowered his voice and leaned toward Sally.

'I have a kit I call the cunning kit that is full of disguises. I have things like a lab coat, clipboard, an expensive briefcase, a yarmulke, a stethoscope, and false identity cards. I use them to open doors that would be normally closed to scum journos like me. That's why I'm *The Truth*'s best journalist. '

'It sounds dishonest. Don't you get sick of prying into other people's lives?'

'Sometimes I wrestle with leaving *The Truth*. Finding out who's fucking who, how often and what fetish is involved can get a little tedious. On the other hand, it's more honest than what politicians and the rich do, although politicians and sex scandals cross paths on occasion. There's nothing I enjoy more than catching a pollie with his dick in the wrong place.' He paused when he heard a nurse walk by on the way to her car. 'It'll probably surprise you to know that after I got nominated for a Walkley award I was offered a political reporting position in London. But enough of me.' Peter stopped talking and went to turn on the car.

'Hey,' Sally protested, 'tell me the rest. What happened?'

'I didn't take it. Couldn't be bothered, I guess. The trouble with me is that I don't have a lot of ambition. Probably be an editor now if I did.'

'Before I passed out you said that you were going after Max. Retracting your statement wouldn't go anywhere or something.'

'Do you want to talk somewhere else?' he suggested, noticing a security guard hovering around the car park. Sally looked at the guard.

'He probably thinks we're druggies,' she said.

'No, Mrs Goodwill. We're Quakers,' Peter grinned as he turned on the ignition. 'Do you want to come back to my place after I take you to your car? To talk. Play some records. I've got a bottle of wine. I'm not...'

Sally cut Peter short. 'I'm fearful of being around men. I've never been able to be close to a man without having an anxiety attack. Even now I'm feeling anxious. I take valium. It helps. You understand?'

'I understand,' Peter replied, a little disappointed.

Just want to be friends. Is it too late for that?

He drove slowly out of the car park.

'Well, maybe just for a little while,' she said sternly. 'I want to know more about what you're going to do with Max.'

Peter replied with a wry smile and kept silent.

Peter was on his second glass of rough red wine before he admitted to Sally that he wanted to cut back his alcohol consumption. They were sitting at each end of the couch with Bindy in the middle. A record was playing quietly.

'I need to cut back,' Peter conceded as he sipped slowly at the wine, noticing that the record was jumping. He got up from the couch and went to the wooden upright record player and flicked the arm forward. Once the record continued playing normally, he skimmed through the records in the cabinet.

'Me too,' Sally responded. 'I can't stop sometimes. I've tried AA a few times. "I'm Sally Enright and I'm an alcoholic" sounds fucked.'

Peter laughed. The record jumped again and he took it off the turntable and returned it to its sleeve.

'We should make a pledge,' Peter said holding up his glass in a toast. 'After this is over we stop altogether.'

'Amen to that, Pastor Goodwill. I'll try. It's awful withdrawing. Awful.' Sally remarked hesitantly as she reached for the bottle of wine on the coffee table and poured another drink.

'In a proper clinic. They have one in Melbourne,' he mentioned vaguely.

'Have you been there yourself?'

'No, although I get invites occasionally. They have great Christmas parties,' Peter smiled. 'Seriously. I've had a few mates get treatment successfully.'

'Are you offering?' she queried as she drained the contents of her glass.

'Are you willing to come to Melbourne for treatment?'

'Don't feel sorry for me, Peter,' she went on quickly. 'Sure I'd like a normal life, a new life. I wish I had the guts to get out of here. I really do. But I'll only leave when I get justice. Only then. So I don't want your pity. I want your skills as a scummy journalist. You know what I want.'

'You have to promise that you won't tell anyone.' Peter lowered his voice, pushed Bindy out of the way and sat a little closer to Sally.

'First you have to promise that you won't run out on me again.'

'I'm going to see this through, Sally. That's what you deserve. It'll be my way of saying sorry.'

'I won't tell a soul,' she whispered looking uncomfortable with his proximity and keeping a close watch on Peter's hand. 'I keep forgetting what you've said or my brain is so pickled. You're going after Max?'

'Sure am. Max has owned this town for too long. You know he's had people killed,' Peter announced.

'Fuck!' she said with shock. 'Who?'

'Billy Johnson. John Tindall. Please…please, this is secret.'

'Cross my heart and hope to die,' she replied as she crossed her heart.

'Your story will be part of it. You'll remain anonymous, of course.'

'Have you started typing up the story? I can't wait,' Sally said. 'Finally someone is listening.'

'I just need another piece in the puzzle.'

'Is there any more to drink? I need another drink. Let's celebrate,' she pronounced, sounding agitated.

'I saw a bottle of sherry that Mum had left lying around. That fine?' Peter replied.

'That'll do.'

Peter left the room and returned with a half empty bottle of sherry. He poured Sally a drink. She gulped the sherry down then looked at Peter.

'You're not drinking?'

'Only a little drink,' he relented pouring a small amount into his glass and taking a sip.

'Tastes like piss,' he shuddered as he put down the glass.

'I've tasted worse,' she grinned. Peter watched Sally pour herself another.

She could be anything. She could be really pretty. If not for that night. That fucking night.

'You know I used to see Noel Gibson around town for about five years after the rape,' Sally recalled. 'Acted like he done nothing. Wouldn't look at me, though. Gutless cunt.' She began taking slow sips of the sherry. 'One day I'd had enough so I assaulted him in the main street. Guess what? I'm arrested and charged with assault. I tell the magistrate that Noel Gibson had raped me and he totally ignores it.' Peter shook his head in disbelief. 'I tried to have the case reopened. I went to the local member, went to the *Bulletin*. Wrote to everyone,' Sally chuckled. 'I think I even wrote to the prime minister.'

'Nothing happened?'

'Quite the contrary. Max starts putting the heavies on me. He says I should leave town. Max said that Noel Gibson had the right to live here and not be harassed. That didn't stop me. I threw a rock through Gibson's window. I'm charged again. Max called me an undesirable and wanted me out of town. I was living with mum and dad at the time. Dad suddenly lost his job at the council and couldn't get a job anywhere in the town. They decided to leave. Stupid old me stayed. Noel Gibson left town eventually.'

'Where did he end up?'

'In Townsville. I found the cunt in Townsville. I saw his wedding picture in the paper.' 'You tracked him down?'

'Shit. I wasn't going to stop until he suffered.' Sally gulped down the remaining contents of the glass. 'No more of that stuff. I can feel my liver hardening.' She pushed the glass and bottle away. 'I found where he lived, and I went there with the intention of killing him. I had a knife. His wife was home.'

'You didn't?' Peter reeled.

'No. She had nothing to do with it. Poor girl. She seemed so nice. I told her that Noel Gibson had raped me,' Sally started to cry. 'I wish now I'd never told her.'

Peter desperately wanted to place his arm around her but thought the better of it.

'Then I read in the paper about a murder–suicide in Townsville two days later. Gibson and his wife were dead.'

Sally paused to wipe her eyes. 'Maybe he snapped after she told him. She might have been going to leave him. She didn't deserve to die.'

'You weren't to know. You don't even know that was the reason,' Peter counselled.

'I didn't start drinking until after that. I couldn't stop thinking about her. I still can't. So here I am. The town drunk. The town undesirable. Max throws me in the cells every now and again for drunk and disorderly. I've been roughed up once or twice. I think Max gets off hitting women. What a psycho. He's told me to fuck off a few times but I'm still here, baby,' Sally laughed. 'Max found me passed out drunk in the park once. I woke up as the Greyhound bus was coming into Mount Isa. Fucking Max was trying to bus me out of town.'

'Time to move on, Sally. This is killing you,' Peter moved to hug Sally. She patted his back and pulled away.

'Sorry. I don't like being touched.'

'Sorry,' he replied as he moved right away from her.

'When Max is implicated I'll start to live. I've promised myself that. I'll move on. I'll stop drinking. I'll breathe. I'll move out of Clarkes Flat.' Sally stumbled to her feet and danced around the room. 'I'll come to Melbourne and start again. I'll get work as a personal carer at an old people's home. That's what I was doing until a year ago when it all got too much. We'll hang out together. Will that upset your wife, girlfriend?'

'Neither,' Peter said sadly. 'I had a girlfriend. We broke up the night I heard about Mum dying.'

'You should make it up to her. Do you love her?'

'She's a nice girl. Didn't deserve me. I miss her,' he admitted.

'You should make up with her,' she repeated, teasing. 'Go on.'

'I'll think about it.'

'I feel like dancing. I haven't felt like dancing for so long.'

'Okay,' Peter said reluctantly as he got off the couch and went to the record cabinet. 'Any requests?' he asked as he took out the pile of records from the cabinet and spilled them on the floor. 'I've got Stones, Dylan, Sabbath, Purple, and Zeppelin.'

'You can't dance to those,' she replied as Peter searched through the record pile. There's one. *Disco Hits 1976*.' She handed him the record. 'This'll be great.'

'Sounds good,' Peter said, rolling his eyes. 'This isn't one of mine. I hated disco. Mum? Can't imagine it.' He put the record on the turntable. *Stayin' Alive* was the first track. Sally immediately went into a disco pose.

'John Revolter,' he chuckled mimicking her pose. She went to the cabinet and turned up the volume further.

'You'll wake the neighbours,' Peter grinned.

'Fuck the neighbours. I want to boogie.'

Peter was dreaming about Michelle. In bed with Michelle. Michelle. Sometimes he had to put a pillow over her mouth when she was orgasming so the neighbours didn't call the police. It had already happened. How embarrassing having to explain that your girlfriend wasn't being assaulted, only coming. Missing Michelle.

I'll take her to Mietta's when I get back.

Best restaurant in Melbourne. So he had heard. *That's if…* Peter felt a wet sensation on his mouth like he was being kissed then felt his neck being licked. Michelle. He reached out just as his eyes opened. Bindy. Bindy tried to lick his face again but Peter pushed her away. As he came fully awake, Peter noticed he was lying on the couch and fully clothed.

'Bloody dog,' Peter growled as he got off the couch. 'Go outside.' Bindy threw him her best look hurt.

'Okay,' Peter relented, 'you can have your bed back.' She wasted no time and was soon curled up on the couch just as Peter realised that Sally had been there last night. She wasn't in the lounge. The last thing he could remember was lying down on the couch as Jimmy Page's masterful fingers caressed Kashmir out of his guitar and Sally was trying to belly dance to it. Peter went into the kitchen and put on the kettle. There was an empty cup and a note written with pencil underneath it on the table.

Thanks for the great night. Didn't want to wake you. I promise I'll come to Melbourne. Keep me updated. Your friend, Sally. P.S. Buy some pens.

Peter smiled. A wrong had been righted.

28

Doug enjoyed having a Monday morning barbecue breakfast at Max's every week, which he called a business meeting. That was the time that Doug kept Max informed on the results of his surveillances. There was a lot to tell Max this morning. A lot had happened since his nosey cousin had come to town. There were the usual routine happenings he'd tell Max — which blacks were causing trouble at their settlement at the reserve on the fringes of town; which boys were drag racing out on the highway. Then there the occurrences he kept to himself: the O'Neil girl who liked to sunbake topless in her back yard; the couple who liked to have sex in their car at the lagoon. Doug loved his job. Max's roving eye. Max's deputy sheriff. Max had given him an important job. Max and Doug ran this town together. Keep the streets of Clarkes Flat safe and free of scum.

Max's wife, Daphne, met Doug at the front door. With her axe-shaped jaw and perpetual five o'clock shadow, she was best described as handsome. She could have been a female version of Max, nearly as tall as him and with the same caustic manner.

'He's out the back,' Daphne said brusquely as she let Doug in. 'He's waiting for you.' She looked down at Doug's shoes and shook her head.

'First of all, you can take those off, Douglas. They're filthy.'

'Sorry, Mrs Hillard. I forgot to clean them,' he replied awkwardly as he quickly unlaced his shoes, removed them and his socks.

'Just remember in future. I don't want my carpet dirtied by your filthy shoes.'

He tiptoed through the lounge. Draped over the wall-to-wall carpeting was a large cowhide, serving as the lounge's centrepiece and surrounded by a plastic-covered pastel leather lounge. The biggest television that Doug had ever seen sat against one wall. The wall was festooned with brass wall hangings and pictures of Max throughout his career. A picture of Max receiving a commendation medal from the premier hung proudly above the television. When Mrs Hillard wasn't around, Doug liked to study the pictures but today she was right behind him, herding him outside.

Max was reading the newspaper at a barbecue table when Doug opened the sliding door. A teenage boy was standing at the barbecue turning sausages. He looked up when he saw Doug, than quickly diverted his gaze back to the sausages.

'I know you?' Doug blustered as he walked up to the boy and examined him intensely. The boy gazed back at him with pale blue, lifeless eyes, and smirked. A mass of blond curls and an angelic, downy-skinned face gave the boy the appearance of a choirboy. He was taller than Doug and wire thin, dressed in a new pair of jeans, sneakers and a T-shirt which said *Police* and sporting a photo of Sting and his band. Doug's eyes darted from the boy's face to the T-shirt and back again, the irony completely lost on him. He blinked first, which made the boy's smirk more pronounced.

'You're Ken Kruger's son. Ken used to work at the abattoir. He was drunk more times than sober. You and your dad left town two years ago. What are you doing back here?'

'Dad killed himself, didn't he? Killed himself in the shed. I found him. Cut his own throat.' The boy giggled in a high-pitched voice as he ran a finger across his neck. 'Sprayed blood everywhere.' His mouth twitched as he recalled the incident. 'I live here with me aunt now. What's it to you?'

Doug watched the boy with revulsion as the boy brushed away a loose blond curl away from his face.

'I still don't know why you're here.'

'Max is helping me get on my feet.'

'So, what happened to your hand, kid?' Doug asked, noticing a crepe bandage wrapped tightly around the boy's right hand.

'I was goin' past someone's yard and got attacked by a dog.'

Doug shook his head dismissively and turned to Max. 'Why didn't I know about this? I'm your deputy, Max,' he asked.

'Stop being so bloody rude, Doug.' Max tossed the paper down on the table. 'That's Corey. Corey Kruger. Now say a proper hello to Corey, Doug,' Max ordered. Doug held out his hand, which Corey refused, the smirk still on his face. Doug returned his arms tightly to his side.

'What if I don't want to?' he sulked.

'Cut the crap, Doug. Do as you're told.'

Doug mumbled something about being pleased to meet Corey although it was obvious that he wasn't, and ended with, 'Why have you got the stupid look on your face all the time, kid? You look like a spastic.'

'You're a fuckwit. Like an old clown,' Corey remarked as he flayed his arms and staggered, as if to imitate a clown. 'All you need is the funny nose,' he chuckled.

'You're fucking nuts, kid,' Doug replied, describing small circles in the air adjacent to his head. 'Too many ants in your picnic basket.'

'Enough boys!' Max roared. 'Get me and you some breakfast and sit down.'

'What do you want, Sergeant Max?' Corey asked quietly, still sneering at Doug.

'Two sausages, two eggs and a fried tomato.'

'I'll get it for you, Max. You always let me.' Doug tried to take the plate away from Corey. There was a brief tug of war, which Corey won. He held the plate tightly against his chest.

'My job, clown,' Corey protested. 'Sergeant Max asked me to.'

'Sergeant Max?' Doug replied sounding perplexed.

'Get your breakfast, Doug, and sit the hell down,' Max barked. 'Stop acting like a little girl.'

Max and Corey sat next to each other, Doug opposite them. They ate without speaking, the only noise being Corey chomping with his mouth open.

'Eat with your mouth closed,' Max corrected quietly. 'That's how polite people eat.' Corey scowled and continued eating carefully with his mouth closed.

'It's hard,' he remarked.

'You're doing better than Doug. He used to eat everything with his hands, even fried eggs,' Max smiled. Corey sniggered in reply, waving his knife and fork at Doug.

'Not hungry, Doug?' Max observed. 'That's unusual for you. You usually eat like a pig.'

Corey grunted like a pig between mouthfuls.

'That's enough, Corey,' Max disciplined. 'Time to act like an adult.'

'He's put me off my breakfast. I don't like him. What's Corey here for?'

'You should be grateful, Douglas, that Corey's here,' Max replied patting Corey on the head. He smiled back, making Doug look away with disgust.

'Why should I be grateful to him? Don't you see he's weird?'

'Corey's going to be your holiday relief. You know you need a holiday. You're long overdue for one.'

'I don't want to go on holiday now. Too much is happening here. I'm still looking for Sam Saturday and my cousin is snooping around that slut.'

'Well guess what, Doug,' Max said with satisfaction as he leant back in his chair, placing his hands behind his head. 'Young Corey found the old coon living at the McConnell homestead. I told you he was staying somewhere.'

'Bullshit he has,' Doug laughed nervously. 'Why has Corey found him when I haven't been able to?'

'You tell me, Doug.' Max replied. 'Maybe Corey has the drive and ambition of youth. Maybe more brain cells.' He smiled at Corey, making Doug wriggle in his chair.

'I know everything that happens in this town. You know that, Max,' he retorted in a quivering voice.

'Not lately you haven't. Not lately,' Max remarked with disappointment.

'But I told you when I found out that Peter was seeing Sally Enright,' he replied defensively.

'Yes. You told about that,' Max returned softly as if he was talking to a child, 'but you made yourself conspicuous didn't you?'

'I hate him,' Doug exploded. 'I want to hit him so much. He's a fucking smartarse.'

'And that's the trouble with you, Douglas. You're too impulsive,' Max replied, choosing his words carefully. 'We can't just harm people because we hate them, can we? We have to be more careful. More crafty. I don't want a repeat of last time. What a fucking mess you made,' Max grumbled. He took a deep breath.

'Did he fuck up big time, Sergeant Max?' Corey tittered.

'I didn't fuck up,' Doug cried. 'I didn't. I just did as I was told.'

Max glanced at Corey and glared at Doug. 'Let's not go into the wheres and why-fors,' he remarked. 'Will you clean up here, Corey?' He continued, 'Take the dirty dishes to Mrs Hillard. Like a good boy.' There was silence as Corey gathered up the dirty dishes. He didn't speak again until Corey had gone inside.

'Listen,' he resumed, 'I don't want a repeat of last time. You can't make the same rash decisions, I won't let you.' He glanced at the sliding door. 'It's all right for you to snoop around but you're not capable of doing anything else.'

'It was such a long time ago now. I wanted to please you, Max. That's all. Those men were upsetting you.' Doug wiped tears away with his hand.

'That's what you thought,' Max replied. 'You're going on holidays. Here are the tickets for you and Gloria.' Max reached into his pocket, pulled out two tickets and a letter. He handed them to Doug. 'You'll need your passports. You're going to New Caledonia.'

'Where's New Caledonia? Is that in America?' Doug asked as he inspected the tickets.

'Give them to Gloria. Just get her to follow the directions I've written out for you. Thank God you've got her.'

'What if I don't want to,' Doug protested as he threw the tickets back at Max. They landed at Max's feet.

'If you don't then I'll have no choice but to arrest you.'

'You can't,' he sobbed, tears running down his face. 'Don't do this, Dad. Please. Everything I've done, I've done for you, Dad.'

'Don't call me dad,' Max growled as he grabbed Doug's arm and wrenched it around, causing him to fall off his seat. 'And stop crying like a fucking girl. It's pathetic.'

'Don't hurt me,' Doug cried in pain. Max released his grip on his arm and he quickly regained his seat, rubbing his arm. Max picked up the tickets and handed them back to Doug.

'Your tickets. You should be happy to be going away to New Caledonia for two weeks for free.'

'I guess I'll get used to the idea,' Doug said meekly. 'Will I still be your deputy when I get back?'

'We'll talk when you get back,' Max replied, rubbing his hands together. 'You'll leave first thing in the morning. And the other thing. I want you and Gloria here tonight for a farewell barbecue for your cousin.'

'I don't want to be around him,' he thumped the table petulantly. 'I don't want to.'

'Settle down, Doug,' Max ordered. 'You'll do as you're told. Don't disappoint me.'

'This is fucked. Really fucked,' Doug replied as he dropped his head and ran his hands through his oily hair.

'It's not, Douglas,' Max touched Doug's hand with a smile. 'It's a bon voyage for you. You should be excited. How many people in Clarkes Flat have ever gone overseas?'

'Hey?' Doug looked blankly at Max. 'A bon av what?'

'It means have a good journey,' Max sighed. 'Good journey.' He gestured for Doug to stand. 'You can go now. Send Corey back out here.'

Doug stumbled to his feet wiping his eyes. He looked forlornly at Max who was engrossed again in the paper.

'I've always done as I was told, Max,' Doug sobbed. 'Always. I'll be loyal until the end. I'll never tell,' he concluded. He walked back to the sliding door and wiped his feet several times on the mat. Corey bounded outside excitedly, brushing past Doug.

'Sit, Corey,' Max instructed patting the chair next to him. 'There's a lot we have to talk about.' Max waited for Corey to settle and to assure himself that Doug had left before resuming.

'I like to keep a register of sorts,' he stated, lowering his voice. 'A book of undesirables who live in Clarkes Flat. Anyone who gets in the book is no longer welcome here.'

'Who's in it? Anyone I know?' Corey asked, sitting forward on his chair. 'What do you want me to do? Can I start with a coon? I hate coons. Smell like dead animals,' he continued as he fidgeted.

'Don't be so eager. Just settle down,' Max replied calmly, placing his arm around Corey. 'You can't lose your head in these situations. Don't get so excited,' he said slowly removing his arm.

'No. I can be deadly calm. Yeah. I've got that. Good. I can do that,' Corey took a deep breath and exhaled slowly and loudly, 'Ninja warrior.'

'Whatever you need,' Max replied, rolling his eyes. 'But stay calm.'

'Yep,' Corey snickered.

'There are two names in the register at the moment. Two names that have been there for far too long.'

'I know who they are,' Corey beamed.

'You tell me,' Max questioned.

'Easy, hey. That old coon Sam, and pisshead Sally. And maybe the guy who's been asking questions?' Corey suggested.

'Peter Clancy is going home tomorrow. He's not on the list. I'm giving him a send-off tonight.'

'So what do you want done with the others, Sergeant Max?'

Max leaned closer to Corey. 'You already know you're like a nephew to me. My right-hand man. What I'm about to say needs to stay between the two of us, right?'

'Right...'

'I worry about the kind of town you're going to inherit from us oldies when your generation takes over, so it's up to you now to make sure only the right kind of people live in Clark's Flat.' Max paused to get himself a drink.

'Where were we?' he drummed the table in thought. 'Yes. Enright and Saturday. They wouldn't be missed, you know. They're taking up precious space. Turning food into shit. You understand?'

'Yes.'

'I don't want to worry about these people anymore. I want a clean slate. I deserve that in my final year before retirement. I want to leave this place a clean town for you, Corey. That's a good legacy,' he looked intensely at Corey.

'You deserve that, Sergeant Max.'

'Of course I do. I've worked so hard to maintain order in this town. When I first moved here, the coons and young no-hopers had just about taken over. There were cattle duffers stealing cattle off good station people. It was a lawless place.'

'They were underisables?' Corey grinned. Max smacked the boy gently on the head and ran his hand through his hair. 'But you sorted it out?'

'Very good,' Max continued. 'You're a fast learner.'

'I'll sort 'em out, Uncle Max. You won't have to worry about them underisables any more,' returned Corey distractedly.

'You know, I believe I won't.'

Peter was dreaming, tossing and turning in the still early morning. He was a child again being chased by a shouting man through morning fog towards the river at Cornish Downs. He couldn't recognise the man. The fog was too thick, although the man voice's was familiar. Peter was going to suffer like he had never done. Suffer severely. Peter stopped at the water's edge. He dipped his foot in. Ice cold. The current tugged at his foot. Trapped. The man gradually appeared out of the fog. Max! Max laughing. Max threatening. Peter walked backwards into the water, slipping over as the strong current pushed him off his feet. Max carrying a pistol. Max raising it to fire. Peter breathless with fear. Paralysed. Dick Clancy appeared and grabbed the gun. The gun fell to the ground. Max and Dick in a tussle, Dick knocking Max to the ground. Max reached for the gun…

Peter was awoken suddenly by the phone ringing on the bedside table. His first reaction was to ignore it but these days he couldn't ignore any phone calls. It could be a lead, a breakthrough. He answered the phone. It was his editor.

'Don't you ever sleep, Bob? You need to check the bladder control,' Peter complained as he rubbed the sleep from his eyes and checked the digital alarm clock. Seven-thirty.

'Don't be a smartarse,' Bob rasped. 'It'll ruin your good looks.'

'I was going to give you a call sometime this morning,' Peter threw off the sheet and spun around to sit on the side of the bed.

'You're still coming tomorrow morning?'

'Sure am,' Peter replied. 'Can't wait to see your ugly head again.'

'Yours too,' Bob replied then coughed. 'Seriously mate. Listen. This story about Christine McGuiness.'

'What's happened?'

'Apart from cocks being cut off?' Bob added.

'By the way, could the surgeon sew the salami back on?' Peter chuckled.

'The wog boy was lucky. Nearly bled to death, though.' Bob diverted then returned to his original conversation. 'I've got bad news for you.'

'What is it?' Peter asked.

'Christine/Rachel topped herself yesterday. So the cops down at St Kilda reckon. We could have got a few more headlines out of her, but now we won't be getting anything at all.' There was a long silence. Peter sighed.

Another casualty of the sleaze paper trade. Another messy ending.

How much longer could the wall hold back the flood of human drama he saw every time he did a story? How much longer could he feed off the carcass before he snapped and became like Bob? Every beer, every sleaze story brought him ever closer.

'You there?' Bob enquired finally.

'Yeah. That's unexpected. Poor Christine,' Peter said softly.

'Sounds like it's thrown you, mate. Did you have a soft spot for the girl? You can't let...' A chortle interrupted Bob's sermon.

'Emotions cloud a good story?' Peter finished off, irritated by Bob's lack of sympathy for Christine. 'I know. I know.'

'So you'll have a clean tab when you get back. I haven't got any leads at the moment. What a pity. So close.' Bob said with a tone of disappointment.

'I told you about something I was working on up here last time you rang,' Peter said in his best professional voice.

'You alluded to something. How far have you got?'

'I've nearly cracked it. A little commando journalism planned for tonight will finalise it.'

'Tell me no more. How you get the story is no business of mine,' Bob wheezed. 'Any sexual deviancy? Sexual misconduct?'

'Fuck's sake,' Peter exploded. 'Can we forget about the sleaze for once. Let's do a straight story. One that we could be remembered for. One that the toffs will take seriously.'

'When did you decide to get on the high horse?' Bob asked defensively. 'I guess everyone in the media business is after a corruption story at the moment. It's a hot topic.'

Peter continued: 'Decorated cop's corrupt empire. Murder and corruption in the bush.'

'It may work. A local cop turns bad. Pity about the sex angle,' Bob concluded with a barking cough.

'So you'll run it?' Peter said as he sprang off the bed.

'I'll look at it. No promises.'

'Good. Good.' Peter caught sight of his reflection in the mirror and noticed that he was overdue for a shave.

'How soon can you send it?' Bob asked. 'Have you got access to a fax? I'll be around the office until midnight. If you get it to me early enough, I may be able to get it in tomorrow's edition.'

'Wonderful. That's great. As soon as I've done my research I'll go to the local newspaper, type it up and fax it to you.'

'You sound like you've hit on something big. Haven't heard that kind of excitement from you for a while. For your sake I hope it's good enough to run.'

'Too many good people have suffered to let it go on any longer. That's how bad it is,' Peter exclaimed. 'I haven't met a more corrupt cop then Max Hillard. Better than anything Victoria Police could create. He's one of a kind.'

'Are you going to be safe? It sounds like the wild fucking west,' Bob remarked earnestly, adding with a laugh, 'Don't get yourself lynched.'

'I should be able to avoid the noose. Just.'

After finishing his call to Bob, Peter went to the kitchen for a quick breakfast. One more trailer load of rubbish to take to the dump, a quick clean of the house, a meeting with the real estate agent and then he'd take what he was going to keep to Maud's for consignment at a later date. Dear old dependable Maud. She had also offered to take Bindy. That had taken a lot of pressure off him; a dog in a flat in Collingwood would end in tears. He certainly didn't want her to go to the pound. Then…Then he would be able to get down to the business end of the day.

Peter felt his pulse increasing, his guts tightening. What did a nurse girlfriend say once? In the event of an emergency take your own pulse first. The final day. The details ran rapidly through his overstimulated brain. He found himself standing at the fridge. He opened the door.

Meet Dave at the hill for a final run through of the plan. See Sally if I have time. Take it easy until tonight. If possible.

Peter saw the six-pack of VB gleaming on the shelf. One found its way to his hand as if by magic. He would check with Jack if he could use his fax tonight. Peter felt the inviting chill of the can in his hand. He licked his lips with anticipation and tore off the tab.

No, don't tell Jack until the last moment.

This was his story. No leaks. Peter placed the can to his lips. Sam Saturday's words of advice flooded into his mind. He was right. Peter went to the sink and poured out the can's contents. He was going to be razor sharp. He had to be.

After breakfast, Peter rang Michelle. The answering machine picked up. Michelle's little girl voice asked the caller to please leave a message, with the emphasis on please. Her innocent-sounding voice made Peter feel guilty. What was a good term for him? Cad? Emotionally challenged? Prick? Peter took a deep breath and was about to say, 'I…' A change of mind. He replaced the receiver. Peter promised himself he'd see her when he got back to Melbourne.

First thing. Maybe.

Bindy ran towards Peter and was preparing to spring into his arms as she approached. Peter put out his arms in anticipation, pushed her away and commanded her to sit. She complied immediately, plonking herself down on Peter's feet and looking up adoringly at him, her tail wagging like a whip. Ever since he had been assaulted, he had begun leaving Bindy outside to guard the house. Before that she had been living comfortably inside on the couch, thank you very much, and she had not adapted well to roughing it. At least the scratching at the door had now stopped although the incessant barking hadn't. Most of it was attention seeking, but Peter didn't care as long as it prevented another break-in.

He walked around the yard checking for dog-baits with Bindy close by his side. He couldn't be too careful. Peter looked up and down the road. For the first three days he had seen Doug's Fairlane coasting past about three times a day. Usual times. Nine, twelve, six. Like clockwork. At first, he thought Doug was merely a bored sticky-beak. Then he realised. Like connecting the old dots. He was being watched.

As conspicuous as a hooker at the Vatican, Doug. You dumb fuck.

Peter checked his watch. It was a little after eight. No Doug. He checked up and down the road again. A white Commodore crept slowly down the road and stopped with its motor still running, across the road from where Peter was standing. Bindy growled and ran towards the fence. She looked at Peter and then turned her attention back to the car. Peter didn't recognise it. The driver was concealed by tinted windows. He could hear the car stereo blaring. *Don't Stand So Close to Me*. The car remained stationary for about twenty seconds and then sped away, the driver blowing the horn a couple of times. Bindy chased the car along the length of the fence until she was stopped by the side boundary.

It was ten thirty when Peter finally loaded the last load of rubbish. Feeling guilty for leaving her outside at nights, he let Bindy make herself resplendent on the back seat of the car as Peter was tying down the trailer. He heard her bark urgently and scratch at the window. He felt a sensation behind him like someone was standing there. He spun around. Max.

'Shit, Max,' Peter said taking a deep breath of relief. 'You startled me.'

'It's all right, son. I should have rung you. I forgot about the assault. You're probably still jumpy,' he exclaimed coming closer to inspect the rubbish on the trailer.

'Looks like you're throwing away the entire contents of the house.'

'Mum kept everything from Christmas cards to broken appliances.'

'You'll keep more precious things, won't you?' he enquired as he took a closer look at a broken record player.

'I'm keeping photo albums. That sort of stuff,' Peter said evasively.

'I remember your mum used to have a camera,' Max laughed. 'Your dad used to get annoyed when she used to shove it in his face. Have you still got that?'

'No,' Peter lied, 'she must have thrown it away when we left Cornish Downs.'

'What a pity,' Max sighed. 'It would have been good to see people again like your mum and dad, even if it was just on film. What a loss.' He picked around the rubbish until he lost interest then turned to Peter.

'Why I called was,' he began slowly, 'we're having a get together tonight and you're invited.'

'Me?'

'Don't sound so surprised,' Max came closer and put his hand on Peter's shoulder. 'We're old friends. I haven't had a chance to catch up with you.'

'I was going to have an early night. I want to leave first thing in the morning.'

Max shook his head and wrapped his arm around Peter playfully. 'That's not what I want to hear.'

Peter tried to pull away but Max's grip was bear-like.

'All my friends want to meet the local lad who made it big in the city,' he joked. 'And the wife would be very disappointed if you didn't come.' He slapped Peter so hard on the back that he was pushed a good half-metre forward. Bindy growled from in the car, scratching at the window.

'And you don't want to disappoint my missus,' Max ended his conversation with a final slap on the back which caused Peter to cough. 'You need to put some meat on those bones, son. You're built like a greyhound,' he laughed. 'All dick and ribs.'

'I guess I could come for a little while,' Peter replied as he adjusted his clothing and moved away from Max. 'Who's coming?'

'Doug and Gloria. Two other couples you probably haven't met.'

'Doug and Gloria?' Peter squirmed.

'I know you two don't get along but this might be time for a truce.'

'Truce,' Peter retorted. 'Isn't that the event they have before a major war.'

'Now don't be like that,' he tried to grab Peter again but Peter made a quick side step and was now out of reach.

'What do you want me to bring?'

'Just bring yourself, son. Six okay?'

'Fine. I'll be finished by then.'

'We'll have a good talk. Like the old days,' Max said as he slapped his hands together with anticipation.

'Old days,' Peter mimicked, wondering what Max really meant.

Peter screeched into the parking area at the lookout aware that he was half an hour late. Dave's car was already there, as expected, but Peter couldn't see Dave in the car or at the lookout shelter. He got out of the car cautiously and crept towards Dave's car. He peered in the passenger window. Great. Dave had rolled back his seat and fallen asleep. Peter threw open the passenger door and got in. Dave awoke with a jolt.

'I could have put a gun to your head and you wouldn't have known it. You have to be more cautious than this, Dave,' he complained as Dave rubbed the sleep from his eyes.

'Anyway, I thought you coppers slept most of the night when you were on nights.'

'I didn't expect you to be so late. Where the fuck were you?' Dave snapped back as he rolled up his seat.

'I would have been here earlier except I had an unexpected visitor,' Peter related.

'Was she nice?'

'Not exactly. It was Max. Inviting me to a barbecue tonight.'

'Shit! The belly of the beast,' Dave panicked. 'You're not going are you? I want to break into the station at ten, when they go out on patrol. Shit!'

'I tried to get out of it but Max put the pressure on me,' Peter replied. 'It starts at six. I'll only stay an hour.'

'That won't interfere with our plans.'

'What's the bastard up to?' Peter said coolly as he looked in the rear view mirror.

'What's wrong?' Dave sprung around.

'Visitors.' Peter observed a car sweep around the car park then leave. 'We must have put them off staying. Probably think we're poofters,' Peter joked. Dave loosened his collar and took a deep breath.

'Why so calm, Peter?' he faltered. 'This is really stressing me.'

'You may not realise it but I'm a bundle of nerves,' Peter replied. 'The best thing we can do is not get so stressed that we make mistakes.'

'Speaking from experience,' Dave added. 'An old pro.'

'Maybe. One day I'll write a book. Any proceeds will help pay for the lawsuits.'

'You were saying?' Dave asked as he took slow deliberate breaths.

'Are you hyperventilating? Peter laughed. 'Don't fucking pass out.'

'Stress relief, meditation stuff.'

'I find drinking a good relief. Or should I say,' Peter paused to correct himself, 'I did.'

'Be careful with Max,' Dave warned. 'He's either going to butter you up or bite you. And sometimes he does both.'

'I have his measure,' Peter winked playfully at Dave.

'If you have, you'd be the first person. What I'm saying is, be careful, mate.'

Peter noticed Dave rubbing his hands.

'Last night,' Peter enquired. 'How did it go?'

'Look,' Dave held out his hands that were covered in blisters and cuts.

'Frigging hell. Soft hands.'

'Hard fucking metal. It took me three fucking hours to loosen the six bars across the window. Wore out the file.'

'Great job,' he patted Dave on the back. 'Any problems?'

'I did most of it after our patrol. I waited until the other constable went to sleep. Except...'

'You didn't get caught?' Peter felt his pulse increasing.

'Nearly. Sort of. '

'Shit.' Peter tapped his fingers rapidly on the window ledge. 'Did the other cop get night terrors and wake up looking for you?' Peter half-joked.

'No. He was dead to the world,' Dave related. 'I was filing away when I heard a noise behind me then a voice.'

'You're making me stressed, Dave.'

'It was a drunk looking for a bed at the watch house. I told him the watch house was full and sent him on his way.'

'He saw you filing?' Peter asked nervously.

'Probably. He was drunk. It was Eddie Terry. He's a metho drinker. He won't remember. Eddie thinks he lives in a mansion in Sydney.'

'We'll have to hope,' Peter fidgeted with his hands.

'We have to go ahead,' Dave opened the car door. 'I'm leaving tomorrow morning and so are you. We won't get another chance.'

'What are you doing with your mum?' Peter questioned.

'Her church friends will take care of her until I get back.'

'Hopefully that won't be long.'

'I've given up on a police career. I'm only staying until this is all settled.'

Peter and Dave fell silent as they watched a small airplane land at the airfield below.

'What'll you do after the police force?' Peter asked.

'Become a journalist,' Dave grinned.

'You can have it.'

'I'd like to own a farm. Run cattle. Look after mum. Maybe get married. I want the quiet life,' Dave disclosed.

'I want this story in tomorrow's edition,' Peter explained 'The sooner the better.'

'So soon. Shit. I'm glad you and I won't be here to see the shit hit the fan.'

'It would probably be ours,' Peter replied softly as he surveyed Clarkes Flat below them. For a moment Peter thought it looked picturesque as it was laid out in the late morning light.

'It'll certainly get the town talking,' Peter added.

'They'll get what they deserve,' Dave leaned out of the door and spat on the ground. 'They're as much part of these crimes as Max and Doug are. Bloody hicks.'

'Just uninformed. Trusting, I guess.'

'The town will want to hang us.'

'If they were allowed,' Peter sighed. 'But that's the danger of being a messenger. People blame the messenger for discovering the truth. They don't want to know it. It's more comfortable not to. Some places operate like that.' Dave closed his car door then turned on the ignition.

'What's wrong?' Peter asked anxiously as he looked again in the rear view mirror.

'I think we've being here long enough. I don't want to attract attention,' he said as he put on his seat belt.

'Where are we meeting? What time?' Peter asked quickly as he opened his door.

'Hobson's Lane at quarter to ten. You know where that is?'

'I know it,' Peter was out of the car and about to close the door.

'No turning back,' Dave said finally as he reversed his car slowly, not noticing that the passenger door was still open.

'Do I wear a balaclava?' Peter joked as he closed the door. Dave looked at Peter but didn't reply.

Peter decided to drive home along the main street. The street was gently bustling with meandering shoppers and people sitting at a row of chairs in front of the town hall, idling away their time in conversation. Country time. The only activity that could be considered to be anywhere near the pace of a city was at the TAB, where a throng of punters were bunched together in their collective addiction, waiting, waiting for their temple of worship to open. A group of young male and female Aborigines walked past quickly and, by the fixed, straight-ahead stare on their faces, full of trepidation. As the two groups intersected, no one made eye contact. This was the world that Max and others of his ilk had created and wanted to preserve; firmly entrenched and ingrained racism that was set like cement in the minds and actions of those who looked to authoritarian oligarchs for their next thought, their next deed.

Joh's world. Max's world. The deep north of Australia. Envying the Sowetos of the world.

Peter reached the top of the street and got out of his car to look back down the road. Even though he had detested this town for most of his life, he sometimes imagined returning as a conquering hero.

Things could change. I can change things.

Peter Clancy Day, a parade down the street on horseback with throngs of admirers waving and shouting. Then meeting the mayor and being given the keys to the town. An inspirational speech, with his proud parents standing on the rostrum beside their son. Award winning journalist. Bestselling author. Humanitarian. Good bloke. The welcome sign would now also read: *Birthplace of Peter Clancy*. The image evaporated as quickly as it came. He got back in his car. After tomorrow he would never again be welcome back here. His life could be at risk if he ever returned.

This is what happens when you decide to tell the truth. The truth is a heavy burden to be placed on your back. Welcome to Clarkes Flat. Do not enter, Peter Clancy and David Tindall.

Did he care? Peter craved recognition but from whom and in what form, he hadn't discovered yet.

The white Commodore was parked across the road from Sally's house as Peter slowed his car down to a crawl. The car's window was wound down. He peered in and saw the occupant, who looked like a young boy. An effeminate boy with long, blond hair. The boy recognised Peter's car and started to quickly wind up his window but not before Peter had caught a glimpse of his hand. It was covered in a bandage. Peter got past Sally's house then sped up when he reached an intersection, glancing in the rear view mirror. The Commodore wasn't following. What was going on? Who was the boy? Where was sticky-beak Doug?

Peter wondered if the injury to the boy's hand could have been inflicted by Bindy. A sickening thought flooded his mind. Was Sally safe? He turned left at the intersection. Was there a back way to Sally's? He continued slowly along the street then spotted a narrow dirt lane to his left. Peter judged that it might run past the back of Sally's cottage. But which house was Sally's? The worst back yard? He could only guess.

He turned into the lane and crawled along in first gear, peering into the back yards as he passed. An old woman was hanging clothes on a Hills hoist watched by her husband, squatting in a fold-out chair, hooked up to a small oxygen cylinder. The old man waved weakly while his wife stopped her clothes hanging to stare. Peter waved back. He continued until he spotted Sally's Cortina parked in a yard, under a mango tree. Peter stopped the car and jumped out, and ran to the fence and nimbly hopped over. *Not bad for a bloke who was useless at sports*, he thought as he readjusted his pants. Peter observed that the old couple were watching him intently from two houses away. Please don't call the cops. The condition of the yard wasn't what Peter was expecting; the lawn was freshly mown, and a vegetable garden looked as if it was regularly attended to. A chorus of birds was feeding at a bird feeder that was freshly filled. This was the other side of Sally, her escape from the demons, her place of solitude.

Peter tapped at the back door and then tapped again, this time more forcefully. He checked the handle. Not locked. He decided to enter, unwilling to announce himself. In case. In case that girly-boy might hear him. He crept through the kitchen. There was no radio or television blaring. The interior of the house looked tidier then last time he visited. He could smell incense wafting from the lounge room. The holes in the wall were still there. But there were the beginnings of order. Of hope.

Peter called out a soft, 'Sally. You there?' several times as he continued to sneak through the house. A floorboard creaked under his weight. He froze. Who was behind him? He turned slowly to face…nothing. He realised what he had done. Still jumpy despite all of the times he had committed the odd act of friendly house invasion. A 'commando', as Peter had termed it. The Toorak mansion break-in flashed into his mind. Nearly caught by a well-known bejewelled liberal ma'am in the kitchen. Luckily, he had been able to fit in a cupboard. He had to stay there with a full bladder, while she had had it off with a man with a Japanese accent on the marble bench top above him. They had ended their tryst happily, her orgasm sounding like a barking dog and his reminiscent of a samurai battle cry. The identity of the Japanese man had since remained a mystery.

Mister Misucumi. Funny. Anything for a good headline. Forget Derryn Hinch being called the human headline. I am the headline. I AM THE HEADLINE.

Peter looked carefully in every room. The mattress in Sally's bedroom was gone, now replaced by a proper bed with fresh sheets. *You can do this, Sally* — but Sally wasn't there. Peter went to the front hallway, opened a tattered curtain and gazed outside. The Commodore was still there. Was Sally safe? Peter beat a hasty retreat and was back in his car catching his breath. The old couple were not in their yard. He heard a car turning into the laneway. If it was the cops? What then? The only way back was to reverse, the lane was only a car width wide. The car drew closer. Now Peter didn't have a choice. Peter started the car and continued slowly down the laneway, unsure whether it was blocked at the other end. What then? He glanced in the rear view mirror. Thank God. It was girlie-boy's Commodore. Then again, maybe the cops pursuing him was a better option.

The lane met another street after two hundred metres. Thank God, again. Peter turned right and accelerated. The road was long and straight. He noticed a sixty kilometre per hour speed limit sign. He could see burn out marks on the road from where the young rev heads had had street races. Peter looked in the rear view mirror. The Commodore was turning right out of the laneway, three hundred metres back. Turning right! It was following him and quickly closing the gap. *Fuck.* Peter wrestled with putting the accelerator right down so he could evade the Commodore, but was what was the point? He wasn't Steve McQueen and, anyway, what exactly had he done wrong? Slow and steady wins the race. Peter stuck to the legal speed as the Commodore bore down on him. He guessed that his pursuer would have been doing double the speed limit to catch up that quickly. He glanced in the rear view mirror. The Commodore was now close enough for Peter to clearly see girlie-boy's face. Girlie-boy was singing and tapping the steering wheel to the beat of the music. Peter maintained his speed, maintained his cool, hoping girlie-boy would grow tired of his play activity and have quiet time. Peter remained quiet and controlled.

After a few seconds of tailgating Peter, girlie-boy sped up and passed him, keeping level with Peter's car for a moment. Peter gave the Commodore a fleeting look. Girlie-boy was holding the steering wheel with one hand and singing into his clenched fist, pretending it was a microphone. *A dangerous manoeuvre*, Peter thought. The Commodore pulled ahead, girlie-boy looking back, laughing.

Peter saw the car first. The car backing out of the driveway onto the road just four car lengths away. *Slow down, you fucking idiot.* Peter blew his horn hard. Girlie-boy looked around, eyes snapped back on the road. One car length away. Peter braked hard and swerved off the road, expecting an impact between the Commodore and the other car. Girlie-boy swung the Commodore hard to the left as if by reflex, avoiding the car, but running off the road and collecting a metal garbage bin on the footpath. The bin hit the Commodore's windscreen, cracking it, then bounced and hit the road. The contents of the bin sprayed through the air like confetti and fell on the Commodore. Girlie-boy neither slowed down, nor did he stop.

An old woman emerged slowly from the other car, clutching her hands to her mouth, surveying the detritus strewn across the road and footpath. Peter fleetingly thought about helping but his mind was elsewhere. How dangerous was this kid? He didn't know. Peter certainly deduced that girlie-boy was a nutter. A village idiot or possibly an average cat-killing psychopath. Cities weren't the only places that bred such a species. Small towns had them too. In some small towns the entire population was made up of them. Peter suspected a limited gene pool, overly close family ties. *Enough. I'm making myself unwell. More pressing events. Where was Sally? Was she safe? Not chopped to little, edible portions by the girlie-boy? But he wouldn't be watching her house if he had done that. She must be somewhere.*

Peter did several circuits around town. He surmised that Sally wouldn't go to the lagoon without a car and he knew she wasn't crashed out at the park, nor was she to be found in any of the pubs. The publican at the Crown said he hadn't seen her for a couple of days. He hadn't been concerned. Sally often had dry spells. The publican joked that his takings dropped when Sally was on the wagon. Peter drove back down the main street. Maybe she was at his house. He was passing the hairdresser's when he spotted a woman who looked like Sally leaving. He wasn't sure at first. This woman was well dressed, wearing make-up with a newly coiffed hairstyle.

He stopped the car in front of the shop and peered out in an attempt to confirm whether it was Sally. The woman laughed as she closed the door to the hairdresser's and glanced in Peter's direction. When he saw her, Peter pretended to look in the glove box. It couldn't be Sally. She would have had a lobotomy before a makeover. The woman approached Peter's car and tapped on the passenger window. Peter looked up. Sally? He quickly wound down the window.

'Were you perving on me?' Sally laughed as she peered in. She looked attractive, Peter noticed with admiration, like she was before. Before that horrible event. All of the furrows and lines in her face had disappeared, erased from her face as if a burden had been lifted from her.

'I wasn't too sure if it was you,' he replied. 'I didn't recognise you with all of the new apparel. You look great.'

'I scrub up okay, don't I?' she said as she stroked her hair. 'It's about time I changed my life.'

'I've been looking for you. I was beginning to get worried. Get in. I'll give you a lift,' he returned seriously.

'Shouldn't we go on a date first,' Sally teased. 'I'm an old-fashioned girl.'

'Get in,' he repeated, 'please.' He was tapping the steering wheel impatiently.

'Okay,' She opened the passenger door a little reluctantly and climbed in, quietly closing the door after her. She leaned forward so the back of her hair didn't touch the seat and didn't speak again until she had buckled her seatbelt. Peter started the car, throwing an occasional glance at Sally as if still not believing her transformation.

'Is there something wrong, Peter? You look worried.'

'I was worried about you,' Peter replied as he engaged the car into first gear. He pulled slowly away from the kerb.

'I was having my hair done. I want to change my life. You should be pleased for me.'

'You're being watched.' He slammed on the brakes as an old man tottered across a pedestrian crossing that Peter had neglected to anticipate.

Peter's car stopped in front of the old man, nearly touching him. The old man shook his fist angrily. Peter leaned out of the car and cried, 'Sorry about that.'

'You should get your bloody wife to drive, mate,' the old man shot back.

Peter waited until the old man had reached the footpath then accelerated.

'Are you all right?' Sally asked.

'No, to be honest. I'm a nervous wreck,' he replied. 'Shit.' The car was revving loudly. Peter realised he had been driving in first gear all the way up the street. He drove into a small park at the end of the main street. A stone cairn commemorating the men from the district who had served in the Great War stood as its centrepiece.

'I went by your place this morning,' he remarked as he switched off the ignition. 'I saw your car in the back yard.'

'I decided to walk into town. I'm on a health kick. You should try it,' Sally joked.

'No way. I heard it could endanger my life,' he snorted.

'You said I was being watched?' Sally asked seriously.

'Some kid in a Commodore was parked across the road from your house,' Peter related as he watched two Aboriginal men wander into the park to sit on a bench.

'The idiot chased me and nearly had an accident passing me. Do you know him?'

'That's Corey.' Sally sighed heavily, 'I know his aunt. Poor kid.'

'Corey?' He repeated, studying Sally carefully. The two Aboriginal men had left the park bench.

'Corey must have been waiting for me to come home. I give him a meal occasionally. His aunt's got psychiatric problems,' she said.

'It must run in the family.'

'Don't be cruel. Corey's had a lot of grief in his short life,' she chastised. 'He only came back to Clarkes Flat six months ago. His mum died in Townsville from a drug overdose, then his father committed suicide soon after. His dad had cut his throat from ear to ear and Corey found him in the shed. Can you imagine?'

'Is Corey safe to be around?' Peter enquired. 'What he did today was pretty scary.'

'Don't worry about him,' she commented, flicking back her hair. 'Corey is special. I don't know the word for it, but he doesn't feel emotions like you and me. He doesn't know social boundaries and he's easily led.'

'Fantastic. He'd make a great Nazi,' he observed.

'He's not like that, Peter,' her voice rising in Corey's defence. 'He's had a lot to deal with. You shouldn't judge him. Corey's an innocent. The trouble with you is that you only deal with the worst members of society. We're not all scum.'

'You're probably right. Sorry,' he said glibly, leaving Sally wondering if he really meant it. 'I guess I don't know who's good and bad anymore. Who's got their pants down and who hasn't.' Peter's hand brushed briefly against Sally's on its way back to the steering wheel. He braced himself for a reaction that never came. 'Maybe I should get out of journalism. Do something else.'

'What would you do?' Sally laughed. 'I think you enjoy what you do. I probably would. Poking your nose into people's lives could be fun.'

'It's a health hazard at times,' he replied with a grin. 'But you're probably right,' he continued earnestly, 'I couldn't work in an office or a shop. I couldn't work at anything else really. It would be too mundane.'

His eyes rested on Sally's face, although it was clear his thoughts had drifted elsewhere. Abruptly he piped up, 'I forgot to say, you look great. You look so young.'

'You've already said that.'

'I did? Sorry.'

'No. I like it,' she returned happily. They fell silent and Peter turned his attention out of the car window. Sally spoke first.

'I don't want to live in the past forever. I want a new start. It will be good to move on. I never, ever dreamed I'd be saying this, but thank you,' she wiped a trickle of tears with her tissue. Peter rubbed her shoulder briefly. His hand fell next to hers but he dared not touch her.

'You shouldn't thank me,' he blushed. 'I'm the one that owes you so much.'

'I've forgiven you, Peter. I realise now that you were a very mixed up boy,' she said as she reached for Peter's hand.

'I should have helped. How gutless am I?' Tears began to well in his own eyes. 'Gutless prick. I left you there to be raped by bastards I thought were mates.' He sat forward, gripped the steering wheel and rested his head on it. Sally wasn't sure if he was crying. A woman pushing a pram on the path adjacent stopped to peer in, and Sally returned her curiosity with a glare. The woman quickly got the message and moved away after first pretending that her real purpose for pausing was to check her baby.

'It's all right, Peter,' Sally consoled him. 'We're going to do something about it. Max is going to be punished and we're both starting again. Aren't we?'

Peter sat back and wiped his eyes with a handkerchief. He blew his nose and replaced it in his pocket.

'Max's shit is going to hit the fan very soon. I just have to do some more research tonight as final confirmation. Sorry about before,' he added, 'you should be the one who's crying.'

'It's all right. I've cried for years. It must have been your turn.'

'I guess I locked it away and forgot about it,' Peter explained. 'Just like Clarkes Flat. Just like my parents. Locked away deep down in a nice, dark place where it could fester.'

'Time to forgive, Peter,' Sally replied a sly grin passing over her lips. 'It's one thing I've learnt recently. If you can forgive the past, no matter how traumatic, you can move on to the future. And that's what you have to do.'

'Time to forgive, I guess,' he repeated loudly as he drummed on the steering wheel.

'So Max's is in for a rude shock soon?' Sally probed.

'Sure is. The chickens are coming home to roost or, should I say, roast,' he joked.

'I can't wait to see him go down,' she smiled and clapped her hands together. 'I can't wait.'

'It would be best if you weren't here,' Peter warned gently. 'Things may turn ugly. I'm leaving tomorrow. Get out of town as soon as you can.'

'But I've got nothing to be afraid of,' Sally shot back defiantly. 'I want to see him without his uniform, without his power, without his arrogance. I'm going to tell him to his face that he may as well been the rapist for all the justice I ever got. Not getting the justice was nearly as bad as having been raped.'

'I thought you told me before that I had to forgive?' he reminded her with a bemused look on his face.

'All right, smartarse,' Sally retorted. 'I'm still forgiving. It's just taking time.'

'That's going to be hard. Forgiving Max.'

'I've forgiven you. I've forgiven the rapists. I'm nearly there. Nearly there.' Sally took a deep breath.

'Please stay out of the way,' Peter counselled. 'I don't know how this is going to play out. Max is capable of doing anything. Promise me you'll stay out of the way?'

'I'm fine.' It was obvious that Sally was miffed by Peter's paternalism. 'I'm a survivor. I shouldn't be here but I am, all right.'

'Don't trust anyone and don't let anyone in the house.' he continued, ignoring the edge in Sally's voice.

'Don't get your knickers in a knot,' she replied, a little softer. 'I'll be in Melbourne before you know it.'

'Are you going to stay off the grog?'

'I've taken the pledge,' she replied proudly. 'I'm sworn off it. What about you, mister?

'Same. It's hard. Really hard,' Peter moaned. 'It's like turning your back on a good friend.'

'We can do this, Peter,' Sally leant across the seat and patted Peter's knee, to his evident surprise. She caught his quizzical look.

'Sorry,' Sally blushed. 'That wasn't an invitation to anything. I'm not ready for romance yet. Or ever. You know how it is. I like you, Peter,' she continued. 'And a long time ago I really liked you.'

'I wish you'd told me,' Peter responded. 'Back in those days I wasn't exactly very good at reading the signs, you know. I was nuts about you to be honest. I even wrote a poem about you.'

'Do you remember how it went?' she laughed shyly.

'No. I just remember the title,' Peter recalled, *'The girl with the smiling face*. Corny or what?'

'That's sounds beautiful. No one's ever written a poem about me.' A solitary tear ran down Sally's face and dropped onto her dress. She caught Peter gazing at her.

'If only for that event, everything would have been different,' he said sadly.

'It changed lives.' Sally took hold of Peter's hand and squeezed it softly. 'But we don't have to stay in the past.'

'I'll be seeing you soon in Melbourne?

'I hope so.'

After dropping off Sally off at her house, Peter had the urge to go to the cemetery, to say goodbye. He felt the sudden need to pay his respects. He wouldn't be coming back here.

Except for those interred, the cemetery was deserted when Peter drove through the entrance. The grounds were bleached free of grass, the headstones appearing to rise out of the bare earth like teeth. A crow sat on a tombstone calling lazily in the midday heat. Why did crows calling make him think of baking hot days, of fallen stock waiting for death, he wondered as he cruised slowly along a narrow road that led to the Catholic section. After calling several times, the crow flew away to the shade of a tree. Peter pulled up under one of the few trees and walked the short distance to the Clancy family plot.

The family tree, Doug's father and mother being notable omissions, was largely represented, starting with Peter's great grandfather Patrick and ending with Peter's father and mother. Peter stopped at the foot of each grave. Patrick's was the most ornate, a towering Celtic cross, a head taller than Peter, covered in Celtic symbols and calligraphy. The cross was the tallest monument in the cemetery. It was an Irish overstatement which basically said, *Here I am, a common Irishman whom you underestimated. I came from Ireland with nothing. Now I'm the richest man in the cemetery. Look at me. Patrick Xavier Clancy. I've got the best grave marker in the place. I'm better then all of you, especially you bloody Protestants down the road.*

After that, the Clancy headstones became more dignified, more Protestant. *We've made it now; we don't have to prove ourselves to anyone. We're above deliberate displays of grandeur.*

When Peter reached his parents' graves he chuckled. Not out of disrespect but for the fact that his mother's grave was still a heap of dirt. The flowers had been removed, making it even barer. Poor Mum, Peter thought, never liked looking untidy. It would be several weeks before the grave 'settled' according to the undertaker, and then a headstone would be placed there. It would say the same as the other Clancys, *Irene Clancy, late of Cornish Downs*. Peter had always wondered why the Clancys wanted to be buried in the Clarkes Flat cemetery when they could have been buried at Cornish Downs, their real home. The Clancys had always loved to party and were renowned for being great hosts. Maybe they thought they could count on having regular visitors if they were buried in town.

Peter momentarily mused on where he would be buried. Not that he'd given it a lot of thought at his tender age. He once had a vision of his ashes being shot over Port Philip Bay from a cannon at the end of the St Kilda pier to the strains of *Whole Lotta Love*, his favourite song. Money would be set aside for lots of drinking, so his friends could enjoy his spectacular departure afterwards at the Tote. They had to celebrate, not get maudlin. Must not get maudlin. And be honest. Don't cry crocodile tears — just don't cry. Tell humorous stories. Say you're here for the free drinks and

you hated Peter Clancy's guts. *And they have to play my favourite music —
Purple, Zeppelin, Hendrix — at ear-melting levels.*

That reminded him. He had to make a will otherwise he would be
buried in uniform fashion, just like everyone else. Born the same way.
End the same way. Of course, this was all dependent on whether anyone
would come to his funeral in the first place. Maybe not even for the free
drink. Death wasn't the end, rather the end of the endless process, from
the crawling beginnings, to the mastery of the walk, the running, to the
occasional fucking, the wandering, to the falling down; that's if you
reached old age. What did James Dean say once? Die young, you'll leave
a good-looking corpse. Poor James neglected to mention the truck.

Peter wasn't planning for that. He'd had the odd close call at times.
Nearly drowning, a machete attack, a pistol fired over his head. He
wasn't ready yet. Fifty could be a good age. Before the rot set in. And
he wouldn't do it himself. Peter didn't like that responsibility. It all
depended on God's good grace.

Despite the layers of accumulated cynicism and nihilist tendencies that
Peter carried around like musty, winter clothing, he still believed in a life
after this one had ended. In the afterlife he'd relax, catch up with friends,
family and finally get to meet his heroes. Again, dependent on God's
grace. He hoped he wouldn't be dancing for the devil in the fires of hell.
He certainly wasn't fond of despots or serial killers. The one thing he
knew for certain was that he wouldn't be buried in this shithole. Being
buried in the Clarkes Flat cemetery would be like being laid to rest at a
truck stop.

Peter reached down to sweep away a heap of dead leaves that had
fallen on his father's grave. A tear came to his eye. Lives were like leaves.
He placed two of them in his trouser pocket. Mum and Dad. He wiped
away the tear before it had the chance to form a droplet. Back to the
leaves. On the tree they are so fresh and yet so fragile. How sickeningly
sentimental. Not his style yet. Not quite. Maybe when he got older he
could get a job as a greeting card writer. Peter could be the specialist in
the sort of maudlin poetry that makes people cry or cringe. Helen Steiner
Rice, but more depressive. Peter got to his feet and did something he had
not done for a very long time — he clasped his hands in prayer and bent
his head and closed his eyes. He prayed, silent at first, in reverence, the
Lord's Prayer, the Hail Mary. Then out loud, as if saying it aloud would
expunge the heaviness Peter felt inside him. That large leaden ball.

'Forgive me for not being the son you wanted me to be. Forgive me. I
wanted to be a good son. I wanted to make you proud,' he paused to look

around. As if someone might be listening. He looked back at the graves. If only they could hear. If only they were still alive.

'I forgive you. I don't want to carry animosity towards you anymore. I pray that you are both happy.' As Peter was opening his eyes, a faint, dusty wind rose out of nowhere and blew into his face carrying with it a scattering of dead leaves. He spat out one that was propelled into his mouth. He snapped his eyes shut and held his head down until the wind passed over him, sweeping along the baked ground behind him, dissipating a short distance away. He wiped away the film of dust from his face, laughing.

'I'm glad you both now have a sense of humour.'

Sam emerged from the shady solace of his shelter to the blistering midday heat. He walked towards the river, barefooted and hatless with a billy can in his hand. Whereas white people would be seeking relief from the heat at this time of day, Sam welcomed it. He liked the stillness and calmness that fell over the country at midday. The country seemed to smell and sound differently; the fragrance of eucalypt leaves as they toasted on the ground, the crow's mournful cry. He walked steadily, his feet not registering the hot ground or the sharp burrs, sensing only freedom and comfort. Touching the country. Feeling its life.

In all his long years, he had never got used to the cramping confines of shoes. He remembered Peter's grandmother, Old Mrs Clancy, trying to put him in shoes when he was a child. He had thrashed and bellowed like a young bull every time a shoe was placed near his feet. Old Mrs Clancy said they were shoes, not snakes, she was trying to make him wear. Good Old Mrs Clancy and very patient Old Mrs Clancy. She never used physical punishment but her bargaining powers were exceptional. In exchange for having as much trifle as he could eat every Sunday lunch, Sam had to wear shoes every time he rode a horse and on special occasions: at Christmas, Easter, her birthday, Old Mr Clancy's birthday, his own birthday and, last but not least, Saint Patrick's Day. That meant a lot of hours in the dreaded shoes but having as much of Old Mrs Clancy's trifle was well worth it. Young Mrs Clancy, Peter's mother, carried on with the same trifle-making tradition but it never quite tasted the same. Maybe it was the bargain with Old Mrs Clancy that made it taste so good.

Sam neared a stand of trees that he knew a mob of kangaroos would be camped under. Always the same number; four does and a joey, just out of the pouch. They never moved when he passed them, only throwing a cursory glance in his direction as he went by. In younger days, he might have speared one to throw on the fire but not now. He was old and tired and well supplied by Dave, who had been doing his grocery shopping since he had arrived back in Clarkes Flat. Sam tossed them a greeting as he passed the stand of trees and then stopped dead. They weren't there. He looked in at their camping spot. The ground was still warm as he walked over it. Just recently scared off. He hadn't heard any loud sounds from his camp. No gunfire. The kangaroo shooters weren't allowed to shoot on this property.

He knelt down when he reached the edge of the river to fill his billy can. He remembered the old days at Cornish Downs when crocodiles had inhabited the river. You had to be careful when you filled your billy. A crocodile could be waiting. You couldn't see him but he'd be sizing you up for lunch. If you stayed too long, that is. Get in quick and get the bloody hell away from the bank.

It was a good day when the last crocodile had been shot by Dick Clancy. It had been a bull croc, about fifteen feet in length. They had cut open its stomach to find an entire bullock's head inside.

Sam looked up and down the river. No change. No change in the height or flow. He looked across at the other side. He could see cattle quenching their thirst at the water's edge. A calf was among them. All looked the same. Sam splashed water on his face and then had a drink from the billy. He could hear crows calling in the tress behind him. Not calling lazily but warning calls. They took off, still calling as they passed over him. He left the water's edge, his walk becoming more purposeful, his senses more heightened. There was a lightness in his walk, belying his near sixty years, as he moved up the bank. His feet appeared to only glide over the ground rather than smacking it, as a white person's would do. He stopped at the top of the bank. Maybe it was Dave, but he would have heard his car coming from miles away. Sam turned upwind. An unfamiliar smell. He put down the billy and crept forward, lowering his body to the ground, getting closer to the scent. Very close. At the camp. He stepped over the ground, making no sound as his feet passed through a heap of dead leaves. Stay quiet. Sam knelt on one knee. Listening. Sniffing. White fella. White fellas smell like rank butter. No disrespect. I like some white fellas; don't understand them. Then another smell. Perfume? White woman?

What was a white woman doing here? Sam stood up. He had nearly reached full height when he saw a flash of movement to his right. On his crook side, as he called it. The white doctor had called it a cataract and he needed an operation. One day.

Sam spun his head around in the direction of the flash. Blond hair. Young white bloke. Holding a shovel. He raised his arms to cover his face. There was a flash. Sam fell. The ground smelt of eucalypt and kangaroo. Laughter. Hysterical laughter. Like a girl. Pain in the head. Extreme pain. A crow call. Then blackness.

29

After meeting with the real estate agent, making final arrangements with Mrs Larsen and packing the car to the gunnels, Peter had fallen into a deep sleep at three o'clock. Only expecting to have a short nap, he was awoken by Bindy barking at the front door as if she had designated herself as his alarm clock. He shot up with a start, realising that the room was dark. He checked his watch after telling Bindy to quieten down. Shit. Six o'clock. Max would be impressed. Then again, why should he care what Max thought. Maybe someone was telling him not to go to the barbecue. Maybe. Peter jumped off the bed, brushed his hair at the mirror and put on a fresh shirt, albeit worn two days ago but only for a couple of hours.

What was Max up to? Peter thought, peering into mirror to squeeze a blackhead on his nose, as if the answer would appear from the other side. For a brief moment, he considered not going. But what would Max do if he didn't? Still intimidated. Maybe Max would break down and confess to everyone at the party. Peter would be there to record history. Highly fanciful. *Imagination runs away on me occasionally. He's up to something, the old Max.* Peter grabbed his wallet and keys off the dresser. *Stay calm, stay alert, and look for signs.*

Peter was welcomed at the Hillard's front door by Max himself bearing a worried look on his face.

'I started to think you weren't coming. We thought we'd have to send out a search party,' Max said, slapping a bear arm around Peter as he stepped through the doorway.

'Sorry. I overslept,' Peter replied sheepishly.

'That's all right,' Max returned. 'You've probably overdone it. Come out the back. Everyone's out's there. They're all waiting for you. Even Doug's wondering where you are,' Max half-joked as he pointed to the large glass sliding back door. He glanced down at Peter's feet.

'You'd better take off your shoes,' he suggested. 'The wife's a neat freak. Doesn't like her precious carpet dirtied. One smudge and it's war. When the wife gets upset. Whew!' he shook his head, pretending to swipe sweat from his forehead.

Peter reached down to pull off his sneakers and left them outside.

'I was wondering why all the shoes were at the front,' he smiled. 'I thought you might have had a large family.'

Doug and Gloria, a tall pinched-mouthed woman Peter presumed to be Mrs Hillard, and a middle-aged, overweight couple who looked like brother-and-sister blobs were seated at a long table. They looked across in unison as Max and Peter came through the back door.

'He's finally here,' Max announced. 'Says he slept in. You know how city people are. Burning both ends of the candle all the time.' Except for Gloria, who smiled and gave a small wave, the others looked Peter over dismissively. Instantly, he felt like a Rabbi going to a Nazi veteran's convention.

'Come and meet everyone.' Max pushed the grim-faced Peter towards the gathering. Peter was never big on socialising with strangers at such occasions. It was always the same inane banter — what do you do, where do you come from, where do you live, blah, blah, ad nauseam. He preferred his own small circle of friends. They didn't care what you were, only that you liked to laugh, liked to bullshit and liked to shout drinks. In situations such as the one he was in at the moment, Peter never disclosed what he did for a living. In these situations he became a humble clerk in the public service. This ensured that you weren't spoken to at all, not even looked at. To the other guests, the napkins were more interesting. *And I care?* He became invisible, which was fine by Peter. And you always have an early exit plan. *I can only stay for a little while, I have an elderly mother,* or, *If I don't take my medications soon I will...* But Peter knew that everyone here was aware of what he did for an occupation. He was ready for the onslaught of mindless interrogation. Gloria slid closer to Doug and patted the empty spot beside her.

'Here, Peter,' she beamed, 'sit next to us. All the Clancy family on one chair.' Peter sat down slowly, noticing Doug scowling at Gloria. She pecked Peter on the cheek.

'That's enough,' Doug spat. 'It's only my cousin. Not bloody Elvis Presley.'

'He's your family,' Gloria argued. 'You should be more welcoming.'

'Okay,' Max interjected with a loud clap, 'those fiery Irish Clancys. Have you met everyone, Peter?'

'No,' Peter mumbled as he looked at the others seated at the opposite end of the table, staring coldly back at him.

'This is the lovely Mrs Hillard,' Max announced as he walked behind his wife and patted her on the bottom

'Call me Daphne,' she announced through pursed lips. She threw a withering stare at Max when he tried to pat her again. It stopped him in his tracks. *That stare could drop a runaway bull to its knees*, Peter thought. Max moved to the overweight couple who were huddled together. He placed one hand on the man's shoulder and the other on the woman's. It looked like a stretch, even for Max.

'Don McMullen and his lovely wife, Janet. Our mayor and mayoress.'

Peter moved to shake Don's hand first. Don stretched his flabby arm across the table. His shake was limp and cold, the mark of a well-fed, well-oiled, pissweak politician. Max placed a stubby of beer in front of Peter. He thought of asking for soft drink but then he'd have to weather the enquiries about why he wasn't drinking alcohol. Besides, one beer wasn't going to do any harm.

'We should be honoured,' Don McMullen proclaimed disingenuously with a broad Australian accent. 'A pioneering family of the north.'

'How come I haven't heard of you?' Janet McMullen added with an affected accent.

'You probably weren't around when the family sold out. It was a long time ago.'

'Those sausages are burning,' Max interrupted. 'Keep talking amongst yourselves,' and he left the table hurriedly.

'Do you want a hand?' Peter asked as an excuse to leave the table. 'I'm the best sausage burner in the business.'

'I'm fine. Make yourself comfortable,' Max replied.

'So you're a journalist, Peter?' Don stated matter-of-factly as he looked Peter up and down.

'I could say public servant but…'

'Afraid to tell people who are you?' Daphne pounced.

Didn't take long. They're not slow in the bush.

'No. Being a journalist has connotations. Like being a police officer. You don't like to tell everyone.'.

'I'm proud of Max and who he is. He's a decorated police officer. He's done a lot for this community,' Daphne looked to the McMullens for support. 'Don't put yourself and my husband in the same boat,' she fumed. 'You're like leeches. Look what your kind is doing to Joh. He's been crucified by the southern papers.'

Peter could feel the anger welling up inside.

Joh's been crucified! Joh's a dickhead but he isn't the Messiah. Always blaming the south.

'Don't blame me,' Peter shot back after a long pause, his voice brisling with irritation. 'I work for the *Melbourne Truth*. We're not interested unless Joh and his mates are into swingers' parties or mistresses.' He glanced at his watch discreetly. *Is it too early for the exit plan? I'm going to be lynched at this barbecue.* He took a long swig from the beer bottle instead and counted how many chins Janet McMullen had. Three and one on the way.

'Isn't that paper banned in Queensland?' Janet McMullen enquired.

'You can buy it here,' Don replied. 'Though if I had my way...'

Peter chuckled.

'What's going on over there?' Max asked as he flipped a heap of sizzling sausages. 'You're making more noise than a bunch of coons.'

'Just talking,' Daphne replied, 'about what the media are doing to Joh.'

'Give it a rest!' Max ordered as he came to the table with a platter of well-done sausages. 'We don't want to hear about Joh every five minutes. I'm sure everyone here wants to have a peaceful dinner, Daphne.'

'It's just a shame,' Daphne continued, ignoring Max. 'Joh's done so much for this state. He put it on the map.'

Max shook his head and sat down next to Daphne. He started handing out plates to everyone.

'For all the wrong reasons,' Peter stated as he glared at Daphne.

'It doesn't sound like you're a Queenslander,' Don observed as he folded his beefy arms across his gut.

'I was born here. I was raised here. I'm proud that my family helped open up this state,' Peter shot back. 'I just don't choose to live here. I live where I can breathe.'

'And where's that?' Janet McMullen smirked, forgetting her accent.

'Melbourne.'

'How could you live there?' Daphne spat. 'Too cold. Too many migrants.'

'Ever been there?' Peter quizzed as he looked around the table. 'Anyone?'

'Okay,' Max sighed heavily. 'Dinner's ready and I would like to eat it in some relative peace.'

'Don't get upset, Max,' Daphne replied defensively. 'We were just talking. Peter should know that Queenslanders are a straight talking bunch. He must have got more sensitive since he went down south.'

'Daphne,' Max growled, 'enough!'

The table fell silent as if a ceasefire had been called. Peter tucked in, choosing not to look across the table, which had been designated no-man's land by the enemy on the other side. He only looked up when he heard the McMullens slopping and slurping at their food. Repulsed, Peter's head shot down and he concentrated on eating his meal and thinking of an ingenious exit excuse.

'Everyone,' Gloria said cheerfully, 'did Doug tell you we're going away tonight overseas.'

'Where to?' Peter asked politely.

'New Caledonia. That's somewhere out in the Pacific,' Doug replied without looking up from his plate.

'We're very excited,' Gloria added as she grabbed hold of Doug. 'Aren't we, Doug?'

'Rather go to Magnetic Island myself,' Doug sulked.

'We haven't been on a holiday since Doug came to the Philippines.'

'Enough, love,' he said loudly as he pushed away an empty plate.

'You should be excited, Doug,' Peter teased. 'You know it's a French colony. You'll get frog legs at every meal and they refuse to speak English.'

'Bloody hell,' Doug thumped his hand on the table. 'No one told me that. I don't want to go.' He crossed his arms and pouted.

'We'll go, Doug. We'll lose all our money,' Gloria wailed. 'Don't listen to Peter. He's only joking.'

'It's not our…' he began.

'You're going even if I have to take you myself,' Max shot in, glaring at Doug until he looked away. Peter studied the exchange between the two. Interesting. Gloria threw her arms around Doug.

'I'll look after you, big Dougy boy,' she planted a kiss on Doug's cheek, making him flinch.

'I have to go,' Peter announced after a polite cough. 'My boss is ringing me in the next half hour.' He was out of the seat before anyone could reply. Lame. Might work.

'But you only just got here,' Max said, looking annoyed. He got up from the table. 'I'll see you out.'

'So soon?' Daphne Hillard lied, nearly as unconvincingly as Peter.

'It was nice to meet you,' Janet McMullen added to the spoken untruths, looking relieved that Peter was leaving.

'We might see you in these parts again,' Don McMullen said, without looking up.

'It was good of you to come,' Gloria beamed and then kissed Peter lightly on the cheek. 'We'll have dinner for you next time you're in town. A family get-together.'

'That's enough!' Doug barked. 'We're only cousins not close family. When are you going to get that into your skull?'

'I couldn't have said that better myself,' Peter replied as he hovered, waiting for Max.

'Sorry,' Gloria said sadly. 'In the Philippines…'

'This is Australia,' Doug interrupted. 'We're not big on families.'

'Okay,' Max remarked to Peter, 'let's get you out of here before you end up putting us in that paper of yours.'

Peter and Max didn't speak again until they had reached Peter's car.

'Thanks for tonight,' he said as he shook Max's hand. 'It was interesting.'

'Don't worry about what my wife said,' Max replied. 'She worships Joh. She'd have his love child if she could,' he chuckled, 'though I think Flo might have an objection to that. And Doug. Well. You know how he is. Not quite on the same page. He's been a good friend of mine. I'm glad he's decided to take a holiday.'

'That's all right,' Peter said as he opened the car door, 'I wasn't offended. We just have different viewpoints.'

'Well you've certainly had an eventful stay.'

'I guess. I thought Mum had a few more years in her.'

'Apart from your mum's death,' Max lowered his voice. He leaned behind Peter and slammed the car door shut.

'Not much happened really,' Peter stumbled, sensing he was being interrogated. 'The funeral, then cleaning up the house. Nothing else happened.'

'You know very well what I mean,' Max returned, staring menacingly. 'I might be a small town cop but I'm not bloody stupid.'

'I don't know what you mean,' Peter matched Max's glare. He wasn't a wet-behind-the-ears teenager anymore.

'Catching up with old friends. Hanging around the no-hopers just like when you were a kid.'

'I ran into Dave Tindall and Sally Enright by chance,' Peter bristled. 'Is that what you're talking about?'

'They must have brought back a few memories,' Max smirked.

'Sally reminded me about the past. That was hard,' Peter continued defensively.

'She must have had a lot to tell you,' Max leaned forward. 'You were at her house.'

'Doug, the nosey…' Peter began. 'But how is that your business?' he resumed angrily. 'I'm allowed to move around freely and speak to anyone I want.'

'I like to know what's going on in my town. My town. My town is a quiet, respectful town where people know their place. Where outsiders like you keep their head low.' He jabbed his finger into Peter's chest with such force that Peter was obliged to lean against the car to keep himself upright.

'If she was trying to get you to write a story about her injustices,' Max continued, 'you'd be a bloody idiot if you listened to her. A drug-crazed mole who's a blight on this good town. She's taken more drugs than the frigging Rolling Stones.'

'I'm not a journalist all the time, Max,' Peter retorted. 'I'd go crazy if I was always looking for a story. We don't run around all the time prying into people's lives, looking for the next scoop. I came here to bury my mother, for fuck sakes.'

'All right. All right. Don't get your knickers in a twist.' Max retreated.

'I buried my mother and then Sally Enright reminds me about the rape,' he went on loudly.

'Why did you go to her place? I wouldn't have gone near her if I were you. It would have been in your best interests to stay away from her. Crazy slut. She could have put a knife in you. She's bloody capable of it.'

'I wanted to say sorry. I wanted forgiveness.'

Max chortled. 'Did she forgive you?' he teased. 'Waved her flaming magic wand and said, "Everything's better. We can be good friends now"? City people!' he concluded dismissively.

'I don't care what you think. I feel better for doing it.' Peter placed his hand on the door handle. 'Can I go now?'

'I'll let you know when I'm finished with you,' Max sniggered.

'Am I in trouble or something?'

Max leaned into Peter's face. His breath reeked of alcohol.

'Now there's no need for that. We're just having a friendly chat. Like old times,' Max slapped Peter across the back. *If only I could do the same back*, Peter thought. *Fucking coppers.*

'And Dave Tindall,' Max asked, 'what did he have to say for himself?'

'What about him? He's an old school mate.'

'I know that,' Max replied. 'I want to know what he had to say for himself. He is one of my coppers after all.'

'What would he say other than, I haven't seen you for a while?' Peter replied sarcastically.

'Don't be a frigging smartarse,' Max whispered threateningly. 'Did he happen to tell you that he thinks his father and his business partner were murdered?'

'Briefly,' Peter countered. 'But it was common knowledge that they topped themselves.'

'Did he want you to write a story on his…*investigations*?' Max queried.

'That wasn't even mentioned. He wanted to tell me how his father died,' Peter replied. 'Once again, I wasn't interested. Because I'm a journalist everyone thinks they have a scoop to tell me. Most of what you're told is bullshit. It's just like every crim telling you that they're innocent.' He paused. 'I came here to bury my mother and get the fuck out of here. I have no desire to stay any longer then I have to.'

'Yeah, I've heard Dave's stories before. What were his theories?' Max scratched his face slowly then grimaced. 'Pray tell.'

'Tom Fry,' Peter blurted out. 'Apparently Tom thought he was back in the war.'

Max laughed heartily, almost sounding relieved.

'That's a good one,' he said after slapping Peter on the shoulder again. 'Dave's a worse police officer then I thought. Where in the hell did he get that from? Poor old Tom.'

'I didn't think Dave was that bright,' Peter added.

'You'd be bloody right about that,' Max said as his laughter started to subside. 'I was right to transfer him. He's a useless prick.'

'Transferred?' Peter asked.

'This is between you and me and the gate post,' Max lowered his voice to a whisper. 'I recommended Tindall for discharge from the force due to mental instability. I've transferred him back to headquarters in Brisbane so he can shuffle papers before he's discharged in a few months. Apparently the shrink diagnosed him with schizophrenia. He hears voices. That sort of stuff. He…' He paused. 'You all right son? You look like you've just seen a ghost.'

'He didn't mention that,' Peter said quietly. 'I guess his medical history isn't my business.'

'I had to basically nurse him for the last two months while they organised his transfer. I tried to keep him away from the public but it's hard when you're short staffed.' Max stopped briefly to cough, then continued. 'If he had to go out he wasn't taking his side arm. That was the shrink's recommendation. Just in case.'

'Shit!' Peter exclaimed loudly.

'Tindall's like his mother. She went nuts after her husband shot himself. Never the same again. Tindall must have inherited her madness.'

'It happens, I guess,' Peter remarked innocuously.

'I'm glad I informed you.' Max briefly placed a fatherly hand on Peter's face. 'I didn't want you to leave Clarkes Flat with the wrong ideas.'

'Thanks.' Peter made another attempt to open the car door. He stopped when Max started to speak again.

'It a shame you're not sticking around for a bit longer.'

'Why would I want to do that?' Peter asked as he managed to prise open the door. *Nearly there. Get me out of here.*

'This is on the quiet again. I don't want you running to the papers.'

'You don't have to worry about that, Max,' Peter sighed with dread, feeling that he was doomed to spend the rest of his life in a conversation loop with Max.

'Don McMullen is stepping down as mayor,' he beamed, 'and is going to become the next state member for the area.'

'Good for him,' Peter said caustically. 'I'm sure the food is better in the state parliament cafeteria.'

'And I'm going to take over as mayor after I retire at the end of the year.'

'Congratulations,' Peter shook Max's hand, hoping this might signal the end of the conversation. 'I'm sure everyone in the town will vote for you.'

'Except the bloody coons, but who cares about them,' he grinned.

'That's good,' Peter commented as he opened the door wider.

'I've looked after this town for a long time. I've helped a few people stay on the straight and narrow. Kept this place largely free of the scum and shit out there. I'm sure the good people of Clarkes Flat will vote overwhelmingly for me. I've always tried to do my best by this place. Protect it like a father would a beloved child. That's it. Like a father. Of course, I had to be hard at times. You know that. You could have ended up in jail yourself, except for my intervention. You didn't know what the future could hold for you, but I did.'

'Who knows what might have become of me,' Peter said, feeling like he had been prematurely listening to a rehearsal of Max's eulogy, delivered by the Great Max himself. Daphne Hillard's shrill voice could be heard calling from the doorway.

'Hurry up, Max. We have other guests here. Come in now.'

'The missus. Where would I be without her,' he said meekly. 'I better let you go.'

Thank God, thank God for the missus, Peter thought as he flung open the car and jumped in. He shook hands with Max from the seat.

'When are we expecting you back in town?'

'Not anytime soon,' Peter replied as he turned on the ignition. 'I don't have any reason to come back here.'

'You're always welcome,' Max leaned in the cabin to give Peter a departing slap on the shoulder. 'You're always welcome.'

Peter drove away from the Hillards' feeling confused, feeling exposed, feeling diminished and feeling relieved. Just like the time he had sat across the desk from Max when he was a teenager. Was Max telling the truth or was he trying to lead him in the wrong direction? Away from the heat. He was a sharp bastard if he was lying. But Peter himself wasn't too bad at the porky pies either. Tom Fry? Where did that come from? Max sounded convincing. Was Dave really mad? Driven to insanity by his mother and his desire to find a killer. Was Sally really the drug damaged rape victim who had misdirected her rage against Max?

Max and Clarkes Flat were one and the same — a façade of small town values but beneath the surface were rumours, illusions, half-truths and fact, all knotted together. What did Churchill say once? The truth is surrounded by a bodyguard of lies. Even if you disentangled the knot you still didn't know the truth or the lies. Melbourne was so much easier to understand. Why did Max tell him about his mayoral aspirations? Was he really just the hard-working small town copper who bent the law so the good folk were protected from the outsiders? The good Max. Hardworking, diligent Papa Mayor Max. Peter knew he wanted answers from Dave and Sally. Final confirmation. He wasn't going to set Sally up in Melbourne or break into a police station without knowing the total truth. Had he been a patsy? Or would he just have to gamble on who was telling the truth in the most convincing way. Sally and Dave, both damaged and bent on revenge versus Max Hillard, the hard, racist but fair small town cop. Peter was still running these thoughts through his head when he pulled up in front of Sally's house.

30

Monday, 7:30pm

Peter could hear the faint sound of a television as he knocked on Sally's door. He waited. No answer. After counting off thirty seconds, he walked straight in. He could hear the programme. *Dallas.* Or was it *Dynasty*? Even if she was annoyed at his sudden visit, he was determined to ascertain what was going on with Sally. He could smell incense. *I'd rather smell a docker's fart.* This was going to be cleared up now. Then again, he probably wouldn't get anything but a curt piss off. He'd never heard a druggie ever disclose their drug history. *Are you fucking nuts?*

Peter called out. This was déjà vu. No answer. *Sally's isn't here again. Probably getting shit faced drunk at her local.* He looked in the bedroom. Sally? Sally was lying on her side away from him, towards the window. Peter knocked at the bedroom door then moved closer.

'Sally,' Peter called. 'Wake up. We have to talk.' Peter leaned across the bed. 'I'll make coffee. After you sober up we'll talk, all right?'

He waited. No reply. Peter suddenly noticed the pale greyish colour of her skin. He took a deep breath. He touched her cheek. Icy cold. Fucking icy cold! Peter reeled back from the bed. He froze for a few seconds. He may be able to resuscitate her. His ex-nurse girlfriend had taught him how, amongst other things that couldn't be mentioned in polite company. He leaned across the bed again, this time turning Sally over. She was rigid. Her lips were blue. He felt frantically for a pulse on her neck. Nothing.

'What the fuck have you done, Sally?' Peter cried. He pinched open her mouth and blew two sharp breaths air into her mouth. There was food still in her mouth. Peter pulled away, dry retching.

'You stupid bitch! Stupid fucking bitch!' Peter yelled. He compressed her chest several times. His mind was a muddle. *Compressions, breaths. Can't remember. I'm not a nurse.* He thought of calling an ambulance, then self-preservation kicked in. How would he explain? He'd call after he left from a payphone. But she was dead. Peter knew she was dead as she could ever be. He'd seen them before. Dead in alleyways, dead in squats. Why would you ravage yourself with drugs when booze was available?

Peter sat on the bed and took hold of Sally's hand, felt the absence of life. The druggies in the alleyways were strangers, someone's child perhaps, but still a stranger. Sally was a friend. He had never seen anyone so close to him dead before. He started to sob. He kissed Sally's hand and placed it across her chest.

As he moved her arm, he noticed a syringe tucked up in the sheets on the other side of her. There was a pale liquid still in the syringe. The needle must be somewhere in the bed. He looked closer at her other arm, the one she had injected. There was a dried spot of blood that began at the veins in her upper arm, ran down in rivulets across her lower arm and onto the bed. There was a large puddle of dried blood seeped into the sheets beneath her arm. There was no tourniquet. Maybe Sally hadn't needed it. The stuff must have been strong. Dead after one hit. Peter knew he couldn't stay any longer. If he'd known someone close to Sally he'd ring them, but who? He covered her body with the sheet as he got off the bed. Silly bastard. Peter pulled back the sheet again. The police would know that she'd had a visitor. He exited the bedroom. The television was annoying. The incense stank like shit.

Peter noticed an opened bundle of fish and chips on the coffee table. She must have been hungry. There was enough to feed three people. Maybe she saved the leftovers. He went across to the television and turned it off. Beside the television was a battered stereo, its lid missing. A record was on the turntable. *Led Zeppelin Two*. A rocker to the end. Peter smiled. He threw a final glance at her small collection of records and cassettes that were scattered on the table beside the stereo. One cassette cover struck him as odd. Spandau Ballet? Had Sally tried to become a new romantic? Sally was a rocker. That was how he'd like to remember her. At least there had been time to make amends.

He was not due to meet Dave for another two hours but he was going there now. He had to confront Dave now. That or he'd go home and get blind rotten drunk. You could forget about the break in. He drove to Dave's in a blur. He was glad there were no traffic lights in Clark's Flat or he would have driven through every red light. Shit! Why is that fucking person riding a pushbike without a light? He blew his horn as the bike swerved in front of him. The rider flicked him the finger as he passed. Peter blew his horn as retaliation and continued. Peter was at Dave's house before he knew it. For a brief moment Peter thought of driving away from Dave's slowly, having a couple of cool beers at home and having a peaceful sleep before waking at dawn and driving like a maniac to Townsville. But there was no challenge in that. A typical Clancy.

Peter flung open the car door and strode to the Tindall's front door. No challenge at all. *Find out what Dave's got to say for himself, assess the situation, and make a decision.* Peter knocked hard several times on the door. Dave answered, holding a cup of coffee and wearing an ensemble of black pants and shirt.

'What are you doing here?' Dave said, his voice betraying his irritation. 'I was meeting you near the station at ten. Remember?'

'Since when have you become the ninja warrior, Dave?' Peter shot back as he looked him over. 'I didn't know we were breaking into Hitler's bunker.'

'Quick, we're not supposed to be seen together,' Dave said tersely as he ushered Peter swiftly through the door.

'Something's happened. We have to talk,' Peter said hurriedly as he followed Dave into the lounge room. Lorna Tindall was seated in recliner chair reciting the rosary. She didn't notice Peter entering the room.

'Mum prays for about four hours a day,' Dave whispered as they walked past her to the kitchen.

'What's happened?' Dave asked as they entered the kitchen. 'Coffee?' He walked towards a still steaming jug standing on the bench.

Peter fell into a chair, placed his elbows on the table and rested his head in his hands. 'I've just come from Sally Enright's place,' he muttered without looking up.

'Sally Enright?' Dave stopped short as he was about to turn on the jug. 'The girl that was…'

'Yes.' Peter's head shot up and fixed on Dave. 'Raped. The same one. The rape that I ran away from,' he continued as he scratched his face nervously. Dave left the bench and sat down beside Peter.

'You've been seeing her? What were you trying to achieve? I thought you would have stayed away from her. For your sake. And hers.'

'I was trying to help her,' Peter said as tears started to sting his eyes. 'I helped fuck her life up. And now?' He hesitated. 'And now?'

'What happened?' Dave probed gently, as he leaned closer in. 'You don't look too good.'

'She's dead. She's dead!' Peter spat out, tears streaming unmanfully down his face. 'It must have been too much seeing me again. I thought I was trying to help. Come to Melbourne. Start a new life. See. I can do it. Address the mistakes of the past. What a fool. She'd still be alive if I'd left her alone.'

'Did you find her dead?'

'In her bed with a frigging needle in her arm,' he wiped his eyes and started to rock in the chair. 'I could do with a drink right now. Bugger Sam and his advice.' He waited for Dave's self-righteous reply. It didn't happen. 'Dave,' he said as he tapped the table. 'Are you there?'

'She's not a druggie, mate,' Dave replied quietly. 'I've seen her charge sheets.'

'What are you talking about?' Peter retorted. 'I saw the bloody needle in her arm.'

'She has no drug convictions,' Dave repeated slowly. 'None. Plenty for public drunkenness, a couple of assaults. No drugs.'

'But,' Peter responded, shaking his head in dismay and confusion, 'what's going on?'

'I hate to say it. You haven't told anyone?' Dave enquired.

'Knowing this place, the cops would probably charge me for doing it.'

'What was that again?' he asked.

'The cops would charge me for doing it,' Peter said looking puzzled. 'Now you're defending the Queensland police? Why?'

'That's it,' Dave said loudly. 'Someone's done it.'

'Come on, Dave, there was no sign of a struggle.' Peter raised his voice in frustration.

'What's going on out there, boys?' Lorna Tindall called from the lounge. 'If you can't play quietly I'll have to send Peter home.'

'It's all right, Mum,' Dave called out. 'We'll play quietly.'

'There wasn't any struggle,' Peter repeated softly. 'All I noticed that was different was a large parcel of fish and chips on the coffee table and a Spandau Ballet cassette cover. Nothing else.'

'Nothing else?' Dave echoed as he rubbed his chin.

'No,' Peter replied. 'Although the fish and chips seemed a lot for one person to eat.'

'Someone she's knows, maybe?' he speculated.

'Shit!' Peter nearly thumped the table but, recalling Mrs Tindall's rebuke, stopped himself. 'Girlie-boy!'

'Girlie-boy?'

'Some effeminate teenage boy she knows, I mean, knew. Said she felt sorry for him. She used to feed him. Bloody hell. That's it.'

'What's his name?'

'Casey? Corey?' Peter replied vaguely. 'Corey. That's it.'

'Corey Kruger. I know of him. He's just moved back into town. Strange kid. Odd. Giggles like a girl. He has nothing serious on him though.'

'I've seen him at Sally's place before,' Peter added. 'He chased me in his car after I went there. He's a nutter. Straight off the farm. But I don't know if he could kill Sally…'

'What would be his motive?' Dave wondered aloud.

'He's the small town psycho?'

'We don't have time to solve it right now,' he declared quickly, 'It'll have to wait. We have to get Max first.'

'I don't know if I can do this break in,' Peter admitted timidly. 'I've had second thoughts.'

'What are you talking about?' Dave fumed. 'We're doing this tonight. I know you've just had a terrible shock but we have to do it tonight.'

'I know. It's not that. I just don't know if we should. I mean, Max is just doing his job…'

'What? I can't believe I'm hearing this. Did something happen at Max's?'

'Maybe.'

'Enjoy yourself? Still feeling indebted to him?' Dave said as he ran his hand through his hair.

'I had to go, remember?' Peter reacted defensively. 'I couldn't wait to get out of there but before I left, Max told me a few things. I just hope they're not true. I hope Max is lying.'

'What were Max's home truths?' Dave asked suspiciously.

'I have to know the truth, Dave. Do you have schizophrenia?'

'You're bloody joking!' Dave broke into a fit of laughter. 'Schizophrenia? I can't spell it let alone have it. Isn't that where you hear voices?'

'It's bullshit?'

'I can show you my medical report,' he exclaimed as he jumped up from the chair. 'Wait here.' His chair fell over, crashing to the ground.

'I'm warning you,' Lorna Tindall called.

'Yes, Mum,' he yelled back as he left the kitchen. 'It was a…oh, forget it.'

He returned shortly afterwards holding a coloured manila folder. He dropped it in front of Peter.

'Read it,' he ordered.

'We don't have to do this,' Peter stared at the folder. 'I …'

'No. No. Let's get everything straight. Right now.' Dave sounded agitated. Peter slowly opened the folder and glanced at the page. He looked up at Dave.

'Read it!' Dave demanded as he hovered over Peter.

'Situational depression,' Peter read slowly, 'exacerbated by current work and home environment. Patient would benefit from cognitive therapy and anti-depressant medication. No suicidal ideations or visual or auditory delusions evident. Okay,' he conceded sheepishly, 'I doubted you. Max. Cunning bastard. Sorry.'

Peter reached around and shook Dave's hand.

'Mates,' Peter said.

'Mates,' Dave repeated then added, 'Trusting mates.'

'Trusting mates.'

'See. I have evidence that I'm sane or nearly. Where's yours?' Dave smiled.

'How did you get hold of your medical report?' Peter asked with a wry grin. 'You're not into the commando stuff are you?'

'The police psychiatrist had left the room after I'd seen him. I told the receptionist that I'd left my keys in there. Walked in, opened the filing cabinet. Easy. Who knows what could happen to this report. I don't trust anyone connected with the police. It's rotten to the core.'

'So we're set?' Peter asked as he rubbed his hands together.

'The truth has to be told. If not now then never.'

'Here's to commando,' Peter laughed. 'If the truth doesn't come to you, sometimes you have to break into a cop shop and steal it.'

'To commando,' they repeated loudly in unison.

'Boys,' Lorna chastised as she wandered into the kitchen, 'that's enough boys. Peter has to go home now.'

Doug had not spoken to Gloria since they had left the Hillards' house an hour earlier. He was at the wheel of the Fairlane, an hour away from Townsville, sullen and morose. Gloria tried to make light banter about the forthcoming holiday. He ignored her, staring at the highway in front of him.

'Doug,' Gloria reached across and grabbed Doug's crotch, 'I make you happy with a little suck-suck. Hey?'

'No,' he growled as he pushed Gloria away. 'Piss off. I'm not in the mood.'

'You love my suck,' she cooed as she stuck out her tongue and ran it sensuously around her lips. Undeterred she tried again. 'Stop the car if you're worried about a crash.'

'Fuck off, I said,' he yelled, backhanding Gloria in the side of the head.

The car swerved off the road, Gloria fell back in her seat, clutching her head.

'Why do you do that to me for? Why do you want to hurt me, Doug?' Gloria howled. 'I want to make you happy. That's all I want to do.'

'I'm upset, all right,' Doug scowled as he manoeuvred the Fairlane back onto the bitumen.

'Why? You should be excited. We can swim, eat, drink and fuck all day. I ride you like a cowgirl.' She grabbed Doug's knee and bounced up and down.

'But I don't want to go,' he cried childishly. 'Max made us go on holidays.'

'Max? What's he got to do with this?'

'He paid for the holiday so he could get rid of me.'

'You should be pleased Max did that. He's rewarding you for all your good work. Good work done by Douglas Clancy, hey?'

'He's getting rid of me,' Doug yelled, punching the dashboard. 'He wants Corey, the girl. The fucking girl!'

'Max won't get rid of you, big cock man,' she soothed. 'Corey's your holiday relief.'

'Max's thinks I'm useless. He thinks I'm a fuck up.'

'Why are you a fuck up?' Gloria asked cheerfully, still massaging Doug's leg. 'Tell me, big cocky cock.'

'Nothing. Just business.'

'He won't replace you. You and him are in business. Big partners. The sheriff Max and Deputy Doggie Doug.'

'I'm going back,' he slowed the car and pulled off at a truck park. He started to turn the car around.

'We're going on holidays, Doug,' Gloria attempted to grab the steering wheel. He slapped her in the mouth with the back of his hand. Blood trickled from her lower lip as she slumped in her seat, wiping the blood away with a tissue.

'Why'd you bash me? I'm a good wife,' she screamed like a banshee. 'I fuck you when no Aussie woman would. I close my eyes so I don't have to see your face. Huff huff. Your tongue hanging out like a dog. You spit all over me. Then, *I'm coming*,' she lowered her voice, mimicking Doug, *I'm coming*.'

'Shut up you fucking slanty-eyed Asian bitch!' He stopped the car completely, unleashing a flurry of wild punches into Gloria's hunched over body.

'If you kill me,' she managed to yell, 'I'll make you pay.'

Doug got out of the car and ran around to the passenger side. He opened the door and pulled her out by the hair.

'You'll pay big time,' Gloria cried as Doug dragged her towards the rear of the car. He flipped open the boot and pushed her in. She tried to kick out but he grabbed her leg and twisted.

'Stay in there. I'll sort you out when I get back to town.'

Peter had decided to leave his car at home and go with Dave to the police station. They sat quietly in Hobson's Lane, contemplating their next move. Lorna sat in the back seat humming a hymn.

'Do you think it's right to bring your mother?' Peter asked.

'I can't leave her at home. What if something happens?'

'Fine,' he replied tersely, 'but can you stop her singing *Nearer My God To Thee*? It's unsettling.'

'Mum,' Dave turned in his seat, 'can you keep it down?'

Lorna fell silent for a moment then started reciting the rosary.

'Well,' Peter said as he undid his seatbelt, 'this isn't giving the dog his dinner.'

'Are you right with the plans?'

'I'll be able to pull the grill off. Climb in. Get the reports. Climb out. Meet you back here in a half hour. Sounds easy,' Peter recounted nervously.

'You'd better take this.' Dave gave Peter a penlight torch. 'I don't know if there's a light in there.'

'Are you sure the station will be empty?' Peter asked as he slowly opened the car door.

'They'll be out doing their rounds.'

'Here's to commando journalism,' Peter added as he stepped out of the car.

'Good luck,' Dave said as he gave the thumbs up sign.

'Bless you,' Lorna said suddenly. 'Remember, God is on the side of the righteous.'

Peter nodded back in vague agreement then walked away from the car briskly, without looking back. Approaching the back of the station, he ducked under the spotlight located halfway up the station wall. He spotted the cellar window and slunk bent over towards it. He glanced behind him. He could see up and down the entire length of the street. The only movement came from a cat crossing the road in the opposite direction.

He knelt down in front of the window and pulled gently at the grill. No movement. He pulled again, applying more force. The grill wouldn't budge. Dave's version of easy wasn't his. He placed a foot on either side of the window and braced himself. Grabbing the grill again with both hands and with all the force his seventy kilo, unexercised body could muster, he gritted his teeth and pulled. What was his father's saying? Blow a fu-fu valve. The grill popped unexpectedly. Peter suddenly found himself on his back with the grill sitting heavily on his chest. He pushed it aside, got up and shone the torch through the opening. It looked like one vast cavern. He turned off the torch and put his arms into the opening. It was going to be a tight fit. Did Dave think he was a ferret? He managed to get his head inside.

Inside the cellar was totally black. Now came the hardest part. One shoulder, then two. Nearly there. More flexible than he thought. He heard the distant sound of a car engine running. He pushed harder. Was the car headed for the police station? Sounded closer. Half of his body was inside the cellar window. Just his behind to come. The top half of his body hung limply as if he was floating in space. His behind was stuck. *Is my arse that big? I've never seen it.* The car passed by without stopping. He clenched his cheeks together. Squeezing. Squeezing his behind through. He could feel his shirt catching then tearing. *If it was going to be so hard to get in, how hard was it…* With one last push, Peter was falling into the darkness, reaching out frantically with his hands to break the descent. He landed on his back with a hard thud and lay there yelping as a shooting pain came from his left hand. He reached into his pants pocket with his right hand and retrieved the torch.

'Great,' he said aloud as he shone the torch on his left hand. It already looked swollen and discoloured. He wriggled his fingers, his fourth and fifth fingers barely moving. How was he going to type? How was… He tugged gently at the fingers. The pain wasn't excruciating but it wasn't pleasant. Tolerable. It had to be.

Peter shone the torch around the cellar. There were three large filing cabinets standing together at the other side of the cellar.

'A lot to hide?' Peter muttered.

The rest of the cellar looked empty except for a broken chair lying on its side. He limped towards the filing cabinets and shone the torch on his legs. The right leg of his pants was torn at the knee. There was an abrasion but it wouldn't need stitches.

'Too easy, Dave,' he commented sardonically as he opened a drawer at random and flicked through the files: *1976*. He pushed it shut and picked the next drawer down. He pulled one of the files out and examined it. It read, *1968 — Mayor*.

Like to read it, but… Next file.

'Found you. Found you,' Peter hissed triumphantly as he pulled out a discoloured folder: *1969 — Billy Johnson*. Then the file behind it. *John Tindall*. He scanned through the files then tucked them into his pants.

Time to go. Peter checked his watch. Fifteen minutes had elapsed. He limped back to the window and shone the torch around the frame.

Fucking hell! The torch revealed that the window was a full arm's length above him. He stood back and thought hard.

'That's it!' He limped back to the filing cabinet and pulled out as many files as his right hand could carry. He took them back to the window and stacked them against the wall. He repeated the exercise until he'd piled the files high enough for him to be satisfied that he'd be able get out without too much pain and effort. The hardest part was going to be when he stood on the stack of files. Would they collapse under his weight?

Peter gingerly placed one foot on the pile, then the other. It supported his weight. Thank God. He was now able to look out of the window and push his arms outside. His left hand started to throb as he placed more weight on it. He turned his head sideways and had his whole head out. Emerging from the womb. *I've done it before. Now I Just have to get the rest of me out.* He pushed harder with his legs. The files started to wobble. *Don't fall, don't fall!* He squeezed. He felt like yelling in pain as he placed ever more pressure on his left hand. The same process as when he got in but now in reverse. He had gotten his torso out when the files collapsed. He was stuck. His legs wriggled wildly in the air as he tried to propel himself out. He ran his feet up and down the wall, feeling for bumps or breaks in the wall that he could use to get leverage. Unfortunately the wall was smooth and he was stuck. He felt like a rat in a trap. Footsteps! *If that isn't Dave I'm well and truly…*

'It looks like you're in a spot of bother,' Dave whispered as he crouched down near the window. 'Let's get you out of there.' He took hold of Peter's hands before Peter could explain his injury.

'Fuck! My hand. My left hand,' he cried through gritted teeth. Dave let go.

'But it's the only way I'm going to get hold of you. I can't pull you out by the head,' he reasoned.

'Okay. Just get me out. Get me out. I can take the pain.'

Dave positioned his feet on either side of the window, grabbed Peter's hands and pulled hard. Peter was propelled forward. The pain in his hand was excruciating but the elation of being freed from the cellar was more overpowering. He popped out of the cellar like a champagne cork, coming to rest on top of Dave.

'Don't say a word,' he cautioned as he rolled off Dave and stood up slowly. 'Not a fucking word.'

Lorna Tindall was asleep when Peter and Dave got back to the car. She woke with a start as they got in.

'What's wrong?' Lorna stammered. 'Peter. What's happened to you?'

'It's all right, Mum,' Dave replied with a wry smile. 'Peter got stuck.'

'Enough,' Peter fumed as he tried to find a comfortable position for his injured hand. 'I think I might've broken a bone in my hand.'

'We could go to the hospital,' Dave suggested as he started the car and engaged first gear. He slowly moved towards an intersection at the end of the laneway. 'Did you get the information?' Dave asked hesitantly.

Peter reached into his pants and retrieved the folders. 'Billy's and your father's.'

'That's excellent. What do they say?' he asked impatiently.

'Don't know yet.' Peter flipped the pages at random and tried to read the typewritten notes by torchlight.

'Good work, Peter,' Lorna said as she sat forward and patted him on the back.

'Where are we going?' Dave asked as he turned right at the intersection and continued along the street.

'The *Miner* office. Just drive normally. Don't attract attention,' Peter said as he opened Billy's file. He turned on the overhead light. 'Let's see,' he continued slowly as he scanned the document.

Dave pulled over in a car park driveway. Peter looked up as the car rolled to a stop.

'What are you doing?' Peter enquired.

'I can't concentrate. Just tell me.'

'Okay.' He continued flicking through the file. 'Let's see.'

'Yeah?' Dave remarked expectantly.

'It was my dear cousin Douglas who found Billy dead at the saleyards.'

'You're bloody joking,' Dave sputtered. 'Tom Fry found him according to Billy's wife. What about Dad?'

Peter opened John Tindall's file. He turned several pages then stopped and stared at Dave.

'I don't know if you want to hear this. It's pretty…'

'I have to know,' Dave shot back.

'What about Lorna?'

'Please tell me, Peter. Whatever it is, David and I need to know,' she said lucidly. 'This has been hidden from us for far too long. Far too long.'

'All right,' Peter said hesitantly and looked down to read from the file. 'According to this, Nipper Coleman found your father.'

'What! How?'

'He had dropped over to pick up a chainsaw. He went in the house and found your father dead in the kitchen.

'What a load of bullshit! Dad barely knew Nipper Coleman.'

'Language, David!' Lorna chastised.

'Sounds like Nipper was paying off a debt.'

'The price for freedom, I suppose,' Peter added.

'What then?' Dave asked.

'Apparently your father…' Peter began and then stopped abruptly. 'I can't believe this. I just can't believe this. In all my years as a journo.'

'What is it?' Dave cried. 'Please, Peter!'

'Your father shot himself twice,' Peter said softly. 'Twice. In the head.'

'Oh, dear God!'

'I remember now, 'Lorna interrupted softly.

'What was that, Mrs Tindall?'

'Yes. It's coming back,' she continued. 'I remember that day. I came back before they had a chance to clean it all up. Max was there when I walked into the kitchen, and he yelled at me — I don't know why. It was my house and John was my husband, after all. I remember all of John's blood was around the sink, but Max seemed to be looking for something over the other side, near the doorway. I remember he picked up something brassy, but I didn't see what it was. I didn't think much of it at the time.'

'That's it. It was probably a spent cartridge,' Peter slapped his hands together. 'Max came back to clean up, I bet you anything. Whoever fired the shots wasn't very competent. He must have shot him from over near the doorway. In my experience, good hit men shoot at close range. Point blank. Make sure it's a clean kill. This guy was an incompetent amateur. Sorry, Mrs Tindall. This must be hard for you.'

'Yes it is,' she replied, 'but it's reassuring to know that my husband didn't commit suicide. He's resting in heaven.'

'And they got away with that?' Dave punched the dashboard. 'Poor Dad. Poor Dad.'

'Are you okay, Mrs Tindall?' Peter asked as he reached around to console her. She was sitting stoically with hands clasped tightly.

'Now I know the truth. God has given me the truth. Now it's time for God's justice.'

Dave suddenly started the car, threw the car into reverse and screeched out of the driveway.

'God's justice, my arse. You're going to pay, Max,' Dave growled as he sped away. He threw the car around a corner, nearly losing control. 'You bastard,' he growled. Lorna began to whimper.

'This isn't the way, Dave,' Peter argued. 'Don't go to jail because of him.'

'Listen to him, David,' Lorna added. 'It has to be Peter's way.'

'Too late. I want him to suffer the same way as Dad.' Dave accelerated, changing gears quickly.

'Listen to your mother!' Lorna reached across the seat and smacked Dave in the back of the head. He was so shocked that he slowed down to a crawl.

'Oww. Why did you hit me?'

'Stop being so angry,' she declared powerfully, 'and start being smart.'

Peter nodded in agreement.

'Mum? You sound…'

'Sane?' she began. 'Oh yes, I'm going to be of sound mind and body when they bring Max Hillard to account. I owe that to your father. I owe that to you. We can only achieve that if we do it Peter's way.'

Dave looked at his mother and Peter uneasily. He finally spoke. 'Peter's way,' he mumbled.

'*Miner* office,' said Peter impatiently. 'Now. No more mucking around.'

Dave stopped the car in front of the *Golden Miner* office. Peter threw open the door.

'I'll wait for you,' Dave said as he turned off the ignition.

'Not here,' Peter returned rapidly. 'Meet me at Anzac Park in thirty minutes.'

'Can you type with your hand like that?' Dave asked when he noticed Peter was still clutching his left hand.

'Fortunately I have the other one,' he replied dryly. 'Now go.'

Peter checked his watch. Eleven sharp. He knocked hard on the door.

'Wake up, Jack. Wake up! It's Peter,' he called. It was a full five minutes later when a bleary-eyed Jack wearing only Y-fronts and a torn singlet answered the door.

'What's going on?' he muttered as he looked Peter over. 'You look like you've been in a fight.'

'I'll tell you later,' Peter pushed past Jack, rapidly scanning the office. 'I need a typewriter and a fax.'

'Now?'

'Please, Jack.'

'Are you filing a story?' Peter ignored Jack's question. He had seen a door with an office sign hanging on it. He rushed towards it with Jack following closely and breathing audibly. Peter pushed open the door.

'You're not still on about Billy and John? Is that your story?' Jack questioned as he closed the office door before Peter could go through it.

'Jack, I can't tell you. Please, I need your help.' Peter tried to open the door but Jack had a firm grasp on the handle.

'You think they were murdered?'

'Maybe. Open the door?' Peter requested urgently.

'It was all their own fault!' Jack exclaimed. 'They were hungry for money. Max doesn't like that.'

'So you suspected the same thing!' Peter yelled. 'You old bastard. You're a journalist. We're supposed to seek the truth.' Peter shoved Jack away from the door and was opening it when Jack raised his walking stick. It came down, striking Peter across the shoulder. He staggered backwards into the office, just managing to slam the door.

'Not like this, Jack. Protecting Max's not worth it,' Peter cried.

'You're a bloody disgrace to this town. Max should have thrown you in jail for that rape. Your father would be rolling in his grave!'

Jack flailed away with his walking stick, striking the door several times. In his frustration he smashed his stick on a nearby desk. He then attempted to push open the door but Peter had already dragged a filing cabinet across it. With Jack out of the way, Peter took a deep breath, sat down in front of the typewriter and started to feed paper into it. He reeled in pain as his left hand touched the keys. Fucking pain. He pulled away. *Got to do this. There is no pain. There is no pain.*

Peter tried again, adapting his typing to place more pressure on his right hand. It wouldn't be his usual one hundred and five words per minute but it wouldn't be school speed. Peter could hear Jack hitting at the door and shouting. Then nothing. Peter was in the story. The pain was gone. Going hell for leather. No time for proofreading. But Peter was renowned for his speed, succinctness and ability to handle pressure. He was the headline. He was the story.

He could hear Jack talking on the telephone. He finished typing, was out of his seat in a flash and gradually feeding the article into the fax machine. It was agony watching the machine draw the paper unhurriedly into its belly, scan it line by line and spit it out equally slowly on the other side. *Fucking hurry up.* If there were a paper jam he'd scream. He could hear voices at the front door. Jack. A young boy. Max. *Max!* Peter tugged at the bottom of the page to make it go faster. Can't do it. It'll either tear or blur. *Shit! Hurry up you piece of shit.*

'Is he in there?' Max barked.

'What'll we do?' the young boy asked.

'Break open the bloody door, Corey,' Max spat back. 'What do you think? But I guess that's my job not yours.'

The last page was feeding through. Peter could hear them pushing against the door and the timber splintering at the lock.

Trapped. How am I going to get out? A window above the desk. Oh yeah, I've got form, I'm used to this.

Peter stood on the desk and smashed the glass with his foot. The last page was through. He jumped down and grabbed the pages. The filing cabinet was falling over as Peter clambered back onto the desk. He dived head first out of the window, broken glass tearing his clothes as he went through. Max was the first in.

'The bastard's gotten out,' he yelled as he looked up at the window then at the loose papers on the desk. 'This is something I don't need.'

Peter staggered back to the car, aware that his shirt and pants were torn to shreds, his legs and arms covered in lacerations, and the pain in his hand getting worse. Dave leapt out of the car to help him as he collapsed breathlessly across the bonnet. He put his arm around Peter and helped him into the front seat of the car.

'What have they done to you, Peter?' Lorna cried, touching his bleeding head tenderly.

'I'm all right,' he replied. 'They're just cuts.'

'But you're covered in blood,' Dave replied urgently. 'I'm taking you to hospital. Now.'

'It can wait,' Peter flinched with pain. 'Max and Corey are after me. Get me home so I can get the car and get out of here before they hang me.'

Dave started the car and was speeding down the street before Peter had time to put on his seatbelt.

'What about Sam?' Dave asked as he pulled up in front of Peter's house. Bindy ran towards the fence barking aggressively. She stopped when she saw Peter ease himself out of the car.

'I'll check on him,' Peter offered. 'I'll take him somewhere else if need be.'

'You're in a terrible state,' Dave replied.

'Don't worry about me. I'm leaving for Townsville straight after I see Sam.'

'Are you going to be all right?' Dave asked.

'Just go. I'm sure Max will come here looking for me,' he continued as Dave leaned across the front seat in an effort to prolong the conversation.

'You'll ring me from Melbourne?'

'Sure.' Peter waved.

'Bless you, Peter,' Lorna said as put her hand out of the window and took hold of Peter's right hand.

'John will be able to rest in peace, Mrs Tindall,' he replied as he patted her hand.

'Thanks for believing,' Dave declared as he gave a thumbs up sign.

'Thanks for getting me into this mess,' Peter laughed. 'Now will you piss off?'

Peter hurried inside as Dave sped off. He raced to his bedroom, threw his belongings into a duffle bag and headed outside to his car. Bindy followed and attempted to jump in as he opened the door.

'Sorry, old girl,' he said sadly, gently taking hold of her collar, leading her to her chain and snapping it onto her collar. Bindy looked up forlornly at Peter.

'Mrs Larsen will take good care of you,' he told her as he patted her on the head several times and then walked away.

The campsite was deserted as Peter limped around looking for signs of Sam. The fire was stone cold and all of Sam's belongings were positioned neatly in their proper place. His car was still there. He shuffled carefully down to the river's edge. There were fresh footprints in the mud but that was all he could notice. *Wish I'd listened when Sam tried to teach me how to track.* He reached down and splashed water on his face and arms, washing off the accumulated dried blood. The wounds were minor and he was sore but the hand was going to need attending to. It throbbed. It would have to wait until he got to Melbourne. To safe refuge. Peter hobbled back to his car. Then he remembered. *Fuck.* How could he forget? *You fucking idiot. The films. I need the films.* Peter limped as quickly to his car as his pain threshold would allow.

'That was fucking good, Max,' Corey yelled cheerfully as he watched Max throw the car into a corner. 'I feel like a Miami cop.'

Max accelerated the Ford to top speed as he reached the highway that led from Clark's Flat to Townsville.

'There's nothing to be happy about yet,' Max yelled as he quickly ran through the gears, 'but we'll celebrate when we catch the bastard.'

'Where do you reckon he is?'

'Buggered if I know. I'd say he's on the way to Townsville. He'll want to get out of town in a big hurry. He'll be shitting himself. Gutless little shit. Should have charged him with drug possession. That would have been easy to arrange.' Max shook his head. 'I didn't think he was going to be this determined.'

'What are we going to do to him, Max?' Corey asked excitedly. 'He deserves to die. We should kill him.'

'Steady on, Corey. Killing will be too easy, boy,' Max said as he narrowed his eyes, 'He'll be getting special treatment.'

'Great,' Corey made a fist with his delicate hand and slammed it repeatedly against the dashboard. 'I can torture him.'

'Control yourself,' Max chastised as the car flew past a semi-trailer. 'This isn't Hollywood. This is real. And it isn't pleasant.'

'Why don't you get the other cops to arrest him?'

'Well, Corey, this is an undercover operation. This has to be on the quiet,' he replied. Max looked at the speedo. One hundred and sixty kilometres. He'd push it harder. He accelerated the car up to one hundred and eighty. He tossed a sideways glance at Corey who was singing to himself and then looked at his own image in the rear view mirror. This kid was trouble. A loose cannon.

Max only caught a glimpse of the white car as it came out of nowhere and ploughed into the rear of the Ford. He heard Corey scream. The wheel was spinning out of control it. The car was spinning. Spinning. Twisting and turning the steering wheel. Out of control. As the car left the road and flipped, Max could see Corey being sucked from the car. Rolling. Rolling over and over. Screaming. Nothing.

Doug had thrown Gloria into the tool shed after he'd tied her hands and feet, taped her mouth and padlocked the door. He didn't want her following. Taking Gloria's Mazda 808, he drove around town looking for Max. Max wasn't anywhere. His car was missing from his house. Not at Peter's. Doug had a hunch. If Max were looking for Peter he'd head for the highway. Catch him on the highway.

Doug sped along the highway, the Mazda's small engine screaming. On a straight stretch of road, he saw Max's car ahead passing a semi-trailer. Doug smiled. *Found him.* Max was going to pay for dumping him. He'd been dumped before. Mum and Dad never wanted him. Corey wasn't going to get Max. Max was his. The father he'd always wanted. If he was going to die he wanted to die with Max.

He passed the semi-trailer and before he knew it he was just behind Max. Nearly touching the rear end. Max wasn't looking. Doug exploded with anger when he saw Corey's head bobbing up and down rhythmically.

'Don't leave me!' Doug screamed as he pressed the accelerator down hard. 'I'm going with you.'

31

It was early morning by the time Peter arrived back at the house. He parked the car in the road at the rear and jumped over the back fence, creeping through a patch of overgrown grass that he hadn't bothered to mow. He was surprised that Bindy wasn't barking. She should have started barking when he was at the back fence. He drew closer to the house. He could see Bindy lying on the chain under the jacaranda tree. Strange. He called. Expecting the worse, Peter rushed forward. He staggered backwards with horror when he got to her. Her head had been bludgeoned to a pulp and her torso had been slashed open in a wild frenzy.

He could see the road from where he stood. No cars parked near the house. He crept up the back stairs. The back door was open. He picked up a broom that was at the back door and brandished it like a sword. A useless weapon but better than nothing. He entered carefully. The first room was the dining room. Despite having no furniture in the house, the tell-tale signs of forced entry into the house were evident. The wall cupboard was pulled off its hinges. A hole was in the wall beside it. Signs of frustration at not finding anything? Peter lowered the broom. The film canisters. He'd left them in the hallway cupboard. The box they were in was lying on the floor. One film had unravelled and was sprawled across the floor. Peter gathered it together hastily and pushed it back in the box. He almost cried with relief. All the films were still there. He quickly picked up the box, knowing he had to get out of there in a big hurry. He heard the sound of footsteps coming up the back stairs. His stomach tightened as he dropped the box and threw the broom up into a defensive position.

'Peter,' Mrs Larsen called as she tiptoed into the dining room. 'Are you all right? I heard all this commotion coming from here.'

'I'm fine,' he sighed with relief as he dropped the broom. 'I was away and just came home. Someone killed Bindy and broke in.'

'Oh dear,' Mrs Larsen held her hands to her mouth. 'How could anyone do such a thing.'

Mrs Larsen moved closer, then emitted an audible cry as she got a better look at Peter.

'You've been attacked!'

'It's all right. I fell over. I had a few too many,' Peter lied. He limped towards her. She stood aside when she noticed that Peter was leaving.

'Are you going to ring the police?'

'Could you do it for me please? I have to leave right away.'

'What's happened? Are you in trouble?' Mrs Larsen asked nervously.

'I can't explain, Mrs Larsen. Trust me on this,' he called from the doorway.

'I just can't fathom what's happening here,' she observed as she leaned against the wall. 'Things like this just don't happen here.'

'Trust me, they do, Mrs Larsen. You just weren't told about it. By the way…Could you bury Bindy for me? She was a great dog.'

'Of course,' she replied, 'I'll…' She stopped abruptly when she realised Peter had gone.

Peter scooted back down the stairs, the box of films securely tucked under his arm.

Get to the car. Get the fuck out of here.

He saw the car at the front gate when he reached the bottom of the stairs. The Fairlane. *Doug. Fucking Doug.* Peter snapped. *This time, no more controlling myself. No more! I've had it with you! I'm going to flog the psycho out of you. Sick fuck!*

Dropping the films, he rushed towards the car, oblivious of the aches and pains that racked his body. When he reached the car he kicked at the door repeatedly, enraged.

'Open up, you sick fuck!' He picked up a rock the size of his hand and started smashing into the driver's tinted window.

'If you don't open up I'll smash your fucking cars to bits.'

The front passenger door slowly opened.

'It's me. Don't,' a weak voice said.

'Gloria?' Peter hurried to the other side of the car.

He reached into the cabin. Gloria was lying across the front seat, her dress torn to shreds, her face a mass of welts and bruises. Peter helped her sit up and noticed rope burns on her wrists.

'My God! You look worse than me. What did that bastard do to you?'

'Doug was raving, crazy like a monster,' she grimaced, clutching her side as she spoke. 'He beat me up, throw me in boot, and then throw me in the shed. Then he takes my car. Wanted to find Max. He's crazy. He's thinks Max is his father.

'Where is he now?'

'I hope he's dead. If he isn't,' Gloria reached into the glove box and pulled out a .45 revolver. 'I blow his brain matter out of his head,' she said contentedly as she waved the pistol around.

'Careful,' Peter warned. 'Just put it down for the moment.'

She obliged and placed the pistol on the seat beside her.

'Why did you come here?'

'I thought he'd come here to kill you,' she replied. 'But God spared you.' She reached again into the glove box and pulled out a large envelope. 'This is for you.'

Peter took the envelope and poured out the contents on the seat. An assortment of tapes and photographs spilled out. He looked at one of the photographs. It was a man lying dead against a cupboard. Peter couldn't recognise the man. The man's face was obscured by blood and brain tissue. Was it John Tindall?

'Doug's a big killer,' Gloria stated. 'He's been doing Max's dirty work all these years.'

'Looks like it.' He looked at another photograph. It was a naked girl aged about ten getting out of a bath. Peter gathered the pile and shoved it back in the envelope.

'That's sick,' he said with disgust.

'He's a big pervert too.'

'How did you find this?'

'When I was locked in the shed. When I got out of the ropes I smashed up the shed with a pick. They were in one of the walls,' Gloria giggled. 'Doug thinks he smart bastard but I'm smarter.'

'What do you think the tapes contain?'

'When I got out of the shed I played one. I hear Max's voice telling Doug to find Sam something. I didn't understand.'

'Sam Saturday. He must have been looking for Sam Saturday.'

'Where's Sam?' she asked.

'Don't know. I can't find him.'

'I reckon Doug bugged Max in case Max fuck him over. Doug didn't like being called dumb all the time by Max. Dumbo this. Dumbo that. Dumbo does this. He wanted to be a cop like Max but he's too stupid.'

'Can I have these?'

'I give it to you. Now you fuck Max and Doug over. You send Doug to jail but you let me shoot him in the balls first. I just want to wound him.' She slid across to the driver's seat and turned on the ignition.

'Where are you going?' Peter asked.

'I get out of this dump. I'm scramming.' Gloria revved the car several times before engaging first gear.

'You need medical attention.'

The car started to move. 'I'm strong. I'm Filipino woman. Doug couldn't break me.'

He quickly closed the door as the car sped away, fishtailing in the gravel.

Peter was at the outskirts of Clarkes Flat a few minutes later. The dishevelled boy he had seen crossing the road with his drunken mother was walking aimlessly in the street, alone, barefooted and wearing a pair of dirty pyjamas. Peter pulled up and got out. The boy stopped walking when he noticed Peter coming towards him.

'Who are you? What do you want?' the boy asked submissively. 'You look hurt.'

'I'm all right,' Peter replied cheerfully as he leaned down to the boy's height. 'What about you?'

'My parents are fighting. I was going for a walk.'

'What's your name?'

'Jimmy Donahue.'

'Well, Jimmy. I have some advice for you. Be strong. Don't let them destroy your dreams. What do you want to be when you grow up?' He counselled as he patted Jimmy on the head and then straightened up painfully.

'Oh I dunno. Rich? A policeman?' Jimmy replied quizzically.

'That's excellent,' Peter responded.

'I want to lock up the bad people.'

'Yeah, although sometimes it can be a bit hard to tell good people from bad. Good luck with that.' Peter stopped and took a deep breath, adding, 'One last word of advice.'

'What's that?'

'Get the hell out of here when you can.'

Peter headed back to his car.

Back to Townsville. Back to Melbourne. Back to my home country. Home.